To Pat,

All the best

Howard Levine

He was just trying to help his cop brother find out who killed his niece, and now he was under government surveillance?

Fowlkes darted from the parking lot and made a left across a double line and three lanes of traffic coming from two different directions, causing at least one driver to lean on his horn.

The truck, judging by its baritone, was an eighteen-wheeler plunging like a giant electric eel through the murky green darkness outside of Fowlkes's passenger window.

"Jesus!" barked Frank. "What the fuck—"

Fowlkes hadn't blinked. His chunky profile, dominated by the mustache and the glasses, stared placidly ahead. "Easy, Frank. I don't think we're being followed. Someone was exiting the lot behind us, but it was a woman in a van, probably a soccer mom. No one entered on this side after we made the turn. But still, safety first."

At this, Frank had burst out laughing and couldn't stop for maybe half a minute, his nerves beginning to unknot. "Right," he managed finally. "So, I'm under surveillance. In a way that just shows that—how long?"

"As of a couple of days ago. Noticed it by chance. Maybe sitting on my ass behind my desk has its advantages. We have classified lists of people under surveillance. You click on the name, all the relevant info comes up. I was looking for this heroin goombah, Texiera, scrolling down, and whose name do I see? Yours and your brother's. You told me, when we spoke on the phone, that you were going to pay that reverend a visit. Did you?"

"Yup," Frank said, his breath catching as Fowlkes ran a light at the intersection of Mamaroneck Avenue, rounded a curve, and made a squealing left.

Frank Tedeschi's niece is dead, one of thousands of victims of a terrorist attack, which has been laid at the feet of "Islamic radicals" by a right-wing US government. Frank—based on a chance encounter—is one of the very few people who question the government's explanation. He's a Vietnam veteran who wants nothing more than to live without further controversy or conflict. Can he and his grieving brother Rob, a detective with the NYPD, obtain the necessary evidence to uncover the truth in the face of scorn and incredulity? Can they overcome their long-term estrangement to work together, given that they are putting their lives in danger?

In *Last Gasp*—a novel that resonates with today's politics—the answers to these questions unfold in a way that mingles personal and societal issues and intertwines the past and present while moving relentlessly forward.

KUDOS for *Last Gasp*

"Howard Levine's *Last Gasp* is a page-turning thriller—one that is very topical, given the current political situation in America. It's also a family drama. Levine's characters are rounded and believable, and my sympathy for them, and for the daunting mission they undertake, made it even harder to put the book down. I recommend *Last Gasp* highly. It's a great read." ~ Bill Stixrud, author (with Ned Johnson) of the national bestseller, *The Self-Driven Child*

"*Last Gasp* by Howard Levine is a fast-paced thriller, filled with unexpected twists and turns in the action and deep insights into the hearts and motivations of its characters—a highly original and skilled blend of literary depth and compelling suspense." ~ Carol Goodman, Hammett Award winning author of *The Lake of Dead Languages* and *The Other Mother*

"For those readers who find today's political headlines as fascinating as they are disturbing (and even for those who don't), fasten your seat belts for a roller coaster suspense plot ride that will compel, inform, and unnerve you. Frank and Rob Tedeschi are unlikely but superbly drawn blue-collar heroes who, in *Last Gasp*, find themselves unexpectedly at war with the highest levels of the US government. Levine, a brilliant creator of character, setting, and plot, masterfully draws on his expertise in areas as diverse as the history of the Vietnam War protest movement and the geography of New York's Hudson Valley to concoct a narrative and perspective that the reader will be drawn deeply into, and never forget—a thought-provoking and spellbinding masterpiece." ~ Lee

Slonimsky, author of Bermuda Gold and co-author of the Lee Carroll *Black Swan Rising* trilogy

ACKNOWLEDGMENTS

The editorial input of my lovely wife Marian was invaluable in the writing of this book. Thanks to Gene Levine and Julia Usatin for sharing their expertise in air conditioning/heating and medical issues, respectively. Thanks as well to Faith, Jack, and Lauri, members of the hard-working staff at Black Opal Books. Last but not least, thanks to my agent, Donna Eastman, whose belief in this book bore fruition.

LAST GASP

Howard Levine

A Black Opal Books Publication

Black Opal Books
BECAUSE SOME STORIES JUST HAVE TO BE TOLD

GENRE: THRILLER/MYSTERY/SUSPENSE

LAST GASP
Copyright © 2018 by Howard Levine
Cover Design by Jackson Cover Designs
All cover art copyright © 2018
All Rights Reserved
Print ISBN: 978-1-626949-83-6

First Publication: SEPTEMBER 2018

Published by Black Opal Books **http://www.blackopalbooks.com**

DEDICATION

To Allyson, Ben, and Jake—the younger generation.

CHAPTER 1

The Bronx, 2010:

Billy Patterson hesitated only briefly. If the guy was that much wasted flesh—packaged in a uniform—that he could sleep even through the "music" of Shove it Up, sleep on the job, when the whole job was to stay awake, to guard two-thousand square feet and one miserable door, then he probably deserved to die, with thanks for making *Patterson's* job that much easier. Besides, it wasn't really Patterson's decision. It was God's. He was just the instrument. A silent one, the antithesis of a screaming guitar, and the more deadly for it.

Not surprisingly, everything was proceeding without glitches. The canister had been just where he'd left it in the wee hours of the previous day. Ditto for the compressible gas mask. His pre-Jesus skills at breaking and entering had not eroded with time. And in the rush of fans to get situated before the "concert" began, to find seats, to load up on beer—as if the vile, mega-amped material flying off the stage would not leave them shit-faced enough—no one had noticed him picking the lock on the custodial closet to one side of the men's room on level one. Dressed in the garb of the maintenance crew, including work gloves, he'd slipped back into the onrushing throng with the mask and canister in hand. The latter resembled a large thermos, silver and innocuous looking. Its gas was highly concentrated, invisible and lethal, divine wrath made manifest.

The intake unit of First Union Arena's central air conditioning/heating was in the basement, along with various circuit breakers, power generators, and the lockers of the unfortunate Event Staff members. The Shove It Up concert would be their last event. This was unavoidable, and Patterson had no real qualms about it. They were not-quite-innocent bystanders, however badly they might have needed the money. Still, those most deserving of a luxury suite in hell, the promoters, were likely nowhere near. The world was large, there was a lot of filth to spread, and only so much could be done via the Internet.

The corners of Patterson's tight lips twitched with unbidden mirth at the thought that the concert would indeed be a gas. But not for the sleeping guard, who would die via a bullet from the plastic gun Patterson had carried in with him. A few simple pieces of equipment—a forged ticket and the gun—and all of the "security" measures in place within the arena, starting with the metal detectors, were worthless. Security, anti-terrorism, kill the Jihadist before he kills you, but let the more insidious terrorists—the ones who poison souls—waltz right into the arena and set up on stage. Provide them with a devil-worshipping audience. Sold out.

When Patterson shot the guard in his temple, the gun's report was like a punctuation mark to amazingly loud snoring. The phlegmy exhalations had shaken the guard's body, much as the bombast of Shove It Up caused the arena to physically throb, even down in the basement. The concert would likely end in a slightly more piecemeal fashion, one or two band members dropping their instruments first, perhaps with a final screech, and keeling over a second or so before the other idiots noticed, before they came crashing down themselves.

Blood poured from the side of the guard's head. Its sudden red brightness was the more striking in contrast with his dark skin, with the dusty dullness of his close-cropped salt and pepper hair. Patterson froze, or the moment did. In his former career as a thief, he'd never killed or even shot anyone, although he employed the threat often enough. Now he'd moved on to bigger and better things.

It couldn't have taken nearly as long as it seemed for the guard, whose head had already been drooping halfway down to his knees, a line of saliva dangling from his open mouth, to collapse over his own fat stomach, to roll off the metal folding chair and onto the concrete floor like some viscous, jellied mass. Fortunately for Patterson, he was the only witness to this implosion of a life. He'd come prepared to shoot his way out of the arena if need be, or to die trying. Neither seemed a likely scenario now. The dimly lit, cavernous basement was largely deserted. Its gloomy expanse formed an echo chamber for death metal, or whatever it was that the mohawked, leather-and-stud clad members of Shove It Up blasted out of their instruments, converting the basement into a metaphor for hell, a harbinger of things to come.

"Bless me, Father Boyfucker, for I have sinned
Stuck a needle into my skin—"

The lyrics—non-melodic ranting superimposed upon instrumentation that evoked a screeching train wreck replayed again and again—impelled Patterson out of his temporary paralysis. He was not a Catholic. But Shove It Up had blasphemed Jesus repeatedly in its so-called music. The idea was to profane everything holy as loudly as you could, and to do it repeatedly, taking advantage of Christian forgiveness and giving a new meaning to the term *filthy rich* in the process. Patterson was sure that neither the band members nor their fans, as they breathed their last, would appreciate the irony that they were following in the footsteps of Christ, who had died for their sins.

Locating the security camera—they were never that hard to find, it was like he could feel their subtle heat on his skin—he faced it and defiantly bellowed what he considered some blasphemy of his own. If they couldn't pick it up over that amplified trash, well, then they could read his lips. Patterson stuck the gun under his belt and laid the canister and gas mask at his feet, a safe distance from the spreading pool of the guard's blood. Then he removed the gloves. Ordinarily, picking the lock on the door of the room housing the intake unit would have been a piece of cake, only slightly more difficult than shifting gears on a manual transmission, if there were any of those left around. But he was a bit shaky, more with excitement than fear. He rarely used two hands as he did now, one to steady the other. Still, the job was done in no more than a minute. He stepped into the room, into the destiny that had been awaiting him his entire life. Of that, he had no doubts.

During his run-through the previous night, Patterson had discovered that the intake unit itself was unprotected. It stood in front of him now like a monolithic oracle of destruction, insatiable, its nonstop inhalation producing a powerful, keening roar which, fittingly enough, all but obliterated Shove It Up's musical mayhem, along with the screaming and stomping of the fans. The roar intensified as he slid the filter out from the unit. Unleashed, it blasted through the vacated slot, evoking the sonic emissions of a turbojet engine at close range.

Patterson would have instinctively fallen back, were he not already staggering beneath the weight of the unwieldy filter. It finally crashed to the floor. A cloud of dust and grit arose from its corrugated surface. He covered his face with both hands and coughed, turning away, nearly gagging. Nonetheless, a smile briefly played at his lips. He was receiving a diluted dose of his own medicine, a humbling reminder of his own mortality, and of the salvation that had been his since he'd accepted the ever-patient Jesus into his heart.

Half a minute late, he donned the gas mask. He'd paid cash for it at a Ranger Surplus store in White Plains. To his surprise, some of the same punk types who'd probably camped overnight to get Shove It Up tickets were clustered around the locked display cases, ogling hunting knives, guns, even grenades. Once home, Patterson modeled the mask in front of a mirror. He was astonished. It was as if he'd been transformed once again by God, his countenance becoming the impartial, featureless face of justice, of a righteous avenger whose eyes were naked windows, a seer, a search-and-destroyer of sin—although he knew that, in fact, there'd been no searching involved.

Lewd posters for the Shove It Up concert, featuring the frenzied, howling faces of band members, had been plastered all over downtown White Plains. The Hot Beef Injection tour, named for their latest CD. No, there was no searching involved. His mission had found him, announced by the lurid posters for a show in the Bronx, Sin City sending its tentacles north. Hot Beef Injection. Well, he had an injection of his own to administer now. And the boys wouldn't feel a thing, at least until they arrived in hell. They worshipped the devil? They deserved a little home cooking.

Still, given his past history of mistakes, and the humbleness that came with the gift of salvation, not to mention the enormity of the act to which he'd been called, Patterson had felt the need to consult with the Reverend Tate beforehand. Maximilian Tate, founder and spiritual leader of the Christian Crusade, had so named the organization with apologies to no one, Muslim or otherwise. After all, Christ had been unequivocal: "He who is not with Me is against Me." And individuals who were not saved were damned. Especially those who defiled His name.

Not surprisingly, the reverend was a powerful man. Even "mainstream" Christian leaders, while publicly painting him as a "fringe" Christian—if a Christian at all—were still obliged to pay attention to his words. He was a self-described Christian Militant. Some called that a contradiction in terms. But it was also an identity that was being adopted by more and more individuals, who were fed up with the flouting of Jesus's teachings in America, a country founded, as the reverend liked to point out, by Christian Militants.

Much to the chagrin of the mainstream—read that "televised from a mega-church"—leaders, Tate's influence was growing. It was only because of Patterson's part-time employment with the maintenance staff at the Holy Church of Christ that he was able to obtain an audience with the reverend, and even then it wasn't easy. But Billy Patterson, especially since his rebirth, was nothing if not persistent.

After finally being summoned, he hustled upstairs straight from one of the fields behind the church. He could barely keep himself still as he was patted down outside the reverend's office by security, on the off-chance that he was wearing a recording device. Patterson was sure that he himself would be recorded, by the reverend's own equipment, but he saw no inequity in this. A man of Maximilian Tate's status needed to exercise all due caution. He was an easy target for the vultures from the liberal media. Their attention was not entirely unwelcome. Still, private audiences with him were intended to be just that. Patterson, champing at the bit, quickly gave his word and scribbled his signature on the form.

The reverend had listened intently as Patterson laid out his idea, its ramifications, and his own qualifications. The words came out non-stop, spring-released, having been stored and suppressed—mostly—for about as long as Patterson could stand it. The path for the second coming was waiting to be cleared. The world needed to see what became of those who blasphemed the name of Jesus. He, Patterson, had picked up some experience with AC units, he'd tried his hand at a lot of things, legal and otherwise, scrounging for that paycheck, hoping for a big haul. Now it was time to render service unto the Lord. And the rewards would be eternal, a limitless paycheck redeemable in heaven, signed by Christ himself.

At this, the reverend's elfin face had creased into a smile. His own words were being offered back up to him, demonstrating again his ability to reach those who before had likely been hopeless, helpless. Clearly, Patterson had been so inspired that he was willing to lay down his life, if necessary—Jesus-like—even if the plan bordered on insanity. Or crossed over the line.

This was not surprising, coming from the wild-eyed Patterson, whose tawny hair was flecked with bits of grass, some protruding as if they had taken root. Still, Reverend Tate's response had been that he'd have to think it over, maybe consult some higher-ups. Patterson's yellowed teeth flashed in a quick smile of his own. He knew that the reverend would pray for guidance, punch in the number of the Lord, to whom he had a direct line.

When he finally heard back from Tate—it only took a few days, but it seemed like forever—Patterson was stunned to hear that the plan had received divine approval. A day or two removed from his initial meeting with the reverend, he'd expected just the opposite. He needed to learn to trust his instincts, to trust himself, now that he was walking in the light of Jesus. And Jesus would surely understand it if he told the reverend a little white lie, in the name of setting his mind at ease.

"No problem, no problem at all," he'd replied, lips set in a thin, grim line, after Tate had warned him to tell no one about the little surprise that awaited Shove It Up and its fans at the concert in the Bronx. But Patterson had, in fact, already run the idea past Frank Tedeschi, his employer and buddy-of-sorts at Tedeschi's Hardware. Patterson worked there part-time, to augment the pitiful salary he received as an assistant groundskeeper at Reverend Tate's church.

If calling Frank Tedeschi his "buddy" was an overstatement, it was still true that Frank was more willing than most to listen to Patterson's critiques of American popular culture.

"Don't take it personally, man," was his stock response when Patterson started getting exercised, and the color began rising in his face.

If Frank was ever really a Christian, he was a lapsed one now, the kind who might make it to church only if it were unavoidable, say for a nephew's communion. *Live and let live* was his creed. *Thy will be done, on the off-chance that You exist.* And that quick laugh, cut short by a customer's approach before its wing-flapping cadence could really get rolling, had been his predictable reaction to the notion of Patterson fumigating the Shove It Up concert. A few minutes later, still assuming that Patterson was joking, Frank had suggested that he "find a gentle woman to curl up in bed with, preferably one with large breasts."

Now, his face inside the gas mask—a fitting metaphor for his separation from other people, even though the only one currently nearby was dead—Patterson approached the AC intake unit with the canister in hand. The gas it contained, highly concentrated and highly poisonous, state-of-the-art, had actually been recommended to him by Reverend Tate. "A maximum cleansing agent," Tate had called it. Patterson mirrored the smile that briefly danced at the corners of the reverend's lips. It seemed that Tate possessed the capability and connections to obtain any information, pertaining to heaven or earth.

Surprised to find himself trembling ever so slightly, Patterson had pocketed the sheet of paper that Tate extended to him over the polished teak desk.

"Two birds with one righteous stone," the reverend declared.

Typed on the plain sheet was contact information for the gas. The contact, Bryan Norton—or whatever his real name was—turned out to be a fortyish Caucasian in a sweat suit that hung loosely on his tall, thin frame. "Patterson?" he said, making a very educated guess as he stepped out of his Ford Escort. His headlights had been extinguished before he drove into the parking lot, this little piece of stealth often being an indication of criminal activity. As it surely was in this case, Patterson knew, at least according to society's laws. But, ultimately, there was only one judge of what was a crime and what was not. Still, crime or otherwise, Patterson was beginning to have second thoughts. He had no desire to fry on a terrorism rap or to go through the attendant vilification and infamy beforehand. Gamely, he tried to remind himself that he was acting in the name of Jesus, who had suffered much worse, and in whose presence he would spend eternity.

Patterson struggled to keep his hand steady as he took

a gym bag from Norton. "The canister can only be opened once, and then it's curtains," Norton matter-of-factly informed him. It went without saying, but he said it anyway: "Have a gas mask on beforehand. You don't wanna breathe in the tiniest leak of this stuff—unless you have a death wish."

Norton, his face overlain by the brim of a baseball cap, took a last look around, quickly scanning the parking lot, although he'd have needed a search beam to see much. He wordlessly ducked into the Escort and drove off. Patterson was left holding the bag. Or so he'd told himself, in a joking attempt to calm his rampaging nerves as he slid back into his own car.

This was for real now. And it was a whole different ball game from petty thievery. The simple transaction he'd just engaged in was the beginning of an upheaval that would radically alter the world. On a more visceral level, what he was really holding in his hands was the extermination of maybe seventeen thousand people. Possibly his own as well. They deserved it, but still…

Patterson just did it. He watched himself unscrew the top of the canister, a job made slightly more cumbersome by the work gloves, which would leave only the invisible fingerprints of the Lord. The gas was barely visible as it seeped out like an exhalation on a borderline January day. It was that innocent looking—mass death in a breath. All of it, maybe twenty seconds worth, disappeared into the intake unit's powerful suction, virtually ripped from Patterson's hands. The poison would now diffuse throughout the system, exit through all of its vents.

As he ran toward the nearest door, which opened onto a loading dock, Patterson felt as if his own body was diffusing, expanding, as if his soul were leaping upward, a process seemingly augmented by the still-blasting music. The giddy rush that he felt was jarred loose from him as he smashed into the door, harder than he intended to, or would've, had he been calculating, and had the gas mask not compromised his vision. The bar latch along the width of the door depressed beneath the force of his body. Patterson burst out onto the loading dock platform. The act of yanking off the gas mask blinded him for a couple of seconds, long enough so that he didn't see his assailants until they'd already gotten the jump on him. But it was his dumb luck—for however long it lasted—that the first blow of a club was absorbed by the gas mask and his upraised left forearm, rather than his head. In recoiling from the sudden impact, he unintentionally ducked a second club, coming from the other side. It ripped the air above him.

A few moments' worth of action, but they seemed to unfold in slow motion. Patterson elbowed the second guy in the stomach. Then he reached inside his pants pocket. Before he could extract the plastic gun, the first attacker landed another blow, this time to Patterson's left shoulder. That side of his body went numb. But this hardly mattered. He'd been supercharged with adrenaline, to begin with. Now he was a wounded tiger.

Patterson slammed a knee into the first guy's crotch. As he reached for the gun again, he was tackled by a third man, who slammed him up against a van that was backed up to the dock. Thug number three ripped the gun away. As Patterson lunged for it, the second guy's club landed against his skull. He went limp, collapsing into the tangle of bodies. Two of the assailants heaved Patterson into the rear of the van. They quickly slammed the doors.

CHAPTER 2

Laureen Tedeschi sat in the upper deck of First Union Arena. She was wrecked, having repeatedly inhaled herbal essence in the front seat of her boyfriend's car, windows shut. Now her eyes were closed, and the music alone existed. It was as if the power chords were erupting from inside of her in rapid-fire succession, blasting her ever upward before she could alight, over and over, each more explosive than the last, leaving her limp, at their mercy, gone, subsumed, *Take me, do me.* And that was just the guitar intro to "Mother Mary," maybe ten seconds that seemed to last forever.

Unwilling to dilute the rush, she kept her eyes closed as Duane Sicko, lead singer for Shove It Up, stepped to the mike:

"Sweet Mother Mary, won't you give me some?" he roared, his gravelly voice riding the chords directly into her skull. "I'll try to pull out before I come. They call me motherfucker not for no reason. This is the time, and this is the season."

Outrage on top of sound, double your pleasure. Shove It Up was all about smashing taboos, screaming, and blaspheming. She fervently wished that Mother Angelica, the headmistress who had kicked her out of Good Counsel High School, was sitting beside her. She could almost see the good sister grooving to the music, crucifix bouncing on her flat penguin chest. The image caused Laureen to laugh out loud. She choked on the succeeding inhalation.

Her last thought was that she had only been joking.

CHAPTER 3

The phone call came at three in the morning. There were two possibilities: a wrong number—likely dialed under the influence—or a tragedy. Someone was dead. When Frank Tedeschi heard his brother's voice through the receiver, laden with grief—that much was obvious from the first syllable—death in the family was his first assumption. Or maybe one looming in the future, a slow, agonizing deterioration, hope dying first. Maybe their mother's breast cancer, supposedly eliminated by a mastectomy seven months previously, had metastasized. The surgery and its grueling aftermath had only served to prolong her suffering.

"Bobby?" he said, double-checking, his usage of his brother's childhood name a reflexive offer of support and sympathy. Of the two of them, Rob would take it harder than he would. All of this was apparent to Frank in the instant after he heard his brother gasp his name, in the nano-second it had taken him to transition from deep sleep to complete wakefulness.

This was the first contact he'd had with Rob—the name his younger brother had adopted, and stuck with, as a plebe at the police academy—in well over a month. As much as possible, they visited their parents, or their mother in the hospital, separately. Outside of family get-togethers, they usually didn't have much to do with each other, by mutual preference.

"What is it?" said Frank, his calm voice seeming to come from elsewhere. He stroked the shoulder of his wife Julie, who'd fairly lifted off the bed at the sound of the phone.

"Laureen—" Rob's voice broke.

"*Laureen*?" Frank repeated dumbly, pleadingly. His niece was a favorite of his. She was also his main regret over his semi-estrangement from Rob. "What happened? Is she—"

"First Union Arena. You didn't hear? Shit, it only just happened tonight. The concert…Shove It Up?"

"Shove It Up? Yeah, right. I've seen the posters up here. All over, actually. Wall to wall."

"Right. Well—" Rob paused. Frank could hear him sucking air, the receiver lending this sound a rasping, desperate quality. "—they gassed the arena. Fucking terrorists. Laurie, she went. She was at the concert."

Frank shut his eyes, as if to meet head-on the pain he felt spreading inside of him, or maybe reverse time, slip back into sleep state, nightmare-less. "No. God, no."

"I couldn't stop her, Frank. I can't lock her in the house anymore. She's eighteen, she earned the money, she…"

The sound of his brother's sobbing through the receiver caused Frank to squirm in bed, as if his skin would soon be incapable of containing his burgeoning grief, the kind of feeling he thought himself to have left behind forever, in Vietnam. "I'll tell you in a minute," he promised Julie in a shaky voice, while his free hand stroked her hair, an action he couldn't recall beginning.

He nodded, swallowing, as she repeated the name, a spreading whisper of concern, a rumor of death: "Laureen?"

Frank gripped the phone tightly. "Bobby, try to…try to hang in, okay? How do you know this? How'd you—"

"I couldn't sleep, for a change. Put on the tube. News bulletin. Fucking Arabs. They—" Rob faltered.

"They know who did it? They caught the bastards?"

"Uh-uh. But who else would do it? Fucking towel-heads—" His voice broke again. "I gotta get over there."

"They probably sealed it off, man. Especially if it was poison gas."

"Frank, I'm a cop."

"That's true. And you're also a very worried parent, who doesn't know anything for sure yet. If this is terrorism, there'll probably be FBI there, what have you. Right? They're gonna tell you that you can't go near the place. And they'll make it stick."

"They can try."

Frank resisted a wayward impulse to tell his brother that he'd probably been watching too many action flicks. Not that this had anything to do with anything. Rob, even though a rapt spectator, had been known to comment on what crap it all was. He was a cop himself, a detective, and this explosion-a-minute bullshit bore no resemblance to reality. Cop work was a grind. That was true, even if a dead body was involved. Of course, it usually didn't belong to one's child.

"Bobby, we don't know how long it takes that stuff to dissipate. Even if you got through, assuming you could find her in the first place, that concert was probably sold out. Besides, you'd need a gas mask, at least."

"Definitely. I'll stop by the stationhouse," Rob said, having apparently thought that far ahead.

He'd been lucky enough to pull duty in the Northeast Bronx, Wakefield, a short distance from where he lived in Yonkers. It was not much farther from Co-op City, where First Union Arena had been constructed five years previously, a belated finishing touch to the transformation of the marshlands at the edge of the Bronx into one of the most densely populated areas in the country, maybe the world, with families of cooperators stacked in buildings a mile high. Add a huge arena filled to capacity, and the density went off the charts. From that standpoint, the place was an ideal target for terrorists.

"Police stations are open twenty-four seven. I'll get one for you too. I need you to come with me."

Frank sighed inaudibly. "Bobby, they must've set up a hot line. Maybe—"

"Fuck that. I can't do this alone. I—" Rob's voice failed him again. It took what seemed like forever for him to get a fresh sob out, to expel a tiny bit of the grief that had robbed him of breath, as if he were briefly channeling his daughter's last moments.

"Hey. Try to, just…we don't know for sure yet. Try to…okay, look, I'm coming. Where do you want me to meet you?"

"Come down the parkway." Having gotten that far Rob paused, his breathing audible, as if he were marshalling his resources. "Bronx River. It's far enough away, I don't think they'd have closed it off. Meet me at the parkway and Two-Hundred-Thirty-Third Street. I'll stick my flasher on the roof. You won't be able to miss me."

"How long?"

"Half an hour."

"Okay. Um, where's Nellie?"

"Maryland. She's visiting her mother. I'm not gonna call her until I know for—"

"Right. Gotcha. And drive carefully. I'll see you soon."

Frank inserted the phone back into its charger and turned to find Julie's brown eyes staring at him questioningly, gleaming as if illuminated in the darkness. Her face, shadowed or otherwise, was one he knew better than his own, an embodiment of his own history, which, he knew, was about to take a hairpin turn, having become bored with relative tranquility, with *The kids are in college, life is good.*

Not that the current situation was about *him,* which was worth remembering. As he related the details of the phone call to Julie—haltingly, as the magnitude of what had happened began to hit him with full force—her hand covered her mouth, as if to stifle any more exclamations of "Oh my God!"

Julie Tedeschi, like her husband and his niece, had offered God nothing, except possibly disdain, tempered by disbelief. It was a little late to start calling on Him now.

Frank leaned over to give Julie a hug. She clung to him. He gently pried himself loose from her arms and jumped out of bed to get dressed.

Julie sat up and turned on the television, her relatively wrinkle-free face furrowed with concentration, with sorrow and rage, as red lights flashed in the background behind the on-the-scene reporter.

Frank kissed her goodbye, promised to call and spun toward the bedroom door. It wasn't until he was halfway down the steps, outside of their townhouse, that he flashed on the conversation he'd had with Billy Patterson regarding the Shove It Up concert.

CHAPTER 4

Bobby. Rob. Frank's biological brother—pick the name. A lot of what they'd called each other over the years would've been unprintable, back in the day. Back when they had a relatively good relationship, big brother Frank not having been inclined toward bullying, getting his combat fix as a high school wrestler who *took it to the mats*, or so they joked, residents of Pelham Bay, Little Italy in Da Bronx. Back before Frank, bored with life in the neighborhood, capable but not especially interested in going to college, had enlisted in the army. He'd shipped out to Vietnam.

Amazed to eventually find himself home again in one piece, if a mite skittish mentally, he'd dedicated himself to protesting the war, wearing his camouflage fatigues and long hair. While Frank was still overseas, Rob had been admitted to the police academy. He became a rookie cop—*piglet,* in the vernacular of the counter culture—whose brother was demonstrating in the streets, and clashing with New York's finest. The rift that developed between them only widened over time.

As he drove down now to meet Rob, jazz up loud, a hedge against drowsiness, Frank tried to distill all of that time, *traverse in reverse*, summon the brotherly affection that he dimly remembered feeling, back in the day. How was he going to console Rob? That was what it would amount to. Laureen was gone. He knew that in his guts, news reports aside. Maybe consoling Rob, somehow, might help him to console himself. As he moved left to pass a tank-like SUV—no easy feat, the guy was well above the speed limit—its taillights shimmered and blurred. Fortunately, traffic was sparse on the Sprain Brook in the wee hours.

Rob was prowling in front of his parked car on 233rd Street, above the Bronx River Parkway, jacket-less with short sleeves in the autumn chill. He waved one thick arm above his head. Frank couldn't possibly miss him, even without the roof of his car flashing red. The way Rob squinted in the direction of Frank's windshield, furrowing his forehead with its receding hairline, that square-shouldered torso, his stomp-walk, all of this was caught in the ultraviolet gleam of a streetlamp. Frank pulled to the curb behind Rob and jumped out.

"You better park on Webster," said Rob by way of greeting, already moving toward his own car. "Some of these assholes who work the night shift at my precinct, it's like quota time for parking tickets, proof that they weren't cooping."

His voice was gruffly matter-of-fact, just another day, or very early morning. A couple of minutes later, Frank slid into the front seat next to him, offering a quick pat on the shoulder. Rob pulled out before the passenger door was completely closed.

"Long time no see," said Frank, as the car sped up 233rd Street, toward the elevated subway station on White Plains Road.

"Right." As Rob ran the red light on White Plains, his horn honking and top light flashing, he swerved around a car that had braked for him, halfway into the intersection. The gas masks—two small masses of straps, wide plastic windows, and protruding metal snouts—rattled on the back seat. "I don't know how I'm gonna handle this, Frank," he rasped. "If she's…"

"We don't know anything for sure." Frank shook his head, dismayed at the hollow sound of his own bullshit. He sneaked a swipe at his eyes with the sleeve of his windbreaker. "And you're a tough son of a bitch—with apologies to Mom. Remember? If you have to, you'll handle it."

As they got closer to Co-op City, the sound of sirens came from every direction, non-stop, as if myriad car alarms had gotten stuck all at once. Fire engines, ambulances, the night was alive with red, white and blue flashing lights. Rob's car with its one winking top light, dwarfed among the speeding emergency vehicles, was like the *Little Engine that Could.* Except that it couldn't. As Frank had predicted, First Union Arena was sealed off for a radius of at least a mile. Rob parked on a side street off of Dyre Avenue and Thayer. He charged Frank with the responsibility of remembering the name, and they started walking past darkened private houses of rectangular brick, metal awnings, car ports, tiny front yards demarcated by chain link fences, *my land.* The streets, never featuring all that many pedestrians even in daylight, became more crowded as the brothers went on, their footsteps audible in the grim silence, as if the distraught parents were automatons, drawn by some otherworldly entity, a spaceship.

Frank and Rob reached the barricades by plowing through a mob of Shove it Up fans' family members, some of them with pajama bottoms showing beneath their jackets, red, white and blue shimmering in their leaking eyes. They made it through with the help of Rob's badge, which he waved in the air like a miniature machete. Still, the fact that he was a cop ultimately counted for nothing.

There were already plenty of cops on the scene by then, along with FBI and FEMA personnel who'd been flown in by a fleet of helicopters. Haz-mat clad FEMA men were already inside the arena, checking to see if anyone was still alive. Radioed indications were not good.

There would be a hot line set up later in the morning. Rob was off-duty and out of his jurisdiction. The best he could do now was to back off. The only thing, unless he wanted to be busted for obstruction. He gazed incredulously at the FBI agent who so informed him. This was after the bastard had actually smirked at the sight of the brothers' gas masks. Fortunately, the guy just ignored the stream of curses Rob unleashed as he wrestled with Frank, who finally succeeded in turning him around in the direction of Thayer Avenue. This process, which cleared a small space in the crowd behind them, was repeated a couple of times before they reached the car.

The sky began to lighten as the brothers drove west on 233rd Street. Rob was beside himself, his face streaming tears as he vowed to take out as many Arabs as he could find—and he *would* find them. Unless he did himself first. As he'd asserted over the phone, it had to be the Arabs, with their fucking *Jihad*.

Frank thought so too. Or, that was where he would have put his money, the other possibility that came to mind being too much to contemplate. In fact, it was only to distract Rob that Frank mentioned his conversation with Billy Patterson. "Bizarre coincidence, no?"

But when Billy didn't show up for work the next morning, or answer his phone, Frank began to seriously entertain the notion that he hadn't just been talking trash. Frank's mind, fogged with exhaustion after having had minimal sleep the night before, cleared as if by magic. In a flash of incredulity mixed with self-recrimination—why the hell hadn't he done this already?—he picked up the stock room phone at Tedeschi's Hardware and called Paul Fowlkes, an ex-army buddy of his who had started working for the FBI a year or so after Vietnam.

Fowlkes—after ragging him about not calling since when…many moons ago—listened attentively. Then he informed Frank that he himself was not involved in the investigation of the mass murder at First Union Arena. Surprisingly, because it seemed like half the bureau already was. Still, from what he knew second or third hand, the focus was on Islamic terrorists. But he would throw the name of Billy Patterson into the mix, see what he could find out. Then he'd be in touch.

Rob had actually gone in to the stationhouse, where he sat "zoning out" on his computer screen, dialing the as-yet-inoperative hot line every five minutes. He barely seemed to remember Frank mentioning some guy who worked for him at the store, who wanted to off Shove It Up himself, a piece of information that had flown by like the run-down bodegas and apartment buildings on the way back from Co-op City. Apparently, Duane Sicko and the boys had friends everywhere. On hearing that Frank thought that this Billy Patterson might have actually done the deed, Rob's initial reaction was, "Yeah, right. Get real." But then a minute later he called back.

"Frank, run that by me again," he said. "Just for the hell of it. Laureen's dead. Barring a miracle. And we both know there's none of those around. But maybe I can still do *something* for her." Rob's voice nearly gave. "I mean, other than ranting about the Arabs. And maybe if I can, then I'll stop thinking about eating my gun. Maybe I can get through IDing her—get through the funeral."

Frank agreed: they needed to find Billy, ASAP. He felt that way even after Fowlkes called him back two days later and said that All for Allah had been identified as the group responsible for the gassing at First Union Arena. He correctly assumed that Frank had already heard this, or seen it. The screaming headlines were hard to miss. And there were only a few TV channels that hadn't carried President Flowers's address to the nation, in which, gazing with steely resolve into the cameras, he'd named All for Allah as the guilty party. Allegedly guilty, of course.

A heroic FBI agent, Michael Scanlon, had infiltrated the organization, only to be brutally killed. His murder had pointed investigators in the right direction. Predictably, All for Allah had subsequently denied responsibility for the death of agent Scanlon, as well as the unspeakable crime at First Union. Either the US government needed a scapegoat or had staged the thing itself. So claimed AFA's Mohammar Khan, clinging to his microphone as if it were a lifeline. He'd added that President Flowers, who considered himself the "designee of God," was capable of anything.

Frank remembered reading about All for Allah in a magazine article about homegrown religious extremists. In the *New Yorker*, maybe. The group's name, with its mixture of English and Arabic, was intended to convey that its members were citizens of the USA, *all* connoting not only body, soul, and anything generated by either, but also an in-gathering of Muslim America, spiritually and geographically. An area of the country, maybe a state or two, in which women were covered head to toe, with every school teaching the Koran, prayer rugs in every business establishment, and restaurants closed until sundown during Ramadan. Infidels tolerated, but not especially welcome.

All of this was to be achieved peacefully, as willed by Allah the merciful and compassionate. The leaders of AFA publicly emphasized that the Koran was anti-violence. While condemning the US Government's "chauvinistic and exploitative" policies toward Islamic nations, they took pains to avoid advocating its overthrow, or the premature death of the president. And despite regular audits, no evidence could be found that they were providing funds to any terrorist organizations, so designated by the government on a list that seemed to expand daily.

In fact, AFA could be considered extremist only because of its precepts and goals, which were no more absolutist than, say, those of Reverend Maximilian Tate's Christian Crusade, but which had emanated from the wrong religion. Especially post-9/11. Beards beneath turbans or kaffiyehs and hidden female faces made the general public uncomfortable. All for Allah's unequivocal condemnation of the attacks on the World Trade Center did little to assuage the paranoia. It was true that assaults on American Muslims, many victims being more assimilated than the AFA members, had created a wing of the organization that advocated responding in kind. Members of this wing were castigated by the "mainstream" AFA leadership. Both factions justified their positions with quotes from the Koran, which was seemingly every bit as malleable as the Bible.

Squeezing the receiver, Frank told Fowlkes that he didn't necessarily believe the government's version of events. That might've been true even had he no suspicions about Billy Patterson—he would believe the time of day if it issued from the Flowers administration, but not much else. Which was generally true of Fowlkes as well, although it was hard for him to buy the idea that they were lying now, about First Union, the AFA and Scanlon.

That would be a whole new level of mendacity. Fowlkes informed Frank that Billy Patterson was, or had been, a small-time crook, one with absolutely no connection to All for Allah, Al-Qaeda, or any other Islamic group. No emails—didn't even own a computer, it seemed—and his phone records were strictly unremarkable. He'd spent his time over the past year working, eating and sleeping. Praying, too.

"Sounds about right," Frank said. "Of course, it's not impossible that Billy is a very effectively disguised Islamic terrorist, one who just has a problem with keeping his mouth shut. Anything's possible. I think we both learned that in 'Nam, and since. Still, Billy a Jihadist? Uh-uh."

"So…file a missing person's report, Comrade Tedeschi."

Well, he'd done that already, with the county cops in White Plains. They duly filled out the forms for a missing ex-con, a drifter gone adrift once more. And his brother Rob fared no better at the Wakefield Precinct where he was based. His commanding officer, fellow cops, and detectives had clapped him on the shoulder, administered manly hugs and offered whatever support they could provide. *Anything.*

The CO had also suggested that the best place for him to be now was home with his family. He totally understood Rob's desire to avenge his daughter's death, even if it was as yet unconfirmed, and even if his suspicions about his brother's vanished employee at the hardware store led one to suspect that his grief was getting the better of him. Regardless, like all the other stationhouses in the northeast Bronx, everyone at Wakefield had been pulling overtime dealing with the fallout from First Union. Pursuit of this Billy Patterson was not feasible—especially since the perps were already known, and most of them were either in federal custody or about to be. Unfortunately, the wheels of justice would have to do their own slow turning before the terrorists could be hung by their balls until dead.

"That's a direct quote. If second-hand," said Frank, capping off a brief summary.

Fowlkes chuckled. He didn't sound at all surprised by the attitude of Rob's CO. "But for sure, let me know if Patterson turns up," he said, his tone leaving Frank with the feeling that he was being patronized. "The bureau'll definitely haul the guy in for questioning if he becomes available. But assigning personnel to search for him? That's not gonna happen."

The conversation had left Frank with the impression that Paul Fowlkes probably had been working for the feds too long. Maybe he'd been co-opted. He had returned from 'Nam several months after Frank. Ex-Corporal Tedeschi, having already gone through reentry, was able to provide some much-needed support. Part of this involved introducing Fowlkes to the Vietnam Vets Against the War. They'd covered each other's backs on a new battlefield, where at least the enemy was identifiable and in plain view—excepting, of course, FBI and CIA infiltrators.

Eventually, Fowlkes, half as a lark, had decided to apply for a job with the FBI himself. He would fuck the system from within. To his surprise, he was accepted as a trainee. It appeared that the bureau's vaunted powers of surveillance had somehow failed in his case. Perhaps none of the photographs of the soldiers-turned-traitors had matched the appearance of the clean-shaven dude who'd walked in for an initial screening.

Currently, he was working on the American end of international drug smuggling, an assignment with which he could live in good conscience. Or so he informed Frank, shortly before they hung up. On hearing that Frank would likely be getting his own feet wet as an investigator, Fowlkes wished him luck and reiterated his sympathy at the apparent loss of Frank's niece.

CHAPTER 5

"If I hadn't reported him missing, I doubt anyone else would've. He wouldn't just not show up and not call. I mean, the guy showed up at work every day on time, like clockwork," Frank said, tapping the puffed arm of his sofa as if counting off a few seconds. "Well, maybe his supervisor at work, head groundskeeper, Sylvester Stout—maybe he would've reported it. Only other person in Billy's life, at least that he talked about, was Reverend Tate. He used to tell me all the time what a holy man the guy is. Direct line to God, but still considered himself a humble servant, a warrior in the 'Christian Crusade.'" Frank shook his head. "Probably one of those warriors who get others to do their dirty work for them. If Billy did this thing—*if*—I'll bet he got some inspiration from Tate. When I spoke to the bastard—at first, they wouldn't put me through—but then when I told them what it was about, bingo, the reverend was on the line. He said no, he understood from Stout that Billy hadn't been to work there, either. He appreciated my concern, natch. But his guess was that Billy had unfortunately reverted to his old ways, probably went off on a bender or something, and never came back. Once a sinner—even if the reverend has laid his hands on you, I guess. He said, 'We tried to help him. Strengthen him in Jesus,' I think that's the way he put it. And the job was supposed to be part of that. 'Tending the Lord's Grounds.' Uh-huh."

Rob took a sip from his can of Budweiser. "And you think Tate's bullshitting?"

"Is the Pope Catholic?" Frank paused. In the two weeks since the death of his niece Laureen, he'd spent more time with Rob than he had in the previous five years. Understandably, he hadn't seen the barest hint of a smile on his brother's face. This inquiry regarding *il Papa's* religion, a reflexive joke between them as teenagers—uttered out of earshot of their mother—did not do the trick now. "Still, it's possible that all that 'religious' zeal that Billy worked up, maybe the effort just got to be too much, maybe he rebounded in the opposite direction. But the timing, he vanishes right after First Union Arena, after telling me—"

"Okay," said Rob, nodding impatiently and taking another sip. "I think we've covered this already. So—first step, we pay the reverend a visit?"

They were sitting in Frank and Julie's living room in Armonk, New York. The brothers were working on a case together, one unauthorized by the NYPD, FBI, or anyone else. This was an eventuality that neither of them would have previously placed within the realm of remote possibility. Still, there they were. Frank's house had become their de facto headquarters since they were very leery of using email or the phone. And a convenient side effect was that Rob had an ongoing excuse to be away from his own place.

His late daughter Laureen had similarly avoided home, except in the wee hours when she needed a place to sleep—so Rob informed his brother while filling up on beer, filling in the blanks that had grown over time. Grounding Laureen had become pointless, unless Rob or his wife wanted to stay up all night to keep her from sneaking out. They'd bitterly joked that she'd become like a ghost, that this was somehow fitting, given her goth/punk clothing and the torture chamber ambiance of her bedroom, where most of her scant time in the house was spent. Now the irony was almost more than Rob could bear.

He saw Laurie everywhere, saw her fingerprints on everything she'd touched, the indentation of her form on the black sheets that still covered her bed. It was like she'd appropriated the place for her tomb, not caring for the one that had been provided for her, spiteful beyond the "end"—not that the term even applied, given her constant presence in Rob's mind. He could see her as a young girl, as a punk person and places in-between. The persona didn't matter, he'd confided a couple of nights previously. Rob had loved her stubbornly, unconditionally, even after she'd become someone to whom his authority was meaningless. She'd known her leverage over his heart and used it to inflict pain, as the spirit moved her.

Rob's wife Nellie had basically been under sedation since their daughter's death had been confirmed. But this had taken more than a week. Beforehand she claimed, in between extensive fits of sobbing, that not knowing for sure was the hardest part. Not that there was much uncertainty that Rob could see. They hadn't heard from Laurie since she left for First Union Arena. It wouldn't have been totally out of character for her not to come home and not to call. But she'd been psyched to go, her excitement was obvious at the rare dinner together the three of them shared the night before, the more so in contrast with her usual veneer of sullen disdain. And after the three a.m. newscast that might as well have announced the imminent explosion of planet Earth, he never doubted that Laurie had gone. Or was gone.

Still, he tried to "humor" Nellie. That was the way he

inadvertently phrased it in conversation with Frank, almost choking on the word as it came out of his mouth. But after Rob and his wife positively identified the body of their daughter—a process that had nearly killed Nellie as well—she seemingly had no further need for him.

Before the Shove It Up concert, their relationship had been rocky at best, arguments over how to deal with Laureen being one large factor. Afterward, dealing with Laurie's death was something Nellie couldn't begin to do. Medications did it for her. Added to the usual antidepressant and cholesterol pills were now two different sedatives, all kept track of by Nellie's spinster sister Fran, who volunteered to look after her. Her husband could've moved out. Frank's house became a way station—and a place to coordinate the only police work that meant anything to Rob now.

The delay in getting to identify Laurie's body was owing in part to the time needed for the poison gas to dissipate. The surrounding area, Co-op City, had been evacuated. Schools in the Bronx and Upper Manhattan were closed to students and were used as shelters for those residents who had no other options. After it was finally deemed safe enough for FEMA and construction workers to enter First Union Arena en masse, it took another several days for them to convert it into a giant morgue.

Their first action was to turn the central air conditioning to maximum. Having served as a conduit for mass extinction, it now functioned as an aid in preserving the corpses of the victims. They were covered with sheets and stacked like loaves of bread on metal scaffolding. Those who had died with identification in their pockets or purses—the large majority—were stacked in alphabetical order. Each was afforded his or her own little rectangle of grating. This left criss-cross marks on the backs of the cadavers as they were placed on stretchers and carried downstairs to the arena floor for identification then returned to the same space pending pickup by a funeral home.

Two young Latino men in dark cotton uniforms and sanitary face masks had turned to carry Laurie back to her "resting place." Their terminology. They'd probably been hired, trained, and begun their temporary employment in the space of a day. They patiently waited as Rob peeled his wailing wife off the stretcher. He bear-hugged Nellie to keep her away, to keep her from collapsing, to prevent himself from doing the same thing. Finally, Rob signed the death certificate proffered by a FEMA worker and indicated on the form the name of the funeral home that would be picking up his daughter's remains. Then he half-towed, half-carried Nellie out of the arena.

As they'd slowly driven away from First Union Arena, Rob tried to focus on the work he had to do, in tandem with his formerly estranged brother. He attempted to sift through the details, starting with a former part-time employee at the family hardware store, a petty crook turned religious fanatic turned mass murderer. Possibly.

Rob drove his Plymouth Blazer past the sawhorse barricades and the flashing lights. All of this "security" was a mite late.

Moving in the opposite direction was a line of hearses that evoked a wagon train, a caravan shrouded by the gathering darkness. Farther along, west on Baychester Avenue, the flashing lights had been replaced by twinkling Christmas decorations in the windows of private houses and soot-brown apartment buildings. They put them up earlier every year. *Laurie*. Even the thundering of the elevated train above White Plains Road couldn't erase her name from his brain. It *had* drowned out the almost unbearable sound of Nellie's whimpering, for maybe ten seconds.

The driveway leading up to the Holy Church of Christ in Katonah, New York, was maybe a couple of football fields in length and lined with trees on both sides. For stretches they were evenly spaced, leading Frank and Rob to wonder if Billy had had a hand in planting them. Probably not, he hadn't been working there long enough. A couple of late-dropping acorns landed with surprising impact on the roof of Rob's car as he drove, fallout from the trees perpetuating themselves. If you wanted to believe in God, which Rob did and didn't, then you had to admire the way He'd set things up. At least until men laid their clammy hands on the world around them.

One thing about which neither brother had any doubts was that if God existed, he could only view with disdain most of the people who claimed to represent Him—men like Reverend Tate, to whom the Tedeschis were about to pay an unannounced visit.

The grounds of the church, headquarters for the Christian Crusade, were surrounded by a gated, iron picket fence, minus the spikes. Rob grunted when Frank suggested that spikes might've given the place too much of a medieval feel, even if the shoe fit.

"Yeah, they would. Plus, they don't even need 'em. Fence's probably electrified, or maybe it's got sensors," he replied. Then he twisted around and talked into a speaker that fed into a metal and Plexi-glass booth abutting the other side of the fence. "I'm Detective Robert Tedeschi of the New York City Police Department. I'm here with my brother Frank, who spoke with Reverend Tate a few days ago."

As he uttered these words, Rob flashed on the staticky drive-through at Mickey D's, himself and sixteen year-old Laureen, to whom he'd reluctantly agreed to give driving lessons. Her bony elbow resting atop the rolled-down driver's window, she'd responded to the query as to how she could be helped by ordering cheeseburgers, fries, etc., with a nonchalance that was belied by the slight elevation in her pitch. Her girlish pleasure in the act was obvious afterward, when Rob playfully rasped, "Good job, kid." Despite her best effort, she couldn't suppress that beautiful smile of hers, only recently liberated from braces…

"About William Patterson?" said Rob now, taking a deep breath and forging ahead. "We'd like to speak with the reverend again. Just to get a little more information."

The uniformed guard in the booth talked into a cell phone for perhaps a minute. Then, his voice gravelly through the wire mesh, the guard asked Rob if he would mind displaying his badge. Rob sighed and got out of the car. Reaching through the fence, he held the gold shield against the glass. The guard jotted down the serial number and spoke again into his phone. Then the gate slid open.

As the brothers drove past, it occurred to Rob that the guy's booth was a little control room, the external nerve center of the church. A Plexiglass periscope. They rode across a parking lot which, if not as extensive as, say, First Union Arena's, was still several times larger than that of the sizable strip mall that had sprung up on both sides of Tedeschi's Hardware. If the Church of Christ, holy or otherwise, didn't rate the prefix *mega,* it came close.

After Rob parked at the front of the near-empty lot, they walked to the main door. The church evoked a columned state house with a huge golden cross on top, the wave of the future. Its name was written in ornate, equally golden letters well above the entrance, likely situated so as to glow in the light of the morning sun. Frank and

Rob shielded their eyes against the glare. This was augmented by the letters in *hristian rusade,* which descended, respectively, from the capital "C's" in "Church" and "Christ," forming two slightly bowed, off-center legs upon which the name appeared to balance.

The mahogany double doors were locked. Rob pressed the adjoining buzzer. It was more of a bell, a resounding one. The doors were opened almost immediately by a slightly paunchy gentleman in a jacket and tie, deep set brown eyes below a receding salt and pepper hairline. He asked both brothers for picture IDs. Apparently, not everyone was welcome in the House of God. The guy studied driver's licenses and Rob's NYPD detective badge. Then he informed them that it was standard procedure for visitors to the reverend to be patted down beforehand for recording devices. Private "audiences" were intended to be just that.

Rob rolled his eyes. "Hey. If I was wearing a recording device, which I'm not, you wouldn't be able to locate it by patting me down."

Tate's screen-man appeared unimpressed. "Detective Tedeschi, it's only out of respect for your status as a police officer—even if you're from another jurisdiction, and even if the local police have already discussed this matter with the reverend, and seen no reason for further discussion—but out of regard for your status, the reverend has agreed to see you without an appointment. That and his concern for Mr. Patterson. I assume you would have shown me if you had a search warrant or subpoena?"

"You assume correctly," replied Rob, mimicking the guy's clipped, officious tone. He was patted down with surprising dexterity, his shoulder holster and gun duly noted. Rob had to suppress an impulse to bring up his knee when the guy bent over to run fingers down both his legs. Later, he was surprised to discover that his normally peace-loving brother had had exactly the same urge.

"So, what's your name?" Rob asked as they were led down a long, carpeted corridor.

"Cavanaugh."

"Somebody taught you how to pat people down?"

Cavanaugh snickered. "It's not rocket science. But yeah, I've done it enough. Had something of a background in security. Way back. It turned out to be useful, though, because as the reverend's prominence grows, as people hear his message—"

"Some of them might take it the wrong way. Or try to deal with that the wrong way," Frank said.

"Exactly." Cavanaugh looked askance at him, as if wondering if the brothers fell into that category. Rob's gold badge was not necessarily a guarantee of anything. He was strapped, and the line between cops and criminals was notoriously thin.

The door to the reverend's office bore no nameplate. Cavanaugh opened it after knocking once. If that was Tate, his gleaming hair catching fluorescent light maybe a foot above the surface of his broad wooden desk, he was more diminutive than Rob would've expected based on Frank's rendition of his grating bass telephone voice.

Rob's attention was still outside. He was listening for the sound of Cavanaugh's departing footsteps. This he didn't hear, but then the hallway was carpeted. As was the reverend's office. Tate's small footprints took life for nanoseconds before vanishing as he strode toward Frank and Rob, hand extended. His hazel eyes, wide and prominent in his fine-featured face, scanned the brothers as if trying to decide which was which.

"I'm Reverend Tate," he said to both, inviting them to make the distinction for him. "Maximilian Tate."

"Frank Tedeschi."

The reverend's grasp when they shook hands was surprisingly strong, as if he were bent on compacting Frank's thick fingers. "Nice to meet you in person, Mr. Tedeschi, after our phone conversation. Has there been any progress in locating Billy? Maybe your dropping in like this is an indication that there hasn't been. This is your brother?"

"I'm Rob Tedeschi. Detective, New York City Police Department, although I'm not on duty at the moment." Tate welcomed him with another isometric handshake. "And you're right about that. Billy Patterson has not been found. According to Frank—" Rob took a fast glance in his brother's direction. "—you were…influential where Mr. Patterson was concerned."

"In a positive way, I'm sure." The reverend flashed a quick smile that could've come off a poster for dental hygiene. With a small sweep of his hand, he invited the brothers to sit in two black leather armchairs facing his desk. Also facing a huge wooden crucifix, with Christ's glazed eyes gazing upward. This was attached to the wall maybe two feet above Tate's high-backed chair. Jesus's tattered clothing presented a stark contrast with the reverend's nicely cut jacket and tie. Maybe Frank had picked this up too, judging from his smothered laugh, masquerading as throat-clearing. It was as if the tangled beard and hair, superimposed on the clean-shaven reverend's neatly parted hair-do, could've served as a before-and-after commercial, extreme makeover Jesus.

"Billy really came a long way," Tate said as he settled back into the contoured leather backrest. "I take a personal interest in the employees of this church, all of whom are members of this congregation. And who view their work as service to the Lord."

"Right. Billy told me as much," Frank said. "Used to needle me that he was working at Tedeschi's Hardware strictly for cash and that by paying him—it wasn't much, but probably more than he got here—I was really supporting the Christian Crusade, whether I liked it or not."

"I'm guessing the answer was 'not.'"

"Well, if I had to pick one, that would probably be it. Although Billy did his job and was likable enough, a little hyper, yeah, but you could feel that he was trying to find his way, stay straight. And he knew enough not to hassle me about Jesus, belief, or my lack thereof." Frank paused, fixing a defiant gaze on the reverend.

"Yes, well, Billy learned that the Lord makes himself known to people in his own time…sometimes with a little help from those who have already been so blessed." The corners of Tate's thin lips briefly lifted. "He was a quick study, and his devotion…he came to see all his trials as having been preparation for being reborn. I don't know how many of the details of his upbringing you know. The foster care in New Jersey, running away for good at age fourteen. The drugs and drinking, stealing to pay for these things and others, the time in jail." The reverend shook his head ruefully, as if he were reciting a catalogue of the all-but-inevitable consequences of faithlessness. "Billy told me that once he tasted the elixir of Jesus's love, the taste of alcohol was bitter indeed."

Frank peeked over at Rob, whose face was unreadable, impassive, a poker-faced detective's. There was no outer indication of scorn or disbelief. But the same could have been said of Frank, who was already convinced that the reverend was a con artist, at the least. Billy was not given to spouting bad poetry—or any kind—unless maybe he'd been looking to impress the reverend with his devoutness, offering up Tate's own words as evidence. The elixir of Jesus's love, on the rocks.

"Yeah, well, Billy told me that he always had the alcohol under control, that it was difficult to pick locks if you were drunk, or your fingers were trembling. Used to amuse me during down time at the store by picking some of the door locks we had for sale, even the ones advertised as super-secure. Could do it with a large paper clip bent straight." Frank paused, again glancing at Rob, who nodded once. "Billy also told me that he was going to gas First Union Arena," he said matter-of-factly.

If Rob hadn't later corroborated that the reverend had flinched on hearing these words, Frank wouldn't have been sure. Tate fixed his face that quickly, rearranging it into a projection of amused incredulity, as if someone had just told him that a woodchuck was on line two.

"Mr. Tedeschi," Tate said, sighing. "This is why you came here? What, you think Billy was—or is—an All for Allah operative? You actually think that instead of teaching the gospel of Jesus, we're secretly promoting Jihad, the creed of heathens? Anti-Christs? Devils?" The reverend's face flushed with heat. "*If* Billy said that, I'm sure it was pure coincidence, and that he was just letting off steam. When you think about Jesus's sacrifice for mankind, and then think about those cretins, Shove It Up, being given a huge arena in which to promulgate their blasphemous filth in front of thousands of impressionable young people—yes, it can make you angry. But Billy Patterson would never do such a thing. Never. And if you've read the papers, watched TV, it's hard to miss. This terrible tragedy was perpetrated by All for Allah. The evidence is irrefutable. They took advantage of our so-called religious freedom—'so-called' because the only freedom is in Christ.

"These people claim that they're peaceful, but from a heathen religion, only evil can come. 'He who is not with Me is against Me.' Al-Qaeda, All for Allah, your local Imam—it's the same soup—they think the route to heaven is to kill Americans. Young ones with a profligate life style, so much the better."

"Mr. Tate," Rob said in a tight, measured voice, "my daughter was one of those 'profligate young ones.' We buried her last week."

The flinch was slightly more perceptible this time, a tightening of Tate's slender jawbone, a compression of his lips, maybe a brief spasm of conscience, empathy or both. "I didn't know. I'm so very sorry, Detective Tedeschi. I will pray for you. And her."

"Yeah, I'm sure you are. And will. Tell me, *Reverend,* was it also a pure coincidence that Patterson disappeared, never showed up for work, the morning after the attack on First Union Arena?"

"As I told your brother over the phone, I can only conjecture as to why Billy disappeared." Tate cleared his throat and shifted uncomfortably in his chair, which swiveled along with him. "My best guess, given his background, is that he relapsed—temporarily, I hope—into his old ways. I'm still hopeful that he'll show up again, hung-over or in whatever condition, to continue his work for the Lord, tending His grounds. He would never, ever, commit such a horrible crime. A crime against humanity, and against Jesus. Especially not since he was devoted to this church and its teachings."

"I agree," Frank said, preempting a response from Rob, whose dispassionate demeanor had vanished. "Billy would never do such a thing, not on his own, even though, like you say, he was exercised about Shove It Up—there were these lurid posters for the concert all over Katonah, White Plains, you name it—and he was part of your Christian Crusade. But then, First Union Arena actually does get gassed, and he disappears. And All for Allah denies responsibility."

"And you believe them." Tate shook his head. "Maybe, despite their brave talk about heaven, seventy-two virgins, or whatever nonsense they spout, they're really afraid that the wrath of God will finally descend upon them this time. But, as near I can tell, you came here because you think that Billy committed one of the most heinous sins in history, right up there with the Nazis and their gas chambers. And you also think he did it with the approval or encouragement of this church. That is a hideous, unspeakable lie. Outrageous, blasphemous, slanderous, and any other word you want to use. Worse. You need to leave now. Both of you."

Either Tate was genuinely irate, or he was an accomplished performer.

"Fine," replied Rob. "At this point, we have no hard evidence, but—" His head swiveled as the door opened behind them and Cavanaugh stepped through. Rob hardly missed a beat. "Gee, Cavanaugh, it looks like you and the reverend here are the ones who are miked. I should've patted you down. One good turn deserves another."

Cavanaugh snorted. "Very clever. I suggest the two of you leave now, peacefully."

"You thought we had other ideas?"

"Hopefully, no. I wouldn't want to have to disturb the local police, have them come out here to remove two trespassers, who are poaching on their case."

The brothers stood up, Frank reaching for his jacket. Despite the warmth of the reverend's office, Rob had merely unzipped his own, probably having judged it unseemly to sit there with his shoulder holster and gun in plain view.

Frank's vision fell upon the crucifix above Tate's desk. Apparently, his coerced participation in Catholicism as a boy had left a residual influence, despite his best efforts. The carved statuette of Jesus made the current scene feel even more bizarre, with its tremors of hostility that threatened to explode under the watchful eyes of the Prince of Peace.

"I'm sure 'the local police' wouldn't give a shit," asserted Rob, moving toward the door.

"Maybe, maybe not. But they'd probably be amused by these insane accusations you're making while flashing your New York City Police Department Detective's badge. Maybe they'd even lodge a complaint with your commanding officer."

Rob laughed, as he and Frank strode past Cavanaugh, who was obviously intent on following them out. "They'd be welcome to," he said.

CHAPTER 6

Julie's elbow gently nudging him in the ribs tipped Frank into a tenuous waking state, the right side of his face and neck lifting by degrees from the thick bed of her hair. Finally, he sat up on their green paisley sofa.

"This is not the subway, sweetheart," she teased.

He rubbed his face, wiping a spot of drool from the corner of his mouth, from his brown mustache. "Juliet," he murmured, "when the hell was the last time I rode the subway? That's your pleasure, riding with the masses."

"I wouldn't call it that."

"Yeah well, best thing to do, if some weary, drugged or narcoleptic person drifts down onto your shoulder—it's so inviting, they can probably tell that you're a social worker—just stand up, that's all. Gravity will do the rest." Frank yawned deeply. "To that, I can testify."

A week had passed since the Tedeschi brothers had visited the headquarters of the Christian Crusade, almost three weeks since the attack on First Union Arena. Understandably, it still dominated the news. It was during a piece on a bereft single mother who had lost twins—two teenaged boys who'd sported identical mohawks, both dyed a fiery orange—that Frank had drifted off.

This didn't mean that he'd become callous. He missed his niece Laureen keenly, more so than he ever had before her death, more than he missed his own children, both of whom had returned to college after her funeral. Maybe this had to do with all the time he was spending with his brother. Rob had sucked it up, he kept his grief to himself, displaying it outwardly only as a fierce determination to have revenge, justice. But it was likely akin to osmosis, genetic transference, something. Laurie kept showing up inside Frank's head.

He vividly remembered the last time he'd seen her alive. It was at his father's eightieth birthday party. Out of earshot of Grandma and Grandpa, she solicited stories of Frank's long gone drug days with an undisguised fascination that rankled Rob, her eavesdropping father—the more so because she'd unintentionally revealed him as an informant. Frank had pleaded the fifth, except for warning Laurie off illegal chemicals, knowing that this was a little late. He could see her pretty face now, as if she were still standing in front of him, her lips pursed with skepticism, dark eyes twinkling mischievously beneath more darkly mascaraed lids: she understood the game he was playing. She didn't say it, didn't have to.

He couldn't help laughing. She joined in, a little moment of collusion between the Tedeschi clan's foremost rejecters of everything Republican and religious.

But if Laurie's death were still a fresh wound, as if she'd just died yesterday, it was also true that Frank was exhausted. This was supposed to be a quiet evening at home, just him and Julie. If he could stay awake long enough.

Frank's preoccupation with finding out, and proving, the truth about First Union Arena was tantamount to a second job, evenings and weekends, on top of the extra time he was putting in at the store, owing to the absence of Billy Patterson. Still, Julie had been supportive. This was just her nature, she'd likely have been so even if the cause were less compelling. And she was compassionate toward her brother-in-law Rob, who'd never been one of her favorite people. Tonight was the first night in several that she hadn't fed him dinner.

At his daughter's funeral, she'd basically held up his wife Nellie, whose tears were camouflaged in the deep blackness of Julie's dress. They mingled there with Julie's tears, most of which had gone unstanched, both of her hands being occupied in trying to comfort Nellie. Laureen's death had brought the two Tedeschi's-by-marriage together, at least temporarily. Julie called Nellie a couple of times a day, from work and otherwise, for the better part of a week after the funeral. Toward the end of that week, most of the calls were taken by Nellie's sister Fran. Nellie was asleep, sedated. It was best that way. And Rob agreed with this—Nellie would eventually be okay, or as okay as she'd been with the help of her anti-depressants, pre-First Union Arena. Doctors might not be able to do much for victims of poison gas, but they sure as hell could handle depression, anxiety, hysteria, and what-have-you. Welcome to La-La land.

Julie had forced herself to hold her tongue when Rob made these pronouncements. From what she'd gleaned, his marriage had been mostly broken before Laureen's death. And she had long since learned that she couldn't fix everything, or even try. This knowledge was essential for her own sanity as a social worker, dealing with child-abuse cases. Even her success at "fixing" Frank, post-Vietnam, might've been deceptive. Maybe she'd been a factor, or maybe he'd have been fine without her. He was a strong person, one who'd always marched to his own drummer. That was obvious enough when she had tried to talk him out of enlisting in the first place…

With a warm breeze off the Long Island Sound splaying her ponytail, the night held the first hint of summer. Actually, it was more like twilight. They'd been sitting on a bench in Pelham Bay Park, necking. Both of their houses had at least one parent present, leaving them with no convenient location for intimacy, no alternative but to keep their clothes on—at least where Julie was concerned. Unsurprisingly, Frank was willing to brave the mosquitoes if she would test out this small clearing he'd found in the woods, which featured a soft bed of pine needles. As they disengaged from an extended tongue-kiss, he breathily suggested, again, that it would be very romantic doing it under the stars. They were actually visible for once, it was like a sign. She had to stifle a smile at his red-blooded eagerness. Still, her response was the same. Frank sighed heavily.

"Julie," he said after several moments, "um, I've been thinking about enlisting."

She wasn't sure she'd heard him right. "In the army?" she replied finally, dumbly. "What, is this my punishment for not going into the woods and dropping my panties? Now that we're doing *it,* it's got to be on demand?"

"Hey, are you serious? You think—wouldn't that be a little extreme on my part? Insane? Julie, I've been thinking about this for a while. It's just…I guess I picked a bad time to bring it up."

His features blurred in the gathering darkness as she studied him, stunned. She brushed away incipient tears and could see him clearly: the earnest face with its small, square chin, wide lips, high cheekbones, broad forehead seeming higher, eyes somehow more prominent, more clear and intense now that he was sporting a flat top, a semi-crewcut. He'd claimed that more than one joker had pulled his hair, in desperate attempts to keep from getting pinned. The first time she'd seen the haircut she teased him about looking like a soldier. She'd never dreamed…

"Did you think there'd be a good time?" Julie managed to say, a note of pleading in her voice, as if he might still crack a smile, apologetically confess to a sick joke. But they'd been together for over a year. She knew him well enough to know that he was dead serious. "Frank, talk about insane—why? How could you even *consider* it?" She slid down her T-shirt, under which minutes previously his fingers had been roaming, caressing her skin. Suddenly, that seemed like a lifetime ago. Julie wrapped her arms around herself against the sudden, unexpected chill of an early May evening. Salt air from the Sound filled her nostrils, condensing, leaking from her eyes.

He gently brushed at the tears. She jerked her head away.

"Julie, I know it's hard to understand. It's just…the only reason I would want to stay here in *da Bronx* is you. We're too young to get married—I feel like I'm still a kid in some ways. I'm not really interested in more school right now, if ever, and I can't even *think* about working full time at my father's hardware store. But it's just something I need to do. Probably after I graduate in June. Someone needs to fight the Commies, stand up for freedom. Might as well do it there, 'steada here. A lot of guys have already gone, you know that. I need to see how I measure up, Julie."

"You fucking idiot!" she screamed, causing a couple of gulls to alight from their perch on a nearby garbage can. "Measure up? You want to see what size body bag you'll fit into?" She paused, trying to collect herself. "Frank," she said finally, in a rasping voice, "suck it up. Go to Bronx Community. You might even get into Lehman. Get a student deferment. Probably they have wrestling at either place. You could get your…combat fix."

He said nothing. His eyes were set on her but already seemed to be focused elsewhere, as if she'd suddenly acquired invisibility. "Listen to me. If you do this, do not expect me to be waiting here for you if and when you get back. And don't expect me to attend your funeral, and bow my head when they play taps and hand your parents that crisply folded flag in lieu of their son. I don't think I could bear it. I don't think they could either."

Pre-First Union Arena, Julie and Frank had watched the evening news if they were too tired to read and there was nothing else worth watching, which meant that they tuned in to the news frequently, even if it was a mild form of masochism. "Flower power" had taken on a most ironic twist. Like twisting the knife, coming off the lips of President Edward Flowers, who milked this little joke when speaking in front of Republican audiences, the only kind he addressed live. They found it uproariously funny. The right to tap, at whim, anybody's phone or email, including retrieval of trashed communications from the hard drive? Flower Power, har, har. The right to "disappear" people, also at will? Torture them? Lie repeatedly to start a war? Drop thousand-pound bombs on the heads of peasants in the name of freedom? *Flahr Pahr*, rendered with the president's endearing southern drawl. And the "Democrat" party couldn't, or wouldn't, do shit about it.

How had this bastard become president? Probably it was his strong arms. He'd waved the flag tirelessly with one, while hefting the cross with the other. The US of A was engaged in a *Clash of Civilizations.* The American Way of Life was being threatened by Muslim terrorists—

really, when you thought about it, the only kind of Muslim there was.

Now, as if to tragically underline that point, the supposedly non-violent All for Allah had been implicated in the heinous mass murder at First Union Arena in the Bronx.

It occurred to Frank that Flowers bore an ironic similarity to those heathen Jihadists, in that he was willing to sacrifice his own people—or, at least, American citizens—in order to pursue his aims, especially if those people happened to be anti-Christs like Shove It Up and their fans, none of whom were likely to vote Republican. Or to join the Christian Crusade.

Of course, it remained to be proven that the Flowers administration and the Reverend Tate were in cahoots. There was no known association between Tate and Flowers, at least none locatable on Google. The president supposedly took his spiritual guidance from some clone of Billy Graham. But it was safe to say that Flowers's MO and Tate's were the same: "He who is not with Me is against Me. And he who is against Me had better watch his ass. Better yet, we'll do it for him. For openers."

Although sitting with his arm around Julie, whose breathing seemed perfectly synchronized with the expansions and contractions of his own torso, Frank felt a chill run through him as he watched the nationally televised address from President Flowers—a nightly occurrence, helping to make the three weeks since the gassing seem like forever.

He had no choice but to watch, even if it meant gazing for extended stretches upon Flowers's face, electromagnetic pollution beamed into his living room. Frank had long been amazed at the ability of politicians to look utterly sincere, even compassionate, while lying through their teeth. Probably the Democrats did it too. Maybe he just saw it more in Republicans because of his own predispositions.

Still, they were so good at it that Frank had to cling almost fiercely to what he knew to be the truth, even while watching Flowers. Despite everything he'd been through in Vietnam and since, his instinct was still to believe what someone told him face-to-face, via the tube or otherwise. It just seemed like part of the human contract, such as it was. Part of getting by day to day.

And it was only because of Billy Patterson's stated plans for First Union Arena, delusional though they may have seemed at the time—and his disappearance after the thing actually happened—that Frank had known that Maximilian Tate was lying, from the moment the reverend sat down beneath his wooden crucifix. Having his constitutionally and professionally skeptical brother Rob with him had been helpful as well.

"…this is extremely necessary for the safety of the American people," Flowers was saying now. Deja vu. "Any *Is*lamic individuals—" Islamic was stressed at the first syllable, with a slight hiss. "—in our country who are not permanent residents must report to their local Immigration and Naturalization Services Center, where their deportation back to their country of origin will be arranged. Failure to do this will be construed as a hostile act against the United States and will result in imprisonment for an indefinite length of time, until such time as the proper authorities deem that the person is no longer a security threat to our nation. Such individuals will then be deported."

"Crutches and wheelchairs will be provided, with the expenses deducted from whatever remains of the individual's assets," intoned Frank.

Receiving no response from Julie, no acknowledgement of his own cleverness, he glanced down to discover that she was now dozing herself, her cheek compressed beneath his collarbone. If he was guilty of cynicism, it was still peanuts in comparison to Flowers's. The president had been unable to suppress a hint of his trademark smirk as he paused from the reading of his teleprompter after pronouncing "deported." The smirk involved a slight compression of his Nixonesque jowls, a slighter flaring of his rounded nostrils.

Caricatures of Flowers by political cartoonists had him resembling a balding wild boar, minus the tusks, or a bulldog. Such caricatures were now actively discouraged by administration officials, who intimated that such a manifest lack of respect for our leader in a "time of war"—Iraq? Afghanistan? The War on Terror?—bordered on treason.

"Under the Emergency War Powers vested in the president, I have directed that any mosques or other Islamic institutions or organizations within our borders be closely monitored by local law enforcement officials, in concert with the Federal Bureau of Investigation. Any such organizations found to be…inciting hatred against the United States and its people, either via speech or literature, will be closed immediately and be obligated to cease operations until further notice."

Flowers cleared his throat and briefly squinted as if attempting to peer out through the camera and scan his audience for Islamo-fascists.

"Mohammar Khan and other leaders of AFA—All for Allah—are being held at an undisclosed location for further questioning. We already have indications that the AFA had ties to Al-Qaeda and other terrorist organizations, which they previously managed to conceal. Once we know that with certitude, any foreign organizations which played any role, financial or otherwise, in the atrocity perpetuated at First Union Arena will experience the devastating consequences of the murder of Americans."

"Should I push the button first, Julie?"

Frank shook his head, realizing that his wife was asleep and he was talking to himself, a not-infrequent occurrence these days. As she softly snored against his chest, her herbal shampoo provided a whiff of sweetness. But on the other hand, Julie's faintly whistling exhalations were eerily reminiscent of the sound of descending missiles. He tried to laugh this notion off. Thankfully, blessedly, he'd had no Vietnam flashbacks for several years. Still, there was a time when even the term *flashback* could trigger one, name and event being one and the same. Now he thought that he might be having a flash forward, exploding fire and vaporizing bodies. *Flower power*. And pushing the button, on his remote at least, seemed like a good idea. Disappear Flowers with one click, get up, peruse the sports section, or maybe stay put, a pillow for his wife, but find a cable station that had the temerity not to carry the president's address. Instead Frank just sat, absorbing. If it wasn't pleasure, it could be construed as business-related, part of the joint venture with his brother the detective.

If that venture could ultimately expose the administration's complicity, or culpability, in the First Union attack, then it was well worth the effort. They would have to start by finding Billy Patterson, extracting him from whatever hole he'd crawled into, assuming he was still alive. Hopefully, that could be step one in nailing the rest of the bastards, Billy's puppet masters. None of that would bring Laureen back. But right now Flowers had carte blanche support from the outraged and frightened American public. If he wanted to nuke Iran or Pakistan, show the world what a tough fella he was, there might not be that many voices raised in protest, before or after the fact. Not that he would necessarily seek anybody's concurrence in the first place.

"It's my sorrowful duty now to pay homage to a brave and patriotic American, FBI agent Michael Scanlon. Agent Scanlon had infiltrated the AFA, and was, in fact, close to uncovering their horrific plans, when his identity as an FBI agent, a servant of his country, was discovered. He was cold-bloodedly murdered. FBI operatives finally obtained this information from Mohammar Khan, via… prolonged, lawful interrogation. Agent Scanlon was tortured before he was—as is the savage custom of these so-called people—was beheaded."

Flowers paused, sucking in his cheeks and clenching his jaw, defiantly holding his own head erect for the benefit of the cameras, milking the moment. "But his spirit lives on, in heaven and in our hearts, and will inspire us to eliminate the evil of Islamic terrorism from our midst, and from the world."

Once more the president silently gazed into the cameras, as if he were delivering the State of the Union and had been forced by thunderous applause to interrupt his address, again. "Our thoughts and prayers go out to the family of Agent Scanlon."

Musical vibes rendering "Lay Lady Lay" announced a call on Frank's cell phone. He finally depressed the TV remote's power button. Then he reached into his flannel shirt pocket for the phone. Before First Union, he rarely even kept a cell on his person. It sat in his glove compartment, to be removed and turned on only if he needed to make a call. Now, he had a new cell phone registered to Phillip Abruzzi, whose fictitious driver's license and social security number had been provided by Frank's former army buddy, FBI agent Paul Fowlkes.

Two days after he and Rob had "interviewed" Reverend Tate, Frank had been stunned to encounter Fowlkes in the parking lot outside of Tedeschi's Hardware. Ordinarily, even though the engine of the Toyota Camry parked next to his own car was running, Frank wouldn't have taken a second glance.

But he was trying to be vigilant, at Rob's urging, and to navigate the divide between vigilance and paranoia. Under normal circumstances even the car's tinted windows wouldn't have given him pause, assuming he'd noticed them in the first place. They were all but obscured by the reflected glare of the lot's ultraviolet lights.

His stomach jumped when the front passenger window of the Toyota silently slid down, and a gravelly voice proclaimed, "Yo, Frank!"

In an instant, he mentally berated himself for having ignored Rob's advice that he start carrying a gun. Frank's right fist clenched around his keys. Moved by some ancient instinct, he quickly braced himself on his spread feet, weight centered—a wrestler poised.

Fowlkes had barked a laugh. "Hey, that's seriously scary, man. What, you don't recognize your old dog without his tags? It's only been what…a couple of years?"

"Paul?" Frank exhaled what felt like several minutes' worth of pent-up air, producing a cloud of vapor. "You crazy son of a bitch. You scared the shit out of me."

Fowlkes, having initially leaned over to poke his face through the open window, grunted as he heaved himself upright. "Yeah? Shit, I can't even scare my grandkid, anymore. FBI should stand for Fat Butt Incorporated. Get in. Quick."

Relieved, Frank had done as he was told. The window slid back up as he pulled open the Camry's door, jumped in, and slammed it shut. He heard the lock click. "You don't look so fat, Comrade Fowlkes," he said, gazing over.

"*So* fat? Thanks, Frank. What, you think it's just this bulky jacket? I need to get out from behind my desk some, while I can still do that with relative ease."

They shook hands. "Get your gear on, and we'll hump twenty miles or so. Whip you right into shape. Seriously, Paul, it's good to see you. But you oughta stop playing spook and call first, let me know you're coming."

"Actually, that wouldn't have been a good idea. They have you under surveillance, Frank."

"*What*?"

He'd studied Fowlkes's face in the ultraviolet light streaming in through the windshield: gleaming tortoise shell glasses above the familiar round cheeks, thin wide lips that stretched across his face, their slight downward arc overlain by a black mustache, no hint of gray, its impressive thickness the more striking given the sparseness of the hair that sat beneath a green woolen New York Jets cap. Fowlkes had cultivated the mustache in 'Nam and worn it ever since, then a little project, an assertion that one day he'd again care about the way he looked. The ends of the mustache pointed to a narrow, tapered chin that had almost doubled itself.

"As of a couple of days ago," Fowlkes replied, as he shifted into drive and began pulling out of his parking spot. "I—"

"Hey, what are you doing? I need to get home. Julie's a mite nervous these days, especially with Rob—my brother?—and me playing detective. If I'm late for dinner…"

"Call her," said Fowlkes, shrugging as he edged his Toyota forward toward the right northbound lane of Route 28/Mattawan Road, the four-lane thoroughfare that ran by the strip mall. It was crowded with suburban holiday-shopping traffic: leave work, grab a bite at Arby's or wherever, pull out your Christmas list. "Tell her, what, there's a traffic tie-up or something. *Don't* mention my name. Remember, Big Brother could be listening. Maybe watching too."

As if to underline this last statement, Fowlkes darted from the parking lot and made a left across a double line and three lanes of traffic coming from two different directions, causing at least one driver to lean on his horn.

The truck, judging by its baritone, was an eighteen-wheeler plunging like a giant electric eel through the murky green darkness outside of Fowlkes's passenger window.

"Jesus!" barked Frank. "What the fuck—"

Fowlkes hadn't blinked. His chunky profile, dominated by the mustache and the glasses, stared placidly ahead. "Easy, Frank. I don't think we're being followed. Someone was exiting the lot behind us, but it was a woman in a van, probably a soccer mom. No one entered on this side after we made the turn. But still, safety first."

At this, Frank had burst out laughing and couldn't stop for maybe half a minute, his nerves beginning to unknot. "Right," he managed finally. "So, I'm under surveillance. In a way that just shows that—how long?"

"As of a couple of days ago. Noticed it by chance. Maybe sitting on my ass behind my desk has its advantages. We have classified lists of people under surveillance. You click on the name, all the relevant info comes up. I was looking for this heroin goombah, Texiera, scrolling down, and whose name do I see? Yours and your brother's. You told me, when we spoke on the phone, that you were going to pay that reverend a visit. Did you?"

"Yup," Frank said, his breath catching as Fowlkes ran a light at the intersection of Mamaroneck Avenue, rounded a curve, and made a squealing left. "You think if anyone was following us, they still are?"

"No way," Fowlkes replied, not without a touch of pride.

"Good. Then why don't you pull over, before we save them the trouble of neutralizing us? Anyway, if someone was waiting in the parking lot, they undoubtedly have your plate number."

"I like it. You're starting to think like a spook" said Fowlkes, as he obligingly pulled to the curb on a residential street that was probably lit five times as brightly as usual. "Man, can you believe the lights on this block? Every single-family, it's like a competition. A giant electric birthday card to Jesus. But the plates?" he added, not skipping a beat. "They're phony."

Frank laughed and shook his head. "Made in prison by counterfeiters. Anyway, yeah, we saw Reverend Tate. Talked to him about Billy Patterson. The guy who used to work for me, who you ran on that all-knowing FBI computer of yours?"

"Right. He also worked for Tate. Assistant groundskeeper."

"You have a good memory. Guess it's part of the job."

"Actually, sometimes I have trouble remembering my own name. But after I saw yours, on that surveillance list, I ran back over our phone conversation and back over what I'd gathered on Patterson. What did the reverend have to say?"

"About what I expected." Frank paused, briefly engaged by the blinking lights that completely outlined one of the houses, as if it were the glowing ghost thereof, the house being otherwise dark. It occurred to him that the Christmas lights must be on a timer. Also, that he was either getting distracted or having a memory lapse of his own, difficulty in pulling the necessary thoughts out of the swirl that had been more or less constantly going through his head since First Union.

Finally, they clicked into place. "He said if Billy talked about gassing the arena, it was pure coincidence, brought about by a waning of Jesus's influence. All those posters of Shove it Up got him upset. And if he disappeared, then it was probably because he'd returned to his dissolute ways."

"Dissolute?"

"Binge drinking, maybe watching porn, I don't know, once a sinner—"

"Impressive vocabulary, Frank." Behind his glasses, Fowlkes lifted his pudgy eyelids in mock admiration, causing his New York Jets cap to correspondingly elevate.

"Right. And, of course, when we—Rob and I—intimated that if Billy did First Union, it was with the reverend's approval, the guy was beside himself with outrage. Had his flunky remove us from the premises, forthwith."

"And then he probably called some administration official. They just put you under surveillance two days ago, which you say is when you visited Tate. It was just pure luck that I came across it so fast. But can you think of any other reason why they'd tap your phone and email, run a background check? Designate you high priority?"

Despite the stuffiness inside the Toyota, Frank felt a chill run through him. *High Priority.* "I don't know," he replied, swallowing. "If it's not Vets Against the War—"

"Shit, that's old history. Like I said, they *just* put you on their little list—actually, it's not so little, you're in good company, Frank—but two days ago? You haven't been involved in anything more recently? Protesting Iraq, maybe?"

"Uh-uh. Call it apathy, I guess. Before First Union, I

was selling toilet plungers, WD-Forty spray. I was an American businessman. Still am. A small-time capitalist pig."

"Congratulations. But if Flowers was so well served by First Union, and he's the darling of the Christian Right, and there seems to be at least a possibility that the Reverend Tate was involved in First Union, with government complicity—"

"Then I become a dangerous person to them. Rob and me. We represent the threat of them being exposed."

"Yeah. I mean, there's no other reason I can think of why they'd put you under surveillance. Not that I'm totally convinced yet. About Billy Patterson doing the gassing, Tate, the whole scenario. But I'm getting there."

Fowlkes paused, unzipping his jacket halfway, lowering the heat. "If Tate has connections with the Flowers administration, it's not public knowledge. Even when I asked around—people I can trust, theoretically—no one could confirm that connection. But the reverend is considered a little extreme, even among the holy rollers, so maybe it's not surprising that Flowers would keep it under the radar. I've been trying to tap into Tate's phone records. Usually, you can do that with anyone, that's the way it is nowadays, even before First Union. But in his case, it may take some doing. Seems like he has his own security arrangements, where his communications are concerned. Which in itself lends credence to the idea of a government connection, and of a high rating on the scumbag scale.

"Anyway, you need to take some security measures of your own. Like getting home and cell phones under a phony name. I can help with that. Or maybe just disconnect the home line. Try to use the cell out of doors, or at least out of the house and car, in the event that both or either are bugged. If you do talk in the car, maybe play loud music at the same time. And change your email account. Ditto for Rob. All of it."

"Jesus. Paul, tell me straight here. What kind of danger am I in? *We,* I should say."

"Um, well, they'll want to see who you're connected with—"

"They?"

"I don't know yet. Someone in the bureau's involved, obviously. CIA? It's even possible that Flowers has his own personal goon squad."

Frank took a deep breath, releasing it slowly, completely, a basic little relaxation technique taught to him by Julie. "And after they've discovered that our connections are minimal? Like, each other and you?"

"Me, they will not discover. Hopefully. It goes without saying that you shouldn't blab my name around. To no one, except maybe your brother. Your wife, if she can be trusted, and understands thereafter not to utter my name. I'd like to keep myself in one large piece, for one thing. And If I come fully on board, I'm a very useful asset, but that goes out the window if—"

"Right. I get the picture, Paul."

"Try to take it easy."

"Sure. Easy." Suddenly, Frank could've sworn he was in a movie, a notion reinforced by the amorphous reflection of blinking lights in the film of vapor on the Toyota's windshield, a blending of colors that tinted Fowlkes's glasses. "It would be nice if you 'came on board' sooner rather than later. Rob and I have been exploring this avenue and that. Or we've started, but even if we wind up with something irrefutable, I don't know where we'd turn next."

"Right. Well, if it's true," Fowlkes said, his mustache seeming to slide a bit down his face as his jaw set, "then not only are the motherfuckers more evil than we could have imagined, but it's a chance to fight a good fight for once. Not that I have a problem trying to help snuff out the heroin trade, even as our buddies in Afghanistan are growing the stuff. But this, if we can nail Flowers and the rest of the bastards—but we gotta be careful."

"*We?* You're still hedging your bets, right? And I'm the one on their high priority list. Me an' Rob. Shit, they've already got the 'h' and the 'i' when they want to change it to *hit list.*"

"Okay, lemme rephrase that. *You* gotta be careful. Although like I said, if it's true, or I become a little more convinced than I am now, I'll be ready to lay my own sizable ass on the line. And you know I'd do it."

Frank had sighed and nodded slowly. Yes, he did know that, assuming that he was talking to even a facsimile of the Fowlkes with whom he'd served in the army. Still, that knowledge didn't provide much relief for the sick feeling in his gut. Neither did Paul's subsequent recommendation that he start carrying a gun, forthwith.

"Shit. After 'Nam, I swore I would never touch one of those again. You know that, Paul. But, yeah. Okay. I can see the logic now. And I'm sure you can hook me up."

"I've got the license and the piece right here."

Frank lifted the cell phone from his shirt pocket, the movement jostling Julie enough that her catnap was ended. She sat up and rubbed her eyes, wide awake in an instant. The ringing of "Phillip Abruzzi's" cell phone, which had come into her husband's possession only a few days previously, was akin to an alarm, the gentle tones of "Lay, Lady, Lay" having been transformed into the sound of foreboding, of "Oh God, what next?" What came immediately next was Frank turning the TV back on, tripling the volume. Julie winced at the noise but stayed put.

"Rob?" Frank said.

"Duh, check your caller ID. It's Paul."

Fowlkes's voice, a hoarse, teasing semi-whisper, caused Frank's synapses to jump to attention. He hadn't heard from Fowlkes since the unscheduled conference in the Toyota with the tinted windows. A week ago? Not a long time, it only felt that way.

"Hey comrade, what's up?" Frank asked, simulating nonchalance. "Can you hear me?"

"Yeah, just barely, which is good. I'm impressed, you're on the ball. You heard this new bullshit, about Mike Scanlon, the FBI agent?"

"Yeah. In fact, I was just watching Flowers eulogize the guy. You think it's bullshit?"

"Well, even aside from the source, I'd have to say, yeah. I didn't know Scanlon directly, a friend of a friend of a friend. But I heard about it yesterday and tried to access Scanlon's reports on AFA. They're inaccessible, top secret, which you could interpret different ways—one being that they contradict the depiction of AFA as a terrorist organization. So, I asked around, discreetly of course. From the little I was able to gather, I'd say that maybe he knew too much, only not from the AFA's standpoint. And, I gotta admit, the rubbing out of a fellow agent by his own government, if that's what happened—and I have a gut feeling, especially with this beheading crap, they're really laying it on—but it's enough to make me very pissed off. So count me in. At least until further notice. When can I get together with you and Rob?"

CHAPTER 7

Vietnam, 1973:

Neither PFC Tedeschi nor Corporal Fowlkes ever figured out who had fired first. No one acknowledged it afterward. Even by 'Nam standards, the shame was too great. As if alert to their stealthy approach, the village had seemed to be vanishing before their eyes, a trick at which the Vietcong themselves were very adept. Assuming that the place was not deserted, the lack of fires was likely purposeful, the desire for the cover of nightfall an indicator of fear, malevolent intent, or both. In that gathering darkness—even the fireflies seemed to have been scared out of town—the flash of weaponry should've been unmistakable. The distinguishing of Charlie's black pajamas from the twilight's last lingering shadows, or from the movement of vegetation stirred by a breeze, that was another matter. Even without the benefit of extreme fright, the eyes could play tricks.

Suffice it to say that someone saw something. Someone fired at something. Then everyone opened up, the night exploding, the intolerable blackening silence blasted to hell by a chain reaction of cathartic, smoking eruptions. It might've taken ten seconds. Maybe five. Then the darkness returned, as if to assert that the whole thing had been an illusion, a brief manifestation of collective psychosis. Except that the silence was gone, replaced by the wailing and moaning of children.

The soldiers in Frank's unit abandoned all caution. Flashlights ablaze, they rushed into the village from its outskirts. Fowlkes, reed-thin in those days, got into the thatched hut first. The kids were screaming and thrashing their arms and legs, blood flying off them, puddling on the packed dirt.

"Oh, God!" Fowlkes cried, his anguished baritone a contrast to the shrill wailing, momentarily obliterating it, much as the unit's weapons, including his, had obliterated four young lives.

The dead kids, including a naked baby, were the lucky ones. As Frank pushed into the hut, he was nearly felled himself by its heat and fetid smell, overlain now by the odor of entrails, of life pouring out from shredded bodies. The intermingling blood of seven children and one old woman was fast turning the floor into purplish mud. Of the three kids who were technically still alive, one's right arm was hanging from his shoulder by a strip of flesh. He might have been four years old—whimpering, eyes glazed beneath a shock of jet black hair that was plastered to his forehead. Frank, his mind inexplicably calm, knelt next to the kid, considering how to help him. He'd reinserted the arm into its socket, intending to tie it there somehow, when the back of his collar was pulled halfway up his neck by Lieutenant Walton, his commanding officer.

Frank jerked his head around. In the next instant, his eyes re-registered the tangle of bloodied flesh and viscera in the hut, the camouflage cloth. Fowlkes was trying to help the old lady. Part of her face had been blown off. He was murmuring repeatedly, "We're sorry, we're sorry," this stream of apology barely audible above the children's wails and the cursing of one of the other two soldiers who'd managed to squeeze into the hut.

"Get up! Get the fuck up!" screamed Walton, yanking on Frank's armpit now.

This had the effect of relocating both Frank and the boy, whose arm fell back out, severing the strip of flesh from which it had dangled.

"Hey!" Frank barked, despite the sudden obstruction in his throat. "You can't see? I'm trying—"

"Fuck that! We need to get the hell out of here. *All* of you. Now!"

"But I'm trying to help the kid!" Frank asserted, elevating his voice in an attempt to penetrate Walton's seemingly uncomprehending brain. "Do *something.* He's too young to be the enemy, right? An' he's sitting here, or he was, in a hut with no weapons, not even a goddamn Vietcong leaflet. We're not supposed to be about murdering little kids—Lieutenant."

Walton's reply—"Get your fucking candy-ass *up*"—seemed to come from far away, as if Frank's helmet had taken on soundproofing capability, a new protective function. He felt almost weightless as he came to his feet, anticipating Walton's next yank, rising above it by a split second. Walton could have been jerking up on a drab green yo-yo.

The lieutenant spun. "Out of here! Right the fuck now!" he shrieked directly into the eardrums of Fowlkes, who was still ministering to the old woman. Of course, Fowlkes might as well have been administering last rites, it would have done her as much good. Maybe it would've given her an additional reason to spit in his face, had she the necessary life left in her.

"But—we should call in the helicopters—medivacs," Fowlkes said, looking up. "Maybe we could save—"

"Are you crazy? Right now, Fucks, we need to save our own asses. If Charlie's in the neighborhood, as usual, we need to get out of here double-time. They can take care of their own. This is a motherfucking war. We don't even have time to have this conversation. And in case you forgot, I'm the fucking CO." Walton fixed Fowlkes with a hard stare, which was returned in kind. "So, at the risk of repeating myself, get your gear on. All of you. We're hauling ass. *Now.*"

Frank, Fowlkes, and the rest of the unit did not encounter "the enemy" again that night. Nor did most of them sleep much, a circumstance that was only marginally owing to tree roots and other protrusions sticking into their ribs.

Concealed by a stand of trees at the edge of an expanse of rice paddies, they breakfasted on C-rations, or tried. The rations were not especially appetizing. Images of the night before didn't help.

"What is this shit?" Jimmy Klesko mumbled, half to himself.

Klesko was a gung-ho enlistee when he first arrived in 'Nam. He'd earned the rank of first sergeant and was technically Walton's right hand man. But the war had dimmed his patriotic fervor. More than once, he'd vocalized his opinion that the Lieutenant was a power-tripping asshole, who seemed to think he was still running boot camp. The night before, per Walton's orders, Klesko had remained outside the hut with several other men. They were to keep watch and provide the initial response to any enemy incursion. Or take the initial hits.

"Pork 'n beans, I believe," said Fowlkes, in between tokes on a fat reefer. "Or it might be beef. Or dog."

"Thanks, bro'. If I throw up, I'll be sure to do it in your helmet."

Fowlkes picked up his helmet off the ground and stuck it on his head, backward. "Sarge, you do that, and you'll leave me unfit for combat. As usual. Plus, Walton'll probably bust *me*, for…I dunno…misuse of army property. Something."

"Yeah, but you might smell better. And cut out that 'Sarge' shit."

Klesko's protest was drowned out by the sound of Fowlkes's coughing, which resulted in the expulsion of a pungent cloud of marijuana smoke. "Dammit, don't make me laugh when I'm inhaling, Sergeant Jimmy."

Frank, seated in the dirt nearby, was not amused. He listlessly stirred dried coffee into a metal cup of water and inhaled second-hand smoke which, if anything, only served to deepen his massive depression.

The arrival of Lieutenant Walton within their midst didn't help either. The lieutenant was battle-ready. His grease-gun dangled from one shoulder. His pack was full, helmet strapped.

"Fucks," he growled, "what have I told you about smoking that shit?"

"Uh…not to?" Fowlkes put the reefer to his lips and inhaled deeply.

"Fucking A," replied Walton.

He somehow managed to snatch the reefer from Fowlkes's fingers and lips without burning himself, no mean feat, considering that it was now little more than a roach. Walton tossed it aside disdainfully. A nod to regs, authority—despite his opinion that getting stoned had no negative impact on a soldier's ability to fight. If anything it obliterated fear, leaving the grunts with a what-the-fuck attitude about the possibility of getting their smoke-saturated brains blown out.

Regs also dictated that soldiers obey a CO's order—which PFC Tedeschi declined to do when Walton instructed him, deja vu, to get up.

"Hey, weren't we just on patrol all night?" Frank gazed up bleary-eyed at the lieutenant's sneering face. Its lupine appearance was augmented by a week's worth of salt and pepper stubble. "And didn't we waste a bunch of kids and one old lady, for the greater glory of Uncle Sam?"

"Tedeschi, get the fuck up. *Now*."

The pouches beneath Walton's eyes resembled, in miniature, the oversized and overstuffed pockets of his camouflage pants. According to Klesko, the lieutenant had not been sleeping much himself, since finding a grenade pin on his inflatable pillow. This was an anonymous gift from one of the men in his unit, a reminder that other commanding officers in Vietnam had been removed from their posts—and their bodies—via fragging, which involved the tossing of a fragmentation bomb into the CO's tent. A token of affection from the troops, from soldiers who'd been dragged out on one too many dangerous missions, or otherwise given to understand that their lives meant nothing where Herr Commandant was concerned. The pin was a warning to ease up, chill out, or the next time it would be live shit. And the tent would become a tattered shroud for whatever remained of Walton.

Other than increasing his vigilance, the lieutenant gave no indication of having been cowed. If anything, the opposite seemed true. "Get the fuck up Tedeschi," he snarled now, pointing his index finger toward the far end of the misty rice paddies in front them. "Once we clear the perimeter of gooks, if any, then you can sit on your candy ass again."

Frank drained his tin coffee cup, craning his neck so as not miss even a drop of its bitterness. "Fuck you, Walton," he said finally, fixing his gaze on the lieutenant. "I mean that in all sincerity. I'll get up when I feel like it. And it won't necessarily be to go fight the *gooks,* as you so charmingly call them."

He shoved the cup into his pack, the contents of which he reshuffled, making no move to snap it shut or lift it. On finally raising his head, he found himself looking into the barrel of Walton's revolver. Its trigger was cocked.

Frank's life didn't exactly flash in front of him. But somehow, in an instant, he could sense the metaphysical presence of his parents, his brother Rob and erstwhile girlfriend Julie, even Hanrahan, his wrestling coach, whom he had considered a prototype for asshole-in-authority until he met Lieutenant Walton.

This convocation actually lifted his spirits, as if it were a celebration of his impending release from the hell into which he'd signed himself. And if the agent was to be Walton, Frank was fine with that too. The lieutenant hated niggers, gooks, and spics. He was an equal opportunity racist, although, after the grenade pin incident, he was slightly more discreet about it. knowing how touchy the niggers and spics in his unit could be. Also, he had little use for most white males who hadn't grown up in the military. Still, it seemed like it would be almost an honor to be murdered by him. A badge of righteousness. The notion caused Frank to laugh aloud.

Walton seemed momentarily befuddled, his sneer contracting. Fowlkes and Klesko, as they took in the surreal scene in front of them, each came to the same conclusion, that Comrade Tedeschi seriously did not give a shit anymore.

"Be my guest, motherfucker," Frank said, with a nonchalance that was beyond absurdity. His words seem to originate from someplace outside of himself, as if he were already gone.

They also appeared to snap the lieutenant back into character. "What, you think I'm bullshitting, Tedeschi? Get the *fuck* up. I'm gonna count to three."

Walton got to *two*. Then his head burst. It took a couple of very long seconds for Frank to realize that the sound he'd heard had not been produced by the explosion of Walton's skull but by the report of Fowlkes's revolver.

In the next instant, the lieutenant's body landed on Frank. He reflexively shoved it aside and jumped up, his face, neck, and shoulders splashed with blood. Slack-jawed, he stared at Fowlkes.

"Friendly fire," Fowlkes said with a tiny smile, as if the whole thing were a joke, as if he could now see through the extended hallucination caused by the powerful Vietnamese reefer he'd been smoking.

CHAPTER 8

Paul is looking for information about that FBI agent who got killed, Scanlon, and his reports on AFA. Some computer stuff. Even if it wasn't intra-FBI, I wouldn't have understood what he was talking about. Told him I'm a computer doofus, but he kept giving me technical details anyway."

Rob nodded. "Yeah, FBI. Probably thinks he's hot shit, wants to flash his—"

"Hey. He's with us, remember?" Frank said, trying to keep the annoyance out of his voice. "Aside from the fact that he saved my ass once." Over the last thirty-plus years, since his return from 'Nam, it hadn't taken much for conversations with his brother to turn unpleasant. Now they needed to keep that *us* together, or try. "This cops-FBI shit? Try to just let go of that. He's not your typical FBI agent, believe me. And you saw how helpful the cops at your own precinct were. Right? Man, that seems like a long time ago. Three and a half weeks."

"'Bout that." Rob suddenly hit the gas, turned on his siren and red flasher, and sped through the intersection of 233rd Street and White Plains Road, against the light.

"Jesus, man. You really think someone is following us?"

"It's not impossible. You heard what your buddy Fowlkes said. And you told me about the little car chase stunts he pulled when you were with him."

"True. I assume you're gonna—" Frank dropped the rest of the sentence, rendered moot as Rob killed the siren and turned off the flasher, the better to disappear into the North Bronx twilight. "And, at the risk of repeating myself, you don't think this car is bugged?"

Rob snorted. "At the risk of repeating myself, no. Not only did I go over it myself—and I know where they'd plant it—but, when not in use, the car sits locked up in the yard at the precinct, behind a barbed wire fence, this being the Bronx. No one's gonna go in there. I only took it now for reasons you just saw. It's unmarked, and it can fly."

"Right," said Frank, bracing himself against the rifle stand between the two front seats as Rob took a sharp left onto the Bronx River Parkway. "Still, it's not impossible that one of your colleagues at the precinct has been persuaded that it's his patriotic duty."

"What, to bug the car? Man, you are getting paranoid. Shit, maybe I am, too. Which is why I went over this baby with a fine-toothed comb. My own car too."

Frank sighed. "Me, paranoid?"

He worked up a laugh. Still, maybe the term applied, as evidenced by a new tendency of his to pat the gun strapped to his ribs via a shoulder holster, as if he were obsessively checking the size of some new bodily growth. *Paranoia runs deep*, he recalled with a flicker of a smile, this phrase from a once-popular sixties counterculture anthem now playing in his head. Foreground music. And an appropriate selection, except that he hadn't selected it, and maybe the term paranoia didn't apply. His fears were probably well founded. Which was why, since his surprise meeting with Fowlkes, the gun was never out of reach, except maybe when he was in the shower. The American bang-bang, don't leave home without it.

He and Rob were on their way to visit Sylvester Stout, head groundskeeper at the Holy Church of Christ. Spiritual leader, Reverend Maximilian Tate. Billy Patterson had alluded to Stout on several occasions, derisively referring to him as "Sly," but if he'd ever mentioned the full name, it escaped Frank. Not so Rob, who'd located the name and address within five minutes. He was not a detective for nothing.

They were planning to drop in on Sylvester Stout at home, knowing that they'd never get past the guard's booth again at the Holy Church of Christ. Their welcome, such as it was in the first place, was more than worn out. And whatever Stout knew about Billy and First Union Arena, Rob was sure that he'd been warned about that crank detective Tedeschi and his brother. Cavanaugh, the reverend's security chief, would've taken care of that. Even were he not auditioning for house dick of the year, they'd antagonized him enough. Plus, they both felt that they stood a better chance with Sylvester Stout away from the church, out from under the huge golden cross that overlooked the grounds, flashing in the sun like a giant camera.

Frank sat staring out at the Bronx River Parkway's leafless trees, their branches shooting past his window, tentacles disappearing in the vapor. Other than requesting that he wipe off the condensation, front and rear, Rob said little to nothing. He stared intently ahead, navigating the twists and turns of the parkway at a much higher speed than the law allowed. They'd already discussed their approach to Sylvester Stout, among other matters. Rob's driving was not an approachable subject, the squealing of his tires notwithstanding.

It intermittently punctured the silence—which for Rob

didn't really exist, Frank knew. His brother had earlier confided that he was still tormented by thoughts and images of Laureen, almost non-stop. Maybe they'd diminish over time. Maybe not. As if hoping to drown them out, Rob turned on his car radio. Country music, WBAR. Rich singers determined to sound like hayseeds, twangy steel guitars, tears in your beer. *You ain't woman enough to steal my man.* White trash/Republican music, the kind of stuff that made Frank want to hurl. He couldn't comprehend how Rob, a city boy and *paisan,* had come to like that shit. Which was more or less the terminology Frank had once used to pose this question…

It was the night of their father's eightieth birthday party. At the behest of their father, who had posed his own questions—"Why the hell aren't you two even talking to each other? You're brothers, remember?"—Rob and Frank had gone out together to Theo's, a bar that was a neighborhood landmark, where generations of Pelham Bay youth had warmed their first bar stool, legally or otherwise. Many became lifelong customers. They could dimly be seen drinking in there even in the morning, through Windex-proof plate glass windows bordering the sidewalk. It was as if the sun never penetrated the smoky interior, the alcoholic fumes.

Sunrise was still several hours away when Rob popped a quarter into the jukebox for the privilege of hearing "Hillbilly Highway." After Frank, in the spirit of reconciliation, had equated his musical preferences with shit, Rob barely batted an eyelash. He was at that stage of inebriation where everything rolled off his back. Rob replied that he'd picked up the country music habit from the last partner he had as a uniform riding in a squad car. Kid name of Scranton, who'd grown up on a potato farm on the Island. And Rob had discovered that the stuff sounded good when you were even mildly drunk, which was more than you could say about Frank's boy Bob Dylan, or Shove It Up, or the rest of the spoiled brats who groused about how unfair the world was while they raked in the cash.

Frank, more than a little soused himself, had taken a few moments to process this comment. "Shove It Up?" he asked finally.

"Laureen's favorite band. Heavy metal. Degenerate shit."

"Ah. Well, I don't how you can lump them in with Dylan. Unless maybe they both have a *fuck you* attitude toward authority. When Dylan was young, anyway."

ᘓᘓ

Now, Frank simply tuned out Keith Urban, Travis Tritt, Faith Hill, et al. It was easy enough to do, the stuff all sounded the same. Besides, it was fitting background music for a trip through rural Westchester, where Sylvester Stout made his home. When they arrived at his place, courtesy of MapQuest and the search beam on Rob's car, it was apparent that the head groundskeeper didn't make much more than the assistant at Tate's church. Christ, whose manger, along with the visiting wise men, took up about half the front yard, seemed to be enjoying only a slightly lower standard of living.

Rob pulled open a squeaky screen door and rapped his knuckles on the wooden one inside, there being no doorbell or buzzer. Sylvester Stout and his address were both identified only on the stand-up mailbox that abutted the curb on Ridge Lane. Its red lever was down, parallel to the grass. Frank, practicing detective-thought, figured this for an indication that Stout had either picked up his mail or received none, assuming it meant anything.

The light from the two curtained windows facing the slightly rickety porch upon which they now stood was a better indication that the man was probably home, a light that paled in comparison with the electric glow from the manger.

A naked bulb on the porch clicked on. Seconds later the door was opened by a tall, thin male, maybe pushing sixty, most notable for his plaid suspenders, hairless gleaming head and the unlit pipe that protruded from his concave mouth. The pipe's angle and shape more or less replicated the shape of the mailbox lever, in three dimensions.

Rob, an authority figure in his own right, flashed his gold badge. "Sylvester Stout? I'm Detective Tedeschi."

"New York Police Department," Stout filled in. "And you're his brother Frank. I was warned by the reverend himself against talking to you." He nodded stoically and looked them up and down, as if contemplating the fact that the reverend had been right as usual, that the Tedeschi brothers would soon be darkening his doorstep.

"I don't know if you have much choice in the matter," Rob said, a surly edge to his voice.

If anything Stout was amused by this assertion. His pipe shifted slightly as the corners of his mouth curled upward. "You got a warrant?"

"I can get one."

"Mr. Stout," Frank said, the porch creaking under him as he bounced slightly on the balls of his feet, trying to stimulate some circulation. They weren't that far north of the city, but it felt a lot colder. "Billy Patterson—you probably know we're here to talk about him. He worked for me too. I'm—we're—concerned about his disappearance."

"That makes two of us. Three." He cast a dubious glance in Rob's direction. The steam from Stout's breath floated up toward the porch light, taking on a faint, evanescent glow. If he was fazed by the cold, in his leather slippers, black denim pants and flannel shirt beneath the suspenders, it wasn't apparent. "Billy actually spoke highly of you, Mr. Tedeschi."

"Frank." He was aware of Rob shooting him a questioning glance.

"Right. Said you didn't walk with the Lord, but neither were you running in the opposite direction."

Frank chuckled. "Okay. I'll buy that, I guess. Didn't know that Billy saw shades of gray."

"He usually didn't." This reply seemed to leave open the possibility that Stout himself did. "But in your case—which I guess shows that, like I said, he was favorably disposed toward you."

"Glad to hear that, Mr. Stout. Seriously. But could we maybe come in? It's cold out here."

"Sure." Stout opened the door all the way and stepped aside. "I don't expect that you'll be reporting on this conversation to the reverend."

"Definitely not. Although even if we had that intent, I don't think he cares to talk to us, or would."

"Not without his lawyer," Rob murmured.

"Excuse me?"

"Nothing. Really."

Rob strode into Stout's foyer, making a little show of cleaning his shoes on the rubber mat therein, as if he were grinding out a cigarette.

The compact living room was dominated by an impressive blaze crackling in the fireplace, the scent of which might've been carried away by the crisp, cold breeze that had greeted the brothers when they'd stepped out of the car. Above this, on the wall, was a wooden crucifix that was a replica of the one in the reverend's office, or close enough.

Frank was briefly taken aback at the sight, which at first glance created an impression of Christ being burned at the stake. Hellfire. The notion made him cringe inside, as if he'd just committed some kind of mortal sin. Watch what pops into your head, especially if you haven't been to confession in thirty-five years, a time frame that can only grow.

Stout indicated a pinewood sofa and armchair placed to either side of the mantle. "I expect you'll warm up in a hurry," he said. "Still, I'd say it hasn't been much of a winter. Groundskeeping at the church used to involve a lot of shoveling snow, clearing the lot, the road. Hasn't been much this winter."

He moved the screen back from his fireplace and used an iron poker to shove a couple of thick branches further in. These he'd surely gathered himself. Store-bought firewood, including the pile outside of Tedeschi's Hardware, came in neatly cut cords.

"Billy told me you all haven't been moving much in the way of ice picks, shovels and the like."

Stout's reference to the store caused Frank to conjecture, with an inward smile, that maybe they'd bugged his mind as well. *Paranoia runs deep.* "That's true," he replied. "Although you couldn't blame him for that. Billy liked to point out to customers everything he thought they needed, that they hadn't asked for. Come in for rock salt, you'd be offered a snow blower, chains for your tires. He had plenty of energy."

"Mr. Stout," said Rob, shifting impatiently in the armchair, unzipping his jacket, half-exposing his shoulder holster. Frank covered his own, using his left arm to keep his jacket flush against it. "You wouldn't have any idea where Billy Patterson might've gone."

Stout shrugged. "Not much. Didn't talk much about his past. There was a foster brother he kept in touch with, or who kept in touch with him, maybe once a year, Christmas. Lives somewhere in Jersey. I tried to find the number, and couldn't."

"Did you tell that to your local police?"

"They never came, or called. And they couldn't connect me with the officer handling the case, if anybody was."

"Actually, I doubt it," Rob replied, shaking his head. "Well…"

"You don't mind," Stout asked, as he used his finger to tamp down the tobacco in the bowl of his pipe then ignited a cigarette lighter.

"It's your house."

"Thank you, Detective."

Stout's sarcasm was laid-back, unperturbed. He exhaled a fragrant cloud of smoke, cherry wood. Frank scanned the living room. On wooden lamp tables to the sides of the sofa and an armchair across the room, framed pictures reflected the glow of the fireplace. He could make out a partially obscured image of a thirty-ish woman who could have been Stout's wife or daughter, or neither. Indications were that he lived alone: one car in the driveway, the spare, utilitarian decor, the silence broken by the crisp snap and crackle of burning wood.

"Mr. Stout," said Frank, as the air cleared at the other end of the sofa, "did Billy say anything to you about First Union Arena?"

A caricature of pensiveness, Stout took another puff and considered this question for a moment. "Well, you know he disappeared the morning after that happened. A Saturday. At least, the last I saw of him was that Friday."

"Likewise. But what I meant was, did he talk about it *before* it happened? About how much he hated the band that was playing that night—Shove It Up? How they were blasphemers and worse? And how he was going to gas the place?"

When the pipe didn't fall from Stout's mouth, when his furrowed yet placid-looking face didn't spontaneously rearrange itself, Frank knew the answer.

"Yes indeed," Stout replied after several seconds. "Letting off steam. He had a lot inside of him. And he did talk like that. So I can only guess, when it actually happened, Billy kind of freaked out. Thought he might be blamed. You know, Mr. Tedeschi, even someone more stable than Billy might've reacted like that. I don't know if you're aware of this, but he was bipolar. At least, that's what the doctor he saw called it. Prescribed medication. But when Billy sought Reverend Tate's counsel about that, early on, the reverend suggested that it was more that he was touched by the spirit, which can sometimes cause…disorientation. The reverend told him that prayer would help as much as drugs, if not more."

"I'm sure," said Frank half-aloud. Billy had denigrated Stout, aka Sly, more than once as a blowhard who liked to pontificate while he, Billy, did the work, for which Stout later took credit if Tate or one of his underlings happened by. Yet it was apparent that Billy had revealed more about himself to Stout than he had to Frank. Maybe he'd spent more hours at the church, or had more down time there. "The bi-polar diagnosis I didn't know about. Can't say it surprises me, though. So, did Reverend Tate recommend that he stop taking the medication?"

"That I can't really say."

"Meaning you don't know, or you won't tell?"

"Both," replied Stout, fixing his slightly puffy, grayish eyes on Rob, the source of the question. "What passes between the reverend and his flock, in private, should remain that way. And maybe I shouldn't have imparted to you what Billy told me about the reverend's counsel. But I'm concerned about his disappearance. And I think what the reverend said possibly sheds some light on it. Troubled people *are* sometimes touched by the spirit. Bipolarity, or whatever fancy name the psychiatrists want to give it, can sometimes involve visions—and swings from moments of intimacy with God to feelings of being completely cut off from Him. It's possible that Billy might have had a precognition of that horrible tragedy at First Union Arena. In his confusion, and his outrage at Shove It Up—the way I understand it, 'blasphemers' is putting it kindly—maybe he thought somehow that *he'd* been called to commit a heinous act of mass murder. And then when it actually happened…"

"He thought he'd really done it," Rob filled in.

"Maybe. Possibly."

"Well, maybe he did."

Stout's teeth clenched on the stem of his pipe, his slack profile tightening, backlit by the smoldering fire.

Frank said, "I guess the reverend didn't tell you about that part of our conversation."

"Actually, he did mention it." With faint whistling sounds, Stout deliberately rekindled the pipe, which could've used a flue of its own. His eyes shifted to Rob. "And he was very sympathetic, Detective—as I am—about your bereavement, and your understandable desire to find some kind of justice for your daughter. Now, given Billy's threats beforehand, and disappearance afterward…but even if the government didn't have incontrovertible evidence against…"

"All for Allah."

"Right. Which I would say should settle the issue then and there. But even without that—Billy was a sinner, like all of us, but one who was trying to do the best he could to overcome his past, to walk with the Lord. He was not a mass murderer. There is no way. None."

"Even if he was off his medication?" said Frank. "Which, again, he never told me he was taking."

"Well, he was. And when he was struggling with his inner demons, or whatever we want to call them, then he was more reliant on the reverend for sustenance, for comfort and guidance. In fact, when he started ranting about what he was going to do on the night of the concert, I told him that he was talking insanity, and that he should speak to Reverend Tate as soon as possible. Which he did."

"And?" The brothers uttered this syllable more or less simultaneously, on the same page for once.

Stout sighed. "Mr. Tedeschi—Frank, Detective—you know how Billy was. Is. When he's devoted to something, that devotion is complete. Mostly. This time, he just told me that private conferences with the reverend are private, even though I was technically his boss. And even though we both knew, or should have known, what Reverend Tate would say—said—to such a deranged idea. And indeed, after Billy disappeared, I was informed by the reverend of the substance of their conversation. He'd told Billy that we don't kill in the name of Jesus. We don't even think about it if we can help it. And that if he'd misunderstood his previous counsel and gone off the medication, he should get back on at once, that, in his case, the prescription would have to be prayer and medication both. I'm telling you this now in the interest of setting your suspicions to rest."

"Okay," Rob said, sighing. "So, Billy Patterson was psychic. He could see that First Union Arena was about to be gassed by Islamic terrorists, but he got himself confused with them, before and after, even though they were anti-Christs, and even though he would never go near a

Shove It Up concert, because they were also anti-Christs or whatever. So he went into hiding."

"Out of shame, I would say. And/or delusion. It's the only thing that makes any sense."

"And despite his devotion to the reverend, he hasn't been in touch?"

"Shame is a powerful emotion, Detective Tedeschi. Especially for one as unstable as Billy. I would hope that he hasn't reverted to drinking, to the self-destructive ways in which he lived before he came to the Lord. Hopefully, he has seen newspapers, watched television, even overheard conversations, wherever he is. The truth about what happened at First Union Arena is hard to miss. Then, hopefully, it will become clear to him."

"Probably it already has," said Rob. "Tell me, Mr. Stout, what's the name of that foster brother of his you tried to contact?"

"Couldn't say. Tried to remember, but couldn't. Kind of eliminated any chance I might've had of finding his number."

CHAPTER 9

She would've come for the calamari, if nothing else." Rob, eyes shut, sipped from a wine glass, his thick fingers wedged between its flat round base and the reddish-purple curvature of the bowl, which he squeezed as if holding the thing together. "She loved the stuff," he added, looking up from the goblet, his voice hoarse. "For that, she would've come."

Julie reached across the table and laid her hand on his arm. "She'd have come anyway. She could've compared notes with her cousin over here. Compared studs and tattoos," Julie said, ignoring the look her younger son shot her as he leaned forward on the other side of Frank. "Plus, even if Laureen acted like it was uncool, she loved her family. Starting with her parents."

Rob gritted his teeth and looked away, thinking that he either needed to lay off the wine or get soused, that he was now inhabiting a dangerous middle ground. Tears in your beer, only substitute wine in a glass that seemed to magically refill itself, to siphon bittersweet vin rose from the carafe. Either the bus boy was very unobtrusive, or Rob was transfusing the stuff himself without really being aware of it.

He couldn't have sworn that Laureen loved her parents, separately or together. Ditto for her extended family. Still, it was Laureen, ironically, who'd brought all of them together. For the second time in a month, no less. They could have left out a glass of wine for *her*, left the outside door ajar like the Jews did on Passover. Except that there was even less chance of Laureen showing up than there was of the Prophet Elijah draining the Manischewitz. Besides, it was cold out, and they were in a restaurant. The place was crowded, noisy, probably bugproof, assuming that the so-far anonymous federal spooks even knew that the Tedeschi clan was dining there. And it was a setting much preferable to that of the previous family get-together, Cascardi's Funeral Home.

Julie and Frank's two sons were on extended winter break, exams having been postponed in the wake of the tragedy at First Union Arena. Sergio, a senior in economics at the University of Maryland, had hopped on a Port Authority-bound Greyhound bus the next day, after hearing that his cousin was likely among the dead. He gazed out at the hardened black snow encrusting the sides of the New Jersey Turnpike and wondered how it could possibly be true. Laureen had been his mischievous accomplice in the house in Pelham Bay when they were little kids, when their families lived within close proximity, and Grandpa Albert was determined to see his sons act as if the same blood ran through their veins, as if being under their childhood roof together again, with children of their own, would surely do the trick. Dinner every Sunday at Grandma and Grandpa's, after which the younger generation had the run of the house.

Sergio's younger brother Carl was either a third wheel or a victim in their fun and games. Once or twice he was locked in a dark closet while the adults downstairs boisterously discussed President Bush's intellect or lack thereof, or the skills of Grandpa's younger brother George in attracting wealthy, philanthropic older women, or other topics, which induced alcohol-fueled, raucous laughter.

Carl's cries went unheard except by Sergio and Laureen, who released him when he finally promised to kiss all four of their bare feet, a promise he broke immediately upon gaining his freedom. Or Carl would trustingly slide down the carpeted stairs into the living room on a pillow pulled by Sergio and/or Laureen, only to have it yanked out from under him after he'd gained some momentum, before reaching the bottom. Undaunted, he'd try it again the following Sunday, by which time his behind was no longer sore.

Sergio's was sore enough by the time his bus reached the Lincoln Tunnel. He'd been obliged to sit next to a seriously obese, musty male passenger whose width had caused Sergio's bottom to be wedged against the iron base of the armrest. But after a while, he'd barely noticed. How could Laureen be gone?

It was true that after they were teenagers and began asserting their independence on Sunday evenings, leaving Carl to the more exquisite torment of being the only kid at Grandpa's, the bond between Sergio and Laureen had diminished. Especially after Sergio graduated to high school. He was a big man on campus by the time she arrived, a jock like his father, putting his muscular physique to use as a catcher on the school baseball team.

And Laureen had just begun to move in weird directions—drugs; punk-goth, whatever that was. When their paths crossed, in school or on the street, they generally exchanged a few sentences, maybe introducing a friend or two before moving on.

On the other hand, at family gatherings, they still felt

some generational solidarity and found enough to talk about. But after Sergio left for the University of Maryland, she rarely crossed his mind. And now somehow she was dead. As was his childhood, something that he thought had happened a long time ago. Only it had just happened again.

At Laureen's funeral, the first he'd ever attended, he witnessed the heart-rending grief of his Uncle Rob, whom he could have never imagined leaking tears, in public or otherwise. It was as if they'd been squeezed out of stone, like the tears reportedly running down from certain statues of the Virgin Mary. Rob's problem child, his only child, was dead.

Sergio was certain that Rob would've thanked God a thousand times for the opportunity to continue having Laureen mock his authority, send his blood pressure through the roof, test his sanity. All he had left now was his wife, Nellie. She was technically still alive. At the funeral, she seemed to inhabit a medication-induced nether world, behind a black semi-veil that was eerily evocative of the facial coverings worn by the women of Islam, whose fanatical men had poisoned Laureen and thousands of others.

"God, help us all," Sergio's paternal grandmother had whispered as she clung to him.

Despite his skepticism where Jesus or any other supposed incarnations of God were concerned—he was his parents' son in that regard, at least—Sergio couldn't help but agree. And he nodded his head and responded in kind each time an all-but-forgotten relative swore that he or she hoped to see him again in happier circumstances.

Now, a month later, officially happier circumstances had arrived, with the metro New York Tedeschis dining together at Sorrento's Ristorante on White Plains Road in the Bronx. The place had been recommended by Uncle

Rob, whose stationhouse was a few blocks away. He dined there frequently when working the four-to-midnight shift. Excellent food, friendly atmosphere, a fine place for the clan to come together, to assert that although one of them was gone in the flower of her youth, they still had each other. Enjoyment of life was still possible.

Theoretically, at least. Uncle Rob didn't seem to be doing a whole lot better. Sergio's mom, having failed to cheer up her brother-in-law, was trying to change the subject, although her choice of topic was mystifying at best. Had anyone seen on the news the protests at Lafayette Square, outside the White House? Sergio had while hanging around at home with his parents and brother.

There were Muslims, in kaffiyehs and burghas no less, along with ACLU types—Mom's ilk—protesting President Flowers's edict mandating the deportation of all Muslims who were not permanent residents, as well as his abrogation of free speech inside of American mosques and other Islamic organizations, which could only be seen as a prelude to their extinction.

They were also protesting Flowers's threats to invade Pakistan and/or Iran, to eradicate the terrorists in their own safe havens, slaughter them like the pigs that they were. The police, Mom said, had performed admirably, preventing an angry mob from tearing the protesters to pieces and refraining from doing it themselves. She had glanced solicitously at Uncle Rob as she said this. No more cop-bashing from Mom, the bleeding-heart social worker. In times of crisis, security came first.

"They've *should've* busted their heads," opined Sergio's brother Carl, looking up from his third piece of buttered Italian bread. He ate like a horse but was still scrawny, Sergio's physical opposite. "See if they were smart enough to put any padding under those stupid head dresses they wear."

"Hey. You're talking sense, little brother. For once."

"Fuck you."

"*What*?" Frank demanded. "That's the way you talk in front of your grandparents?" He fixed Carl with a hard stare. The kid just looked away. Then Frank glanced over at Rob, who had a faint smirk on his face. Brotherhood. Us. Their parents, if nonplussed, at least didn't seem overly shocked. But then that would've taken a lot, after First Union Arena.

Besides Rob, the only other person in the family who knew anything about Billy Patterson, Reverend Tate, and the mission the brothers—plus Fowlkes—had undertaken was Julie, who didn't really need to be sworn to secrecy. Frank and Rob had quickly agreed on the wisdom of this, even before learning that they were under surveillance. The older and younger Tedeschis were better off innocently going about their business. And Nellie was not especially stable. Lest anyone wonder why on earth Frank was wearing a gun, he'd left it home. This was Julie's idea, but he'd quickly seen the logic—just as she'd understood the necessity for him to arm himself in the first place, even though the sight of Frank's .38 special made her almost ill. Not so with her occasional glimpses of the hardware attached to Rob, now overlain by his sweater. For better or worse, he was a cop. It was part of the packaging.

"You know, boys," said Frank, his voice dripping sarcasm, "all of this war-mongering, by old men, *that's* about as old as the hills. And who do you think is gonna wind up getting killed, or maimed? Kids your age. Poor slobs from the ghetto or whatever. Cannon fodder, to our brave president."

Sergio said, "Hey, if *I* have to defend—*you* went, right? Enlisted."

"Exactly. So maybe you should assume that I know what I'm talking about. You don't wanna do that, Sergio. And believe me, I'm not saying you're not man enough. That's not it."

Sergio shrugged, as if the notion of aspersions on his manhood were too ridiculous to be taken seriously. "Okay. But if we have to protect this country, protect ourselves—I can't speak for little brother over there, but I'm willing to go."

"My hero," Carl sneered, resolutely apolitical except possibly for the nihilistic attitude he was lately trying to project. His eyebrow stud and nose ring glinted even in the subdued light of the restaurant. Carl hadn't pierced his face merely to be down with the latest fashions. You could look at him and tell that he was not the same person. Leaving home, and/or a few months at Stoneybrook University, had done wonders for him—not. With their parents between them as a buffer, it was easy enough for Sergio to ignore him. The kid was just trying to compensate for his own fecklessness.

"Um, Serge? You think Flowers's son, or daughter, or Vice-President Mayberry's son, you think they're gonna go? How many rich Republicans you think will be getting their heads blown off in Iran, or Pakistan? These guys are really tough, with other people's lives." Frank bit through the crust of a piece of bread and sank his teeth into its buttered center, while reminding himself to keep it down, keep it level. "For the record—" he said, immediately wishing that he hadn't. He was ninety-five percent sure that he wasn't, in fact, on record, courtesy of the latest in surreptitious taping technology, but still… "—and I know this may shock you, but I don't believe what Flowers says about anything, including what happened at First Union Arena. And once they get you in the army, it's like they own you. You wanna talk about the government controlling people's lives—"

"Hey, Dad, better watch that," Sergio interjected. "If I didn't know better, I'd think you were a member of the Vast Right-Wing Conspiracy."

Frank chuckled. Sergio's participation in the Young Conservatives Forum at the University of Maryland had more or less lapsed, that was true. So his son had indicated over the phone. But Frank and Julie's incipient hope was short lived: Sergio added that his political convictions hadn't changed, at all. He'd simply reshuffled his priorities. It turned out that Serge was head over heels for a pretty junior from Ohio. She'd actually caused him to attempt the first unassigned poetry of his life. Then there was baseball, still a priority, if no longer numero uno.

"The Vast Right Wing Conspiracy? Yeah, I've heard of that," Frank said, wondering how on earth he and Julie had managed to raise a son who'd actually voted for Edward Flowers with his first and only presidential ballot. Youthful rebellion had claimed him for the party of rich white men. Not only had the apple fallen far from the tree, it had rotted. "They're against government when it suits their purposes," he continued, "like if government wants to infringe on their right to rip people off, pollute the environment, rig elections, what have you. And they're all for war, which usually helps them and their friends get richer. The populace gets all fired up and patriotic. Republican incumbents get reelected, and their opponents get vilified as traitors. It's like, tighten the screws on the rest of the world, or at least targeted areas, where we drop those smart bombs and deploy the other little toys that keep the military-industrial complex humming.

That's what Dwight D. Eisenhower called it, a Republican president no less. Then tighten the screws at home, on anyone who doesn't like it."

"Relax, Frank," Julie counseled.

The conversation had been moving back and forth along one side of the table, as if only that side were wired for sound. Frank's parents' politics lay somewhere between his and Sergio's. Over the previous couple of years, they had been nudged leftward by the Flowers administration, which by now they basically agreed with only on abortion. Albert and Maria Tedeschi gazed across the table in dismay.

It was bad enough that one of their two remaining grandchildren appeared wired himself, between the glitter of his facial metal and the scraggly goatee that looked like static electricity personified. This gathering at Sorrento's was supposed to be a night for healing. At least for a beginning, insofar as it was possible, a night on which to be fortified by the bonds of familial love.

"Okay, sure," Frank replied. *Relax. Presto.* He took a deep breath, let it out slowly, almost audibly. "It's just…believe it or not, Serge…Carl, your mother and I would be crushed if anything happened to either one of you. It's the last thing this family needs." *Another child killed by the government.* "And you can take it from me, war, being in one, is horrible beyond anything you can imagine. That's why so many ex-soldiers refuse to talk about it. It's like a whole other realm, and the last thing you want to do is bring it out into this one, especially if you're lucky enough to have survived with your sanity still intact. You could be the most morally upright person in the world, but put yourself in a situation where *anyone,* even a child, could be the instrument of your death at any time, could have a bomb strapped to them—you're almost guaranteed to do things you'll regret the rest of your life."

He paused, conscious of every eye in the family being fixed on him with a mixture of trepidation and expectation. Frank was one of those ex-soldiers who had refused to talk about it, except once to Julie, after he returned from Vietnam. He couldn't help but spill his guts then, the sight-memory of entrails literally spilling being too painful to contain.

"Case in point," he said, even as half of him rebelled against what he was about to do. He gazed at Sergio as if channeling himself at that age, as if that was what it would take to make himself tell it with conviction, with certainty, with the knowledge that he wasn't talking about a once-recurring nightmare that he'd managed to leave behind over the past ten-fifteen years.

"We shot up this hut," he declared finally, his voice croaking slightly. "It was full of little kids, and one old woman. Not a weapon, not a knife, not even a Vietcong pamphlet. Someone in my unit opened fire. Probably thought he saw something. That was all it took, we were that scared out of our minds, that much on edge. We all started shooting, call it a chain reaction, whatever, it was impossible *not* to shoot. Sergio, if you could see what I saw inside of that hut afterward, you might become a pacifist. If everyone in the world could see it, there might not be any more wars.

"Actually, I take that back. People like my commanding officer—" Frank couldn't bring himself to utter the name. "They'd say it was collateral damage, unavoidable. Part of the price you have to pay—or that those kids and that old woman had to pay, for being born Vietnamese, I guess. Anyway, the next day, when he told me to move it out, to go on patrol, I just refused. I'd had it with the war, I felt like I was done. Period. So he pointed a gun at my head. And he would've shot me, wouldn't have hesitated—if someone hadn't intervened."

Frank probably would have stopped there, even had he and the rest of the men in his unit not made a promise, a non-disclosure agreement regarding the identity of that "someone." He'd broken that promise only once, with Julie. Now he scanned the table. The slack skin around his father's jaw was trembling. His mother's rouge was streaking with tears. She'd been emotionally labile since having a mastectomy eight months previously, more so since First Union Arena.

"Sorry." Frank's voice was compressed by the blockage in his throat. "Maybe this wasn't the time or place. But if it makes my sons think twice, or ten times, before becoming soldiers…"

Sergio and Carl were both looking away. Hopefully, something had registered.

"You know, Pop," Frank said, gazing across at his father, anxious to change the subject, "that's why I wound up going in with you at the store, despite once having sworn to myself that I never would, that I wanted to make my own way, or some sh—something—like that. I knew you weren't on a power trip, and that, eventually, I'd be my own boss. After dealing with the army's command structure, I couldn't handle the idea of having to work *under* someone."

"Well, you made a good decision," Albert Tedeschi said, his eyes shining with pride. He still helped out at Tedeschi's Hardware on occasion, more so recently, since his wife was feeling physically stronger and Frank was short-handed at the store. "And you built up the business. That whole paint wing, the potted plants—"

"Hell, the business built itself up, especially after all those subdivisions started popping up around Armonk. Like plants. Don't know what made me think of that. But dealing with employees, being more than just my own boss, *that's* been interesting. Trying to be diplomatic. Make suggestions, 'steada reaming someone out."

"Billy Patterson still hasn't turned up?"

"Nope. It's been a month and a half. And I don't believe I'm gonna go looking for him, either." Frank glanced over at Rob, a party to this unnecessary little lie. "'Course, I was brilliant enough to hire him in the first place. Hopefully, I can replace him with someone who has his head on straight. It's—"

He paused as the waitress arrived with their food, impressively matching each dish with he or she who'd ordered it without needing to have her recollection refreshed, laying down fragrant eggplant parmigiana, spaghetti carbonara, scungilli, baked ziti, chicken cacciatore, food for the living.

The next evening, Frank and Rob drove to meet Paul Fowlkes at a public library in Forest Hills, New York. This was the same area of Queens in which a functionally furnished apartment, including a computer and back-up that linked him to the FBI's data system, served as Fowlkes's base of operations.

The building's Mutt and Jeff doormen and two or three neighbors he'd chatted with in the basement laundry room, or while stuck in an occasionally balky elevator, were under the impression that he was "in computers," and often worked out of his apartment.

Fowlkes was able to give enough technical-sounding details to make this seem believable, on the off-chance that someone was paying more than cursory attention.

And yes, he lived alone. His ex-wife and daughter, a college junior, lived in Jersey.

Bill Summers—aka Fowlkes—also had a son in college, who worked as a chef part time, trying to pay off his student loan. Fowlkes had discovered that the unused college money that had been available to him via the GI Bill was not transferable to his offspring.

The family details were more or less accurate, excepting the names. He'd toyed with the idea of using his ex-wife's maiden name, just as a goof, since she'd kept his, even though she pointedly informed him that she was, in fact, keeping the *kids'* last name.

Fowlkes had laughed and rolled his eyes, a maneuver that his teenaged daughter had elevated to an art form.

Forest Hills was populated by well-off Italians, Jews, and other ethnics, including a recent influx of stereotypically hard-working Koreans, who lived in luxury high-risers or custom-made homes protected by security gates. Two of the area's residents were heroin kingpins, jacket-and-tie professionals whose mantle of respectability was well established among their neighbors.

Even though each served all five boroughs, plus Long Island and New Jersey, they'd so far managed to avoid a suicidal turf war. In the best tradition of American corporations, they were busy extending their tentacles outward, vetting their employees, establishing chains of command that began and ended in Forest Hills.

Fowlkes hoped that they were less vigilant about vetting their customers, including Bill Summers. In any case, his placement in the metropolitan New York area had made feasible his extra-curricular project with the Tedeschi brothers. He didn't necessarily believe in fate, but he was willing to in this instance.

Frank and Rob were driving across the Throgg's Neck

Bridge. Down below, the black expanse of the Long Island Sound was dotted with points of light. Boats, but they could have been inverted stars, or luminous fragments broken loose from the Bronx or Queens. The edges of the two boroughs were outlined in random configurations of windows and street lamps interlaced with headlights, glowing faintly on the distant, opposite shores.

Frank had no idea why anyone would be sailing or motoring across the sound on a cold January evening. But the idea seemed appealing—all concerns temporarily dwarfed by the elements, at once vast and insulating. Surrounded and soothed by the ancient murmur of lapping waves. Of course, he didn't vocalize these musings to Rob. They sounded hokey enough in his own head, even if much preferable to worrying that any one of the myriad pairs of head lights behind them might belong to a vehicle whose driver had in mind to run them over the side, a tactic against which his gun would likely prove useless. Theoretically, the bridge's guardrails had been built to withstand the impact of vehicles much larger than Rob's—or the NYPD's—Ford Taurus. But still…

"Frank." Rob's voice almost startled him, neither of them having spoken or even reached for the car radio's power button since getting onto the New England Thruway, off of the Cross County Parkway in Westchester. "I sorta felt guilty about not serving."

Frank gazed over at his brother, who was likely by now ninety percent recovered from the hangover that had resulted from the dinner at Sorrento's. Rob had driven back to Pelham Bay, with his parents and wife in the car, keeping a watchful eye out for his fellow cops. His badge probably would have caused most of them to ignore the fact that he was DWI, unless it was a uniform who relished busting a detective. The intent look on Rob's face now was softened somewhat by the strobe effect of the conveyor belt of headlights moving toward the Bronx and points north and west.

"Not serving what?"

Rob shook his head. "In Vietnam, man."

"*What*? Are you fucking crazy?"

"So I've been told, on numerous occasions," replied Rob, with a grunt intended as a laugh. "Still, a lot of people went through that shit, you know, they didn't have a choice."

"Unlike your stupid-assed brother. It's like…Rob, if nine people go through hell, that's better than ten having to do it. But, hey, I forgive you, man. Really. For getting a high number in the draft lottery, like a punk."

"Fuck you."

Frank studied his brother's profile—their mother's rounded jaw, father's high broad forehead and prominent nose—against a backdrop of the bridge's ultraviolet-lit cables, which ran vertically in diminishing lengths, harp-like. Their illusory motion was evocative of riffled pages as the car descended toward Queens. Or of the many years gone by, seemingly just as fast, since he, then Rob, had been obliged to register with the Selective Service System.

"Hey, relax. I was kidding, man," he said. "You didn't know that? And I was not talking about 'Nam last night to make you feel guilty. Why the hell would I want to do that? I was trying to scare the shit out of my sons. Not that I was making anything up, but—"

"I know that. And I'm sure they heard you loud an' clear, even if it didn't stop them from stuffing their faces then ordering cake and spumoni for dessert."

Frank laughed. "Yeah. Well, Grandpa was paying. But correct me if I'm wrong, but you've put your ass on the line for how many years now, as a cop?"

"It's not the same thing. And since when do you… since when are you a fan of cops?"

"Always. Seriously, man, now that I'm not dodging nightsticks anymore…and that time the store got robbed? The cops up there were helpful. Actually caught the bastard, too."

"I remember." Rob checked over his right shoulder as he came off the bridge then shifted lanes and accelerated. He was a Bronx man, making his way in a foreign land, navigating one of the hydra-headed exchanges for which Queens/Long Island highways were famous. Frank provided guidance, reading his MapQuest sheet with the help of the cruiser's overhead lamp, barking directions as if Rob were hard of hearing.

When they were safely on the Van Wyck Expressway heading east, Rob said, "And Fowlkes was another hero."

Frank pursed his lips. "What? We're back on that? Man, I never said *I* was a hero. *Au contraire*, which I think means 'to the contrary,' which might be all the French I know, since I took *Espanol* in high school. But in 'Nam, I was just trying to stay alive. It was instinct, even though a lot of times, before and after, it was hard to see the point. But hero? I was trying to keep from getting hurt, man. Period. You put a gun in a total coward's hand, and if running away is not an option, he'll shoot that thing 'til the trigger falls off. Shoot at anything, blindly. Anyone."

"Okay. But Fowlkes, you told me he 'saved your ass,' when you were talking about what a fine partner he would make, FBI man, tough son of a bitch. That story you told last night, about how your CO would've wasted you if someone hadn't intervened? Was that someone Fowlkes?"

Frank sighed and gazed out at the rectangular red-brick houses of Elmhurst, Queens, lit by street lamps and porch lights, row after row of them.

The cross streets kept them from merging into one, a sooty red wall regularly punctuated by doors, awnings, and windows, fronted by brown patches of earth littered with lawn chairs left out after the summer, lying on their sides.

"You'd have to ask him that," he said finally. "I'm not really at liberty to talk about it."

"Hey. This sounds interesting."

"Yeah, I suppose. But it's not some juicy piece of gossip, or some shit like that. Take my word for it."

"O-kay. 'Scuse me," said Rob, shooting his brother a look as if the sarcasm in his voice needed a visual, bringing his eyes back to the road just in time—or so it seemed to Frank—to avoid ramming a car stopped for the light at the intersection of Utopia Parkway and 119th Street.

There was a poetry reading in progress at the Forest Hills branch of the New York Public Library. It featured a slender, forty-ish woman in a turtleneck sweater, upon which her Adam's apple appeared to make a larger impression than her breasts. The thickness of the sweater highlighted by contrast the severe shortness of her haircut, as did her gold hoop earrings. The woman—Sarah Janowitz, according to flyers posted on both of the library's glass outer doors, and at several locations inside—looked the part, based on Frank's very limited experience with poetesses.

She was reading from a paperback on a wooden lectern, something about cosmic vertigo, starlit eons, her rapid cadence adding to the elusiveness of the lines. The rest of the poem escaped him altogether as he scanned the audience of seven or eight people seated in metal folding chairs. Paul Fowlkes was indeed among them. He actually seemed rapt, almost a caricature of attentiveness, his lower lip having parted slightly from his mustache as he gazed upward at Sarah Janowitz.

Frank stood to one side of her, futilely attempting to catch Fowlkes's eye. He finally did so after the poem was over. Given the size of the crowd, the applause was impressive, delivered on the other side of a few seconds' worth of silence. Fowlkes was clapping as he slid from his seat, nodding and smiling apologetically at Ms. Janowitz.

With a mere inclination of his head—this was either out of deference to Janowitz, who was introducing her next poem, or borne of a spy's habitual discretion—he indicated the rear of the library, where there were several "silent study" rooms. These were sometimes used for tutoring or group research projects being carried out by AP high school students, Children of the Successful in Forest Hills. One was fortuitously empty. As Rob shut the door behind them, enclosing the three men in what seemed like a hermetically sealed silence, Frank clapped Fowlkes on his broad shoulder.

"Poetry?" he inquired. "The bad-assed FBI man has a sensitive side, which he keeps from his fellows because, otherwise, rumors will circulate that he is queer, which will endanger his job."

Fowlkes laughed. "Fuck you, Comrade Tedeschi. It was something to do while I was waiting for you. It's not like I knew she was gonna be here beforehand."

"Yeah, but you really seemed into it."

"Actually…yeah. Not that I understood half of what it was supposed to mean, but it's much preferable to listening in on drug goombahs' phone conversations, discussing their problems with constipation and other such fascinating stuff. It's like, you listen to three hours of bullshit before you get maybe thirty seconds of something that might be useful, down the line."

"Hey, I was kidding, Paul. Poetry's cool. It can be like its own kind of detective work, trying to figure it out. But—oh shit, sorry Rob. Paul, this is my brother Rob. Rob, Paul Fowlkes."

The two men exchanged rote pleasantries and shook hands, a conjoining of thick flesh that produced a moist, sucking sound. "Good to finally meet you, Detective," said Fowlkes as they disengaged.

Rob chuckled. "Yeah, we're sort of in the same racket. Even overlap, sometimes. But I've heard a lot about you too. Frank says you saved his ass in Vietnam."

Frank gave a soft whistle, as Fowlkes sent a narrow-eyed, questioning look his way. "Rob doesn't beat around the bush, as you can see. I…um…didn't supply any details."

"Ah. Well, still, Frank is prone to exaggeration," Fowlkes said, fixing his gaze on Rob now. "At least in this instance. And…um…I wanted to say that I'm sorry about your daughter."

Rob was momentarily speechless, as if caught off-guard by the sudden subject switch. "Right. Thank you," he replied, tight-lipped.

"So, why don't we sit down, discuss this research project we're working on?"

Rob and Frank both nodded. The round metal disks at the bottoms of wooden chair legs scraped against the floor. The brothers sat facing Fowlkes across a darker wooden table that was carved or inked with various teenaged endearments—Sonja & Kyle 4-ever, The Bone is in the House, Fucketh Thee Brother, etc.—surprisingly, this being Forest Hills, where graffiti was not in vogue, or at least not in evidence on the sides of buildings, trucks and other such inviting surfaces.

"If we hurry up, maybe we can catch the end of the reading. Joke," added Fowlkes, when neither of the brothers cracked a smile. The weight of their little project had seemed to settle almost palpably on Frank as he sat down, unzipping his jacket but leaving it on, this having become almost second nature. He'd been relieved to discover that the library had no metal detector, that the sensors in the parallel metallic uprights in the foyer were apparently for the purpose of preventing the liberation of books, CDs or videotapes that had not been checked out. "You guys paid a visit to Billy Patterson's supervisor. Stout, his name is?"

"Yup," said Rob. "Mid-to-late fifties, lives alone, devoted to the church, and to keeping it looking pretty." He recited these words in a clipped tone laced with quiet disdain, Sergeant Friday with a dose of latter-day cynicism, a world-weary cop moved by his own brand of devotion. "Patterson, before he disappeared, bragged to Stout about his plans for First Union Arena. Seems like he had a really hard time keeping his mouth shut. Stout thought—like Frank did—that the guy was just, ranting, letting off steam. According to Stout, Patterson was bipolar. One variety of nut case. And he was probably off his medication, on the advice of Reverend Tate, who told him that prayer was all he really needed."

Rob shook his head. "It's probably cheaper, at least. Anyway, Stout claimed that Patterson was really touched by the spirit. Had visions. The way I understood it, the idea is that some people who are whacko actually have a direct line to God. Sort of as compensation, I guess. So, Patterson's rantings were the result of his premonitions of what was going to happen. Then, when it actually *did,* he freaked, thought *he* was responsible. Skipped town. All of this according to Stout."

Fowlkes absently tugged on one end of his mustache, at the same time retracting that corner of his mouth, creating the momentary impression that his hefty face was elastic, constructed of putty. "And you think he actually believes that? Or do you think he's really an accessory? He's kind of a link between Patterson and Reverend Tate, isn't he?"

"No and yes," replied Rob, short-circuiting his brother. "I don't think he's involved, although the reverend warned him about us beforehand, that we might come around asking ridiculous questions, making ridiculous accusations. The only reason he agreed to talk to us was that he's concerned about Patterson, which I believe. Plus, Patterson spoke highly of Frank—"

"Ah. *Must've* been off his meds."

"You're a riot, Comrade Fowlkes," said Frank, laughing even as he made a mental note to dispense with the "Comrade" jazz. Rob was not about to play the role of third wheel, perceived or otherwise. And if his Republican proclivities were at a low ebb, adopting Pinko terminology, even in jest, was probably a bit far in the other direction. "But I agree with Rob. Just, on a gut level, there was no sleaze factor with Stout, unlike Maximilian Tate. Stout seemed totally blind to what a scumbag Tate actually is. Like the fact that Billy was being counseled by his Holiness meant that it was completely impossible that he could've done First Union. And, I got the impression Billy was like his—Stout's—protege, sort of a project, a good soul in need of a little nurturing, the kind of person who would never dream of murdering thousands of people."

Frank turned to his brother. "You agree, no?"

"Sure, Frank." Rob's voice was suddenly hoarse. "Yeah," he said to Fowlkes, a trifle loudly, as if the constriction in his throat could thereby be dispelled. "Stout told us he called the local cops to get information. Frank filed the missing person's report, although Stout was under the impression that Tate had. And maybe he did call in to do that after Frank, I don't know. That would probably add to his…what, profile of innocence? See, I care about my hired help. No chance that Patterson has been whacked, now that he's done their dirty work for them. Anyway, Stout got nothing from the cops. Same as we did. He also tried to reach a foster brother of Patterson's. Lives in Jersey, as far as Stout knew. No luck. Not surprising, since he couldn't recall the name."

"Right." Fowlkes shifted uncomfortably in the hard wooden chair, trying to get centered. He cast a fast glance out, in the direction of Sara Janowitz, who was still reading her poetry to mostly empty chairs now, her animated delivery inaudible inside the study room, the sounds of silence. "Finding Patterson…like you said, Rob, they've probably eliminated him, like they did Scanlon."

Both brothers nodded.

"But if Patterson's still alive, then finding him's gotta be priority numero uno. Not that a confession from him would necessarily fly, even if it was an up-and-up investigation. Not without corroborating evidence. A crime of this magnitude, this high a profile, even with the Bureau claiming that they already know who did it, I bet they've still had plenty of head cases offering up confessions. Without evidence, they'd say he was one more. Even if he could give them details—the kind of gas used, whatever—all of that is known, it's been all over the news forever. Even if Frank testified that Patterson had announced his plans for First Union beforehand. And imagine how frustrating *that* would be. Commit mass murder in the name of God, and no one will even give you credit."

"We will," offered Rob.

"Corroborating evidence," said Frank, while using his thumbnail to try to deface or obliterate an ink drawing on the table of a swastika with a maniacally grinning head attached to its upper branch, muscular arms extending from either side, and equally bulging legs extending from the horizontal line on the bottom. "Such as?"

"Well, first there's the guard who was posted by the air conditioning intake unit, the one who got shot. Died a 'hero's death.'" Fowlkes was quoting President Flowers directly, from an address he'd given subsequent to the one in which he eulogized agent Scanlon. Like Scanlon, John Laurent had been profiled widely in the media. He was depicted as a Jamaican immigrant who gave up his life for his adopted country, while attempting to thwart the most heinous crime in American history.

"If we had the gun that Patterson used—assuming he was working alone—we could match it with the bullet they took out of the guard's head. I know someone in ballistics. That should be all we need, assuming we can find an honest official high up enough in the bureau, and/or the administration. Someone willing to stick his own neck out. I have a couple in mind, in the bureau. We'll cross that bridge when and if we get to it."

"What about Klesko?"

Fowlkes shot Frank a quizzical look. "What about him?"

Behind the gleaming tortoise shell glasses, which reflected the room's neon lighting, his gaze shifted over to Rob, whose face indicated that they'd lost him. "This is the guy who was the commander of our unit in 'Nam," Frank said. "Stayed in after the war, to both our surprise.

Then he took officer training and is now a high-ranking general. Who'd a'thunk it?"

"This is the same guy who pointed a gun at Frank's head?"

Fowlkes's eyebrows lifted. Frank didn't need to be clairvoyant to read his mind. *I thought you didn't supply any details.* "No, the one who replaced him. Who, technically at least, is under the command of our douche bag president. You spoken to him lately, Frank?"

"Not for maybe five years. At least."

"Well, I don't see what good he can do us now. So…where were we? Corroborating evidence. I—"

"What about security cameras?" interjected Rob. "That intake unit was in the basement. You figure afterward, Patterson would've hauled ass for the nearest exit. There's a loading dock nearby. Gotta have a security camera there." He turned to Frank. "Loading docks are one preferred area for jokers who like to boost things off trucks. Even if Patterson was wearing a gas mask, he might've ripped it off outside, on the dock. They're not all that comfortable and impede visibility, and he'd have been in a serious hurry."

"Rob, you should come work for the bureau."

"I'll pass. Shit, I can retire in a year. Although I'd pass anyway."

"Hey, you can have my job, man," said Fowlkes, as if he hadn't heard Rob's last words, or the understated disdain behind them. "It's basically part-time, although my supervisor in DC has not been apprised of that. But, yeah, some of that 'incontrovertible evidence,' that Flowers says they have, might involve doctored images, either from the loading dock or the basement, assuming there were cameras down there. Still, the real images might be around, somewhere, on somebody's hard drive.

"We need to find out which company wired the place. Also, try to find out who in the bureau—and maybe the CIA—-who's in on this thing. It can't be many, that'd be too risky for them. But it would be good if I knew who can be trusted, as much as possible, anyway. If I poke around too much, or too indiscreetly—"

"That's your ass," Rob said.

"My large ass, yes. You saw what they did to Scanlon, who probably just knew too much. Speaking of which—I paid a little visit to his widow. See if I could come up with any useful information. Yesterday. I told her I hadn't made the funeral because I was on an assignment. Didn't tell her that I didn't really know him, and also there were like two thousand people there, including Flowers, which would've meant a long day, a media circus, and participation in a charade. The motherfuckers seriously have no shame. It's like they killed the guy and then stuck his head on the wall like a trophy, exhibit *A*. These A-rabs are savages."

Fowlkes shook his head. "Believe it or not, she actually told me that the funeral home did a 'miraculous' job of reattaching the head. Seamlessly. It was an open casket, people filing by. She—Florence her name is—really opened up to me. I came armed with enough details that I'd gleaned about him to make it seem like we were indeed associates, a while back. It didn't take much. She was eager to talk. You know the way it is. At the funeral, everyone's there, 'if you need anything, don't hesitate to call,' and then after a week or two, you're alone. 'Like, totally,' to coin a phrase."

If Rob could relate directly, he gave no indication. "You did this in a day?" he asked. "Where's she live?"

"Connecticut. Half a day. I sort of took a chance that she was home, she works part time, or was. She's in the process of packing up the place. Anyway, you're not supposed to discuss the secret shit you're doing, even with your spouse, but Scanlon did. Not uncommon. And yeah, All for Allah was disappointingly free of terrorist involvement, even rhetoric. In fact, anyone who seriously made noises like that was invited to leave the organization. But she took that as evidence of how devious these people are. Mike was taken in, despite all his experience. I didn't suggest that maybe it was evidence that someone else did the deed and wanted to make sure he didn't contradict their version of events. Someone like the government he worked for, which probably doctored his reports after killing him. Even aside from my desire to keep my own head joined to my neck, she was crying, man. I really didn't want to upset her any more than she already was.

"In fact, I was comforting her. And I started getting these urges, made me feel like…I don't know…I was already there under sort of false pretenses, and here I am getting all yanged up. Her husband's dead a month and a half. Still, she's not bad looking at all—not that it would matter. It's been a while. A serious while." He paused, scanning Rob and Frank's faces, evidencing no embarrassment. "Sorry," he said nonetheless. "Too much information, I know."

"Nah," replied Frank. "That's cool. It's good to know you can still get it up, Paul."

Rob shot his brother a wide-eyed look. Fowlkes laughed, but there was a hint of blush on his face.

Frank wished that he'd kept his mouth shut. "Sorry," he said. "I shouldn't assume that we're all members of the Viagra generation."

This was met by a resounding silence around the table.

"So," said Rob, moving right along, "assuming the cocksucker is still alive—a big assumption, but we've gotta at least find out one way or the other—it seems like locating Patterson is priority number one."

"I agree. And, I was thinking maybe you guys should handle that," Fowlkes said. "I'll assist in any way I can, pursue other avenues, like the reverend's phone and email messages, security camera images, try to find out who deals in sarin gas on the black market, try to access Scanlon's original reports. Also, depending on where and when they killed him, he might've been wired, although it's likely that any incriminating shit has long since been erased. A lot of this stuff I can do on the computer, which is where I spend a good amount of my work time, anyway. You'd be amazed—or maybe you wouldn't—at how easily your government, including the FBI, can tap into supposedly private communications. Maybe it'll turn out to be the monster that devours itself. Even though the reverend's communications have proved more difficult, so far. But, yeah, Rob, you got that right—Patterson, if we can find him alive."

CHAPTER 10

"Take evasive action."

That had been the advice of both Rob and Fowlkes. Each had already demonstrated his own NASCAR skills, pinning Frank back against his seat while eluding hypothetical pursuers. But there was nothing hypothetical about the SUV that was tailing him, probably since he left Tedeschi's Hardware. Frank had just noticed it a mile or two down the road. Its high beams were glaring non-stop in his rearview mirror. He tried turning his head and looking mainly out of his right eye, but there was no getting away from it. The blinding white light of death? A preview?

His heart pounding, he took a squealing U-turn on Mount Kisco Road, intending to double back eventually and catch the Sprain Brook Parkway, his usual route home. Home was no secret. His was still listed in the Westchester County phone book. There was nothing to be gained, in terms of useful information, for the motherfucker—or fuckers, he couldn't even see their outlines for the glare in his mirror—who were tailing him. But information was obviously not their goal. Otherwise, they'd have been more discreet. Hopefully, they were just trying to scare the shit out of him. If so, they were doing an excellent job, the gun strapped to his ribs notwithstanding. The SUV was back on his tail within half a minute of his having reversed field.

Take evasive action, even if you have only faint suspicions that you're being tailed, and even if they'd only be following you to the supermarket and back. If nothing else, losing the bastards will be a moral victory. Eat my dust. And if you can't shake them, and they seem serious—they're threatening to ram you, shoot you, or otherwise convert your car into a coffin—then turn the tables on them. You know your next move, and they don't. Plus, you have a gun. And whatever you do, don't panic.

No, I wouldn't think of it, even though my hands are trembling and clammy on the wheel, even though I'm sweating with the heater off and the windows down—they were totally steamed when up—and frigid air whipping through the car. It occurred to Frank to call Julie, just to let her know what was going on, tell her he loved her in case…

But instead of reaching into the glove compartment for the cell phone, he attempted a ninety-degree left turn at seventy miles an hour, action preceding thought.

He careened into a residential street in some blurry township, likely still in Westchester County, his car going dark as the glare vanished from his mirror. And he could no longer hear the growl of the SUV's engine over the whine of his own. Both sounds were gone in an instant, having been replaced by the squealing of his tires as he slammed on his brakes and took the left.

His car spun out, 360 degrees plus, vaulting a sloped curb and coming to rest on somebody's lawn. This he understood, with a tiny flicker of gratitude, after he clicked open his seat belt with one hand and the door with the other. He flung himself out of the car—or was catapulted by the jolting stop. He landed in dirt, narrowly missing a white plaster birdbath that loomed in the darkness.

Frank scrambled to his feet, reached into his already-unzipped jacket and pulled out his gun. It had gone from being a burden to being his most precious possession in the space of minutes. Crouching behind his car, he saw the SUV's lights illuminate the yard of the house to his right, spotlighting a male resident who'd come running out to investigate, drawn by the sound of screeching tires.

In the next instant, Frank saw the SUV come tearing around the corner. He took aim and fired twice, bracing for the recoil from distant memory. His first shot punctured the front tire on the driver's side, pure luck. The second hit metal, maybe the engine through the SUV's grille. Careening out of control, it gouged bark off of a curbside tree before coming to rest, front half embedded in some shrubbery several yards from the curb, rear tires barely remaining in the street.

There was enough light coming from the house across the road from the SUV to allow Frank to note its license plate. He had the mental wherewithal to do so even as he scrambled back into his own car. Its engine was still running. Somehow, he'd put it in park, an action he couldn't recall. As he threw it into drive, he heard the barking of dogs. A door slammed at the house to his right. He saw a flashlight beam from the porch of the house whose shrubbery had been violated by the SUV, a second's worth of impressions back-dropped by darkness.

Thankfully, no lights had gone on in the house directly behind him—commuters not yet back from their white collar jobs in the Big Apple, Mom and kids off at Mickey D's, whatever. Frank was gone. His tires flung dirt on the way out, adding new ruts to the mess he'd already made on the lawn, leaving evidence of his escape as he tore off in the opposite direction from the SUV. For a few seconds, he was literally flying blind, driving with his head ducked down below the top of his dashboard. He lifted it as he hit the corner, executing a screeching right, finally exhaling as it became apparent that no bullets would be piercing his rear window, tires, or head.

Frank made himself keep the car to a moderate speed, suppressing the impulse to floor it, even as his mind raced. Someone might've called 911. Tearing ass down the road was the surest way to attract cops on their way to investigate. Had it been necessary to fire? Maybe the SUV would've kept on going, trying to pick up his tail again. Except that he'd left his lights on when he bailed, having been in a major hurry to get out, get down. Pros that they undoubtedly were, they'd have noticed his headlights shining at an angle from somebody's lawn. Duh.

Had anyone seen his license plate? Unlikely. The whole thing had probably gone down in a minute or two, plus the street was dark, out here in the 'burbs. He actually knew where he was now and was amazed that he'd traveled so little distance from work. These were supposed to be quiet streets, at least until cowboys in cars started shooting the place up, vaulting their Ford Bronco, or whatever it was, over people's hedges, turning them into innocent bystanders in their own homes.

Sirens. How many people within range of the sound of his gun had picked up their phones? And how eager would the cops be to sink themselves into some city-type action, guns going off, maybe drug dealers bringing their heat north? Instead, the cops would find at least one thug, likely more, changing a flat tire, assuming they'd managed to back the Bronco out of the hedges. Frank's pursuers would probably flash their FBI, secret service, or whatever credentials at the cops and tell them no sweat, the situation is under control, *even if it doesn't look that way at the moment*.

They'd promise to cover the landscaping bill for the shrubbery and also take care of the son-of-a-bitch they were tailing, the one who shot at them. Or maybe they'd just hand the cops Frank's license plate number and possibly the bullets, traceable to his gun, and have him arrested. Maybe they would figure that it was better just to get him out of circulation now, rather than wait until he led them to whatever other subversives he was working with. Frank was dangerous. He was a bad motherfucker, had a gun, and knew how to use it. He felt a surprising flicker of pride at the notion, even as the sirens got louder, closer, sending his adrenaline level through the roof.

Still, when the wailing cop car with its top lights flashing approached, forcing several vehicles to pull onto the shoulder of the lane opposite Frank's, he didn't panic, didn't really have time to before the cops sped past. He felt himself start to breathe again. Soon he'd be getting on the Sprain Brook Parkway. Homeward bound, sweet normalcy. Except that he could just as easily wind up jail bound instead, pending bail. Reckless endangerment? Attempted murder? Could he prove that he'd been menaced, assuming that the cards weren't already stacked? At the least, he was deep in the shit now, with both feet. Rob and Fowlkes would both need to be apprised of his little adventure immediately. So would Julie. That was the part he couldn't bear to think about.

Julie had been instrumental in reclaiming him from the wreckage of Vietnam, forgiving his two-year desertion and nursing his wounds, including those engendered from the nightsticks of patriotic cops. That phase of their lives was supposed to be history now. Of course, the fact that they'd even found each other again in the first place was a small miracle. Neither of them had really been looking.

Frank, one more uncelebrated Vietnam vet who'd returned to the states technically alive—in the days before *PTSD* made it into psychiatric lexicon—was at first just looking to get his head on straight, or to get drunk enough that it didn't matter. Unfortunately, even in bars, images from the ongoing war flashed on the tube. *Bring the War Home.*

Or so the demonstrators chanted, also on TV. His parents quickly learned to switch channels if he was in the vicinity, even though he swore that 'Nam was just like a bad dream he'd had in another lifetime. Most of the time he did feel that way, detached from the war and everything and everyone else. He had no idea what to do with himself, or how to avoid those embarrassing moments when a truck's backfire, or the sudden screech of the Number Six Train's brakes, caused him to dive for cover, scraping his knees, palms, elbows and/or face on the sidewalk. This was purely reflex, a blast from the past.

For his parents, hearing him stumble into the house late at night was disturbing, but not without its silver lining. At least he was home. He was not on the other side of the world being measured for a body bag. Nor was he out puking in the street, or being mugged by those brave young souls who liked to roll drunks. And if he was soused, that meant that he would sleep it off, rather than wake up screaming from a nightmare involving severed limbs, skewered babies, exploding land mines, items they'd gleaned from him before he was fully awake.

Unfortunately, Rob could hear as well, his vaunted ability to sleep like a stone having deserted him. And he wasn't particularly empathetic, or tolerant of being woken even before his alarm clock went off. It was his first year at the police academy. In keeping with the quasi-military structure of the place, they started *early.* Plus, Rob was still half a kid himself. He was not equipped to deal with the reality of his formerly rock-like brother as a basket case, or close enough. Fortunately, the academy engendered its own social life. Even as trainees, cops mostly hung with other cops, plus the number of female recruits was growing. Rob was a busy person. And when he was home and Frank was also, they were blessed to live in a large house.

Their parents, on the other hand, stepped instinctively into the role of being Frank's *safety net,* a term he was introduced to at his first Vietnam Vets meeting. Albert and Maria Tedeschi couldn't have done otherwise. He was their son, their firstborn, the glue that had cemented their marriage.

Also, they'd known him pre-war. Frank was a casualty of Vietnam, the kind that didn't register in the statistics. The numbers that the bastards issued tenaciously everyday were issued as if they were evidence that there was a system, a logic to their precious war, a reason for it.

Even Frank's father, patriotic to the core, joined MPAW—Military Parents Against the War. The before and after of his son was reason enough. Even on Frank's relatively good days, the horror of the war was in his eyes, in the way they flitted whether or not anything was moving in front of him, in the way he worked his square jaw as if trying to unfreeze the corners of his mouth.

Albert Tedeschi offered his son flexible hours at the hardware store. "Just like the old days," he said, mustering a laugh. Frank just shrugged and agreed. *What the fuck, ya gotta be flexible.* If he'd learned nothing else…

His mother, part-time bookkeeper for Tedeschi's Hardware, part-time housekeeper and gardener, jumped with both feet into the more compelling job of being an advocate for her son—even if he wanted no such services. When she told him that the US Army seemed to finally be acknowledging that the wounds of discharged soldiers were not always physical, that free counseling was available at the VA hospital, it seemed to focus his vision. He glared at her and said, "Thanks so much, Ma. But A, I do not need to see a shrink, and B, I want absolutely nothing more to do with the fucking army."

"Does that include fellow veterans?" his mother asked, masking her reaction to his cursing, his vitriol, having had plenty of practice by then. Apparently, many vets were, ahem, having trouble readjusting to civilian life.

At this, Frank had snorted. "Is that what it is, Ma? Shit, why don't you sign me up for AA too, while you're at it?" Still, he agreed to go. His parents were putting him up rent-free, putting *up* with him, and hanging out at a Vietnam Veterans Against the War meeting or two seemed preferable to one-on-one sessions with some shrink who'd read all about the war.

To his surprise, Frank wound up bawling his eyes out at his first VVAW meeting. He was not the only one. The place was packed, and a good portion of the ex-GIs in the room shed tears. This was precipitated by a former corporal, assuming that the rank indicated by his well-worn camouflage top was accurate. The guy was gaunt, wild-eyed, disheveled, his pony-tail a spray of filthy hair behind him. He stood up in the middle of a discussion about veteran's benefits and the daunting bureaucratic roadblocks one had to navigate in order to obtain them, or at least stand a chance.

"I killed babies," he'd said almost matter-of-factly. His head swiveled as he scanned the room, perhaps anticipating that this confession would bring about the lynching he so richly deserved. "They fucking made me kill babies!" he announced again, his keening voice echoing in the stilled basement, his bloodshot eyes overflowing.

Another vet stood up and wrapped his arms around the guy. "I hear you, brother," he said, rocking him like a child. Former soldiers, supposedly battle-hardened, quietly wept in their seats.

The meeting was transformative for Frank. If the self-confessed baby-killer, wigged out though he was, could stand up and bear witness, then he himself jolly well could. It was time to get his shit together. He used GI Bill funds to start attending New York University, where he agitated against the war and attended introductory classes in a variety of irrelevant subjects. And it was in a sociology seminar that he laid eyes, for the first time in three years, on his ex-girlfriend, Julie D'Millio.

From his vantage point in the last row of the lecture hall—he liked to be near the exit—he wasn't sure if it was her at first. She was seated to the side of the podium from which Leon Rosenberg, PhD, was holding forth on the sociological ramifications of single parenthood in urban communities. Her head, bent over a clipboard, was covered by short, blonde-tinted, frizzy hair. Gone was the shoulder-blade length brown hair into which he used to sink his face, nuzzling her, inhaling the flowery scent of her shampoo. A long strand of coral beads dangled from her neck. Eventually, she looked up from the clipboard, removing all doubt about her identity, even before she was introduced as a teaching assistant near the end of the lecture.

Frank's heart jumped, pogo-sticked, a reaction that seriously surprised him, given all that he'd been through. He was sure that he'd long since written her off, after she'd done the same for him, literally.

"You've come a long way, baby," he said, resorting to a cigarette ad line, blind-siding her as she scanned the list of students who'd been assigned to her small-group recitation.

Julie looked up, and her jaw dropped. She was speechless for several seconds. "You're alive," she replied finally. "I…um…Frank, I really don't mean to sound…flippant or whatever. I'm kind of, shocked? So…you're a student here now?"

"Affirmative," he said, reverting to military-speak. "GI Bill. If you make it home alive, and with your brains still intact, Uncle Sam pays for your education. But I didn't expect to see you here, Julie. Obviously. Small world."

"Frank—"

"How come—why didn't you write back to me?"

She sighed and glanced behind her, where Professor Rosenberg was snapping shut the clasps on his briefcase. "I did, Frank. Once. And I explained—I thought you must have received it, based on what you said in the next letter that came. And the one after that."

He gazed back at her, unwilling to acknowledge that he'd been given fair warning in her letter, and beforehand. Since returning, he'd been on one blind date. This was courtesy of Rob, who thought that a little nooky might help Frank to get his head straightened out. But Frank discovered that he seemed to have lost his mastery of the art of suave conversation, if he'd ever possessed it.

"Yeah, I got the letter, Julie. Took a while, you know, army helicopter, across the rice paddies—"

"So you know why—and Frank, I told you that night in the park, when you informed me that you were leaving, to go find out what a man you are—"

"That was the worst mistake I ever made, Julie. Gotta be the worst one I ever will."

"Well…" She hesitated, sucking air. "However you mean that, I've moved on. Or, at least I thought I had," she added, her voice nearly giving. "You hurt me deeply, Frank. Like I said in the letter—and the park—I had to let go. Call it self-protection. And along the same lines…"

She paused again, her eyes misting over. "I need to go now." She reached for her clipboard and handbag.

"You seeing someone, Julie?" he ventured, his heart sliding back into his throat.

She gave a bitter laugh. "Actually, at this very moment, yeah, someone I never thought I'd see again in this life, or any other. A ghost? But, yeah, I guess I am. Sort of."

Now, decades later, Julie gazed at him in disbelief as he related the story of his adventure with the SUV and the gun.

"No. Uh-uh," she said finally, shaking her head as if dislodging the words. "Frank, even with you toting around that gun, this still seemed unreal. Some kind of game…cops and robbers? Rob's always acted like he thought he was John Wayne, and you were just humoring him. Maybe that sounds stupid, but it's kind of the way I've dealt with it in my head. But now it's very obvious that it's no game. Laureen's dead. As we may all be, before Flowers and his merry band of lunatics are through. But still, I've tried to keep all that at some remove. Go on with the daily routine. Try to keep believing I'm 'making a difference'—to coin a phrase—like these kids' lives are gonna—Frank, you could have been *killed.*"

She clenched her teeth and inhaled sharply. Her reading glasses, dangling from her neck, rose with the intake of breath then slid several inches back down the front of her red University of Maryland sweatshirt.

"Hey. If they wanted to kill me, they could've easily enough. They were right on my tail. They could've rammed me or shot me. They must have had guns. But they were just trying to scare me, Julie. Scare me off."

"Well, *that's* not gonna happen, is it? You'll just whip out that rod of yours and let 'er rip." She stood glaring at him then looked away, brushing at her eyes. "Look, Frank, I understand, intellectually at least, that you have to do this. I really do. This time, you sort of got drafted. By events. And this time, I will stand by you, no matter what. Maybe I should get my own fucking gun. Stick it in my bra, whatever those tough broads do, the ones that you see nowadays on TV and in the movies. In case they decide to threaten your family."

"Shit. Yeah, I've thought about that. Haven't wanted to, I've tried to…what…compartmentalize, like this is one sphere, this is another. A little moonlighting before I come home? But believe it or not, I'm actually hungry." He made a little show of sniffing the air. "Spaghetti sauce? All that car chasin' and gun slingin' can work up an appetite. Sorry," he said, pre-empting. "Not funny. Look, let's sit down and eat, and we'll talk everything through."

Julie's distress had evoked in him some strength, some calmness, although if that was what it took—

"Talk it through? That's gonna make the boogeyman go away? Frank, the cops can connect the bullets to your gun, no? Didn't Paul Fowlkes register the thing? And how could you prove these guys were menacing you?"

"*Paul* will do fine," Frank pointed out in a delayed reaction, forcing himself to speak gently. "I mean, on the off-chance that we're bugged. The alarm on the house has not been tripped, and there's no indication that anyone's been in here, but…yeah, he got me a license for the gun, I guess that means…but Julie, I really don't think they want me arrested, whoever *they* are. I got their plate number, if it's not a fake, maybe Paul can track it down. I'm guessing they probably flashed their credentials at the cops, told them to forget about it, that it was a federal problem. Something. Like I said, I think they were trying to scare me off, or maybe trying to scare me into an urgent consultation with my cronies. So they can maybe see who I'm connected with. Actually, I do need to run this by Paul and Rob, see what they say. Use my trusty new cell phone. Lemme write down the license plate number before I forget it. I've repeated it in my head a hundred times."

"Sure, go ahead. And then we'll have supper together. Who knows how many more opportunities we'll have left?" Julie fairly tossed the utensils onto the kitchen table. They landed with a sharp metallic ring, which caused Frank to jump slightly in his seat.

"*Jesus,*" he said through clenched teeth. "Listen, Juliette, try to take it easy. Okay? I understand that it's easier said than done. For both of us, it's kind of uncharted territory. But there's the situation, and there's how we deal with it. Freaking out is definitely not gonna help."

"Yeah, I *know* that," she snapped, looking away from him, exhaling slowly. "Fine. Okay, yeah, you're right. Obviously. And I'm not exactly freaking out anyway. Like I said, I know you have to do this. And you could wind up being a hero, saving the world. But Frank, all I care about right now is you. The boys, yeah, but they're probably safe on their insulated little campuses. If you wind up dead, then I don't care if the world is saved or not. Because as far as I'm concerned, it's *over.*"

"Julie…" He stood and wrapped his arms around her, and she returned the favor. "Listen, we both need to try to be strong. Any kind of luck, another few years, I'll sell the store, settle with my father, we'll both retire. Live where the ocean's blue."

A quick laugh discharged itself from her stomach, causing a tremor to run through the center of their embrace. "Are you patronizing me?"

"Um, not exactly."

"Not exactly. Well, okay, Frank, sure, I'll try to be strong. Spaghetti and meatballs, that oughta do it. But you need to unhand me."

While he searched for a pencil and paper, she dumped the pasta onto their plates with an oversized *spork*, serving herself half of what she gave him. Even were she not trying to lose a little weight, her appetite had deserted her. After several minutes of silent ingestion—she nibbled, but his lips and the bottom of his mustache were quickly coated in red—Frank came up for air.

"I'll, um, consult," he said, before inhaling several more marinara-coated strands. "Obviously, Rob and Paul are more experienced, knowledgeable. But…I hope you understand that I feel the same way about you. You're the one thing I'm not willing to risk. As much as possible, given the dangers involved in visiting the neighborhoods you visit, walking down the street, crossing it, riding the subways, spending most of your day in the Big Apple, which the terrorists would supposedly like to puree—"

"Very clever, Frank."

"Sorry. What can I tell you? But I meant what I said. About you. I hope you know that."

She sighed. "Of course, I do."

"Good." He gave her hand a squeeze. "So, Juliette, I…um…I guess I'll make those calls. Then I'll clean up."

"You're done eating?"

"Um, no, but I don't think either one of them will mind me chewing in his ear a little."

Frank turned up some jazz on the kitchen radio, fished his cell phone from his pocket and punched in Fowlkes's number, surprised at how quickly and spontaneously he had committed it to memory. Fowlkes had "recommended" not entering the number on the phone's contact list.

Not that the technologically challenged Frank knew how to do that in the first place.

Paul picked up on the first ring. "Yo."

"That's how you answer your phone?"

"Sure. When my homies call, like Phillip Abruzzi."

"Phillip…oh, yeah, right."

"So, what's up? Since you tore me from that poetry reading in Forest Hills last night."

Frank worked up a laugh. Then, absently twirling spaghetti on his fork, he related the story. Fowlkes just listened. Frank didn't leave much space for him to do otherwise. Once begun, the narrative poured out.

Finally Fowlkes, after jotting down the plate number that Frank gave him and confirming it, said, "Good thing I got you that gun."

"Yeah, I guess."

"Well, okay, I'll run the plates, although they're most likely phony, but who knows? These guys are probably…there's rumors, you know, a *secret,* secret service, sort of like Nixon's dirty tricks squad, only way beyond that. Mercenaries, basically, who do Flowers's bidding, as it filters down through the chain of command. And it's probably a very short chain. These bozos might not know, or care, anything about what really happened at First Union, or why they're chasing you. You're the bad guys. It's their job, that's all. And they probably enjoy the action. Get off on it."

"I hope not." Frank shook his head. "But even if they're just trying to scare me off—for now—they seem to know how to go about it. And I'm worried about my family. Still, I'm not about to quit, and I *know* Rob isn't, but if there were some way to get them to call off the dogs…"

"Actually, there might be."

As if attempting to lend extra strength to his efforts to chew the huge forkful of spaghetti that he'd stuck in his mouth, Frank nodded intently as he listened to Fowlkes's suggestion, and subsequent reassurances. Several minutes later he hung up and told Julie that he needed to call Rob now, promising her that he would indeed clean up, eventually. She'd already begun emptying the dishwasher.

"What'd Fowlkes say? About getting 'them' to call off those SUV-driving dogs."

"Well…"

"Okay, that's worth a try," Julie allowed when he was finished, feeling a dawning sense of relief, of hopefulness. Maybe, possibly, a cease-fire would be in the offing.

"I agree," Frank said while punching in the first few digits of Rob's cell phone number, another that had quickly embedded itself in his brain in the wake of First Union.

Rob, fortunately, had worked day shift and was home, although he probably would've picked up anyway, maybe with limited freedom to talk, a detective moonlighting as a detective.

"My brother Phillip," he said drily.

"You home?"

"Yeah."

"And you can talk?"

"Sure. Nellie's in bed. Seven-thirty."

"Right. Sorry, man. Really. But I had an adventure tonight."

After hearing the story, Rob was duly impressed. "Shit, that's my line of work, even though I haven't shot my gun for real in two or three years, at least. You're a fucking gunslinger, man. My brother the ex-liberal."

"I think not…brother. I spoke to Fowlkes, and he

thinks that if these guys wanted to set the cops on me, they'd have done it already." As Frank imparted this information, it dawned on him that Rob might not appreciate his having called Fowlkes first. Rob didn't vocalize this, but still…

"Well, yeah, your buddy Fowlkes knows what he's talking about, in this instance. They probably wanted to see how you handled the pressure, and see your next move, who you're moving with."

"Yeah, well, I'm not real anxious to see *their* next move. And along that line, Fowlkes had a suggestion as to how we can get them off our backs."

"Really? Hit me."

"Well, you and I, separately or together, we apologize to the Reverend Tate for the outrageous accusations we made. They came out of our bereavement, our blind desire for revenge, to do *something*. With a little time for reflection, and seeing just the evidence against All for Allah that's been made public, we see how ridiculous the notion of Billy Patterson's having done First Union was. Is. We hope that Billy turns up, for his own good. And on reflection, given what Billy has told me, maybe we mention Stout too, I don't know…we realize that the good reverend has been trying to help Billy right along, has his best interests at heart. So, Rev, again, we apologize. With heavy hearts. And we've abandoned this fool's mission we were on."

"'Heavy hearts'? That much is true, Frank. But, yeah, although that jazz about the reverend's noble efforts to help Patterson, that might be laying it on a little thick. Still, we apologize, then we do nothing, go about our pre-First Union routines for maybe a week, while Tate notifies his buddies in the government that we are no longer a threat. We've seen the light."

"Hallelujah."

"Hallelujah, if it works. It's a candy-assed idea, recanting, apologizing to that scumbag, except that I can see the logic. It's worth a try."

"Good. Meantime, Fowlkes will be running down leads, mostly with his trusty computer. Including that foster brother of Billy's, etcetera, the stuff we discussed in Forest Hills."

"Then, after the heat's died down, we go looking for Patterson," Rob said. "Assuming he's still alive, I'd love to make his acquaintance."

CHAPTER 11

"Felipe, you don't need to try to sell people things they don't necessarily want." Frank said this with a quick smile. The kid was twenty-one, the same age as Sergio, but the similarities ended there. Felipe was eager to please, and not just because he needed the job. At least that was Frank's sense of it. Regardless, Frank needed *him*, maybe fulltime in the near future, if the Tedeschi brothers went off in search of a mass murderer.

"Gotcha, Frank," Felipe replied immediately. "Toilet plunger, *sí*. Toilet auger, Drano, toilet handle and arm, Three-in-One Oil, bathtub appliqués, no." He rattled the items off with a staccato flair, hardware hip-hop.

Frank couldn't help laughing, while he took a fast glance up the aisle to make sure that the customer in question—a middle-aged suburban housewife whose jet-powered Toto toilet had improbably become stuffed—was out of hearing range. "Not that we don't make suggestions. People are gonna *ask* for your help. They'll assume that because you're working here, you know what you're doing."

Felipe flashed that wide smile of his, wispy mustache doing a quick dance atop his slender upper lip. "Hey, 'nother week. I'm a quick study, you know?"

"Yeah, you are. Seriously." Also, the kid had a lighthearted vibe about him—unlike Billy Patterson—and plenty of energy. During occasional down time, he helped Frank dust the cobwebs off the Spanish he vaguely remembered from high school. Plus, Felipe was an asset with the Latino customers who were coming in with greater frequency, having migrated north from the Bronx and elsewhere. "And it's not like we're not here to sell—in fact, that's the whole idea—but we want people to feel comfortable, like they're not gonna be pressured. *Comprende*?"

"*Claro que sí.*"

"Good. And don't be ashamed to ask me where something is, or anything else, even if you've asked the same thing before. It took *me* a while to learn the ropes completely. It wasn't always that you could blindfold me, and I could walk to the mini-drawers back there and immediately fish out half-inch ribbed sheet metal screws or whatever." He shook his head. "Man, I been here too long."

Thirty-five years, on and off, before and after returning from 'Nam. The recent turnover in his assistants was one more reminder of the passage of time, of its evanescence—real and immediate now, eventually gone and forgotten. Except that Billy Patterson fell into neither category. He was the ghost of the future. Felipe notwithstanding, Billy's absence was almost palpable, a reminder that Frank might soon be in for more of the kind of adventures that he'd once sworn off forever, guns and smoke, fear of what might lay around any corner, inside of any vehicle. Fun and games.

He tried not to think about this during his breaks. At least he could *take* breaks now, thanks to Felipe and the store's original owner, Frank's father, who'd been helping out some of late. With Dad in the store, Frank could even vacate the premises for half an hour. Today he took his afternoon break in the garden implements section—things being relatively dead back there during the winter—so as to be available should Felipe need him up front. Moira, a heavyset eighteen year-old, had hours today also, but she mainly worked the cash register, got paperwork ready for his signature, chewed gum, and answered the phone.

Frank parked himself in one of the plastic lawn chairs that were stacked in the back and put his feet up on another. They were good for that. It occurred to him that maybe he should keep two and return the rest, cut his losses. The chairs not being especially stable, he leaned back just a little while perusing the *New York Times.*

Maybe this was not the best way to spend his break. Page one detailed a rush hour evacuation of the subway in Manhattan, owing to a gassing threat. False alarm, surely the work of another head case inspired by First Union, there seemed to be no shortage of them. Thankfully, Julie had not been affected. She'd begun taking the express bus down from Armonk, although she was still obliged to use the subways in the course of her job.

Also on page one, American aircraft carriers were massing in the Persian Gulf. Hello, Iran. Or goodbye. President Flowers was bent on "Eradicating terrorism at its source." Hopefully, the alleged terrorists would hang around long enough for the smart bombs to land on their heads. Hopefully, the peasants in the neighborhood would evacuate their homes in time.

Also hopefully, the US Air Force could obliterate Iran's rumored nuclear facilities without unleashing radiation across the Middle East. Page two, architectural designs were being accepted for a massive memorial to be constructed at the site of First Union Arena. The arena itself was slated to be razed, its viability as a venue for concerts and sporting events having been fatally compromised. Rob had already stated his unwillingness to attend the memorial's dedication. He needed no help in remembering.

Sometimes, Frank was amazed that people still came into the store looking for hose clamps, ice chippers, duct tape, and the like, that they still carried on with their daily activities as if the world weren't going insane. Carrying on, he located the sports section. He attempted to fold the paper accordingly. After what seemed like several minutes' worth of fumbling, he muttered, "*Shit.*"

Bad timing, since Felipe had picked that exact moment to walk into the garden section. His angular jaw clenched.

"Hey, man, that had nothing do with *you,*" Frank said, holding up the *Times* as evidence. "This paper, it's like trying to fold Jell-O or something."

"Oh. Yeah, that's cause it got all the news fit to print, or some shit like that, right? Double-sized. You need to get one a' them trashy little papers, like the *New York Post.* Anyways, Frank, someone out front wants to see you."

Frank sighed, resignedly dropping the paper into his lap. "Is it a vendor? Someone who—"

"Nah. I know what a vendor is, Frank. He said it was 'personal' business, and he could only speak to you."

"Ah." Frank's throat tightened. Ostensibly scratching his rib cage beneath his oversized flannel shirt, he felt for his gun. "Well, okay, bring him back." He sat upright. The *Times* slid to the floor, where it formed a ramshackle mini-tent.

In short order, Felipe ushered in Sylvester Stout. Stout's head was covered by a woolen navy watch cap, so it took Frank a second or two to place the face. "Mr. Stout, how you doin'?" he said, standing and offering his hand, surprise mingling with relief. "Please, sit."

He disengaged from Stout's grip, using the same hand to indicate the chair that had previously been his footrest, then thinking better of this and detaching the top chair from the stack, placing it in front of his guest then quickly turning to Felipe: "Thanks, Amigo." *You're dismissed,* he signaled unnecessarily with an inclination of his head. Felipe took the hint. Stout folded his tall, thin frame into the new chair, not looking especially comfortable.

Frank shifted his chair around, its plastic legs scraping on the concrete floor. "You might want to open your jacket, maybe take off the hat," he suggested. "Back here in the garden section, it's unseasonably mild."

Stout didn't crack a smile or otherwise indicate recognition that Frank had just attempted a little joke. He unzipped the jacket. "Mr. Tedeschi—"

"Frank."

"Okay. Then I guess you should call me Sylvester. But maybe we should just get to the point, since I'm sure you're wondering why I'm here. Last night, I was visited by two FBI agents. They wanted information about Billy Patterson. They said that they were looking for him in connection with interstate trafficking in stolen goods. At first, they wouldn't even tell me that. It was as if the badges they showed should be enough for me to tell them anything they wanted to know about Billy and his whereabouts. Or as much as *I* knew."

Frank nodded, all ears, fixing a steadfast gaze on Stout, even as his mind attempted to absorb and sift through what he was hearing—were these "FBI" agents the same guys who'd stalked him in the SUV?—and envision the phone conversation he would have with Fowlkes and/or Rob immediately after Stout left.

"When I asked them what kind of stolen goods they were talking about, they more or less told me it was none of my business. I did not care for their attitude, at all.

Now, between his work at the church, and at your store here, I think that Billy's time was pretty much taken up. Whatever life he had outside of work—a lonely one, I suspect—but, given what I know of Billy, and the fact that he was working two jobs, I find it impossible to believe that he was also trafficking in stolen goods."

Stout paused to remove his woolen watch cap and wipe sweat from his glistening head and brow. Then he put the cap back on and readjusted his glasses, which had slipped halfway down his slender nose. "Jeez, that car of his, which is also nowhere to be found, according to the county police who are supposedly investigating his disappearance—driving that across state lines? Would that make it to New Jersey? I was amazed that he even made it to work in that heap."

Frank laughed at Stout's uncharacteristically animated delivery as much as the memory of the car. "Yeah, I know what you mean. I'm not an expert on cars, but I'm guessing it needed a muffler, shocks. Probably a new engine."

"Probably," agreed Stout, nodding as he offered a quick smile. "Still, these…FBI agents claimed that they searched his apartment and found the evidence. Nothing they could or would show me."

"I see."

Frank and Rob hadn't found anything of use when *they'd* searched Billy's "garden" apartment two nights previously. It was part of a complex that was a small island of semi-poverty on the outskirts of Mount Kisco, sort of like servants' quarters, the rest of the "village" mostly featuring mansions and houses that aspired to that status. The brothers had gained entry via Rob's lock-picking skills, which were almost as impressive as Billy's.

The place was a total mess. Rob's opinion, which

made sense to Frank, was that Billy had left in a rush, taking whatever he needed to flee after gassing the arena. But maybe the place had in fact been ransacked by the same gentlemen who visited Stout. If so, that also explained the scarcity of mail the brothers found when Rob violated federal law by picking the lock on Billy's mailbox.

There were a couple of solicitations for charities and one brochure from *The Heavenly Host,* picturing the pricey crucifixes, bibles, etc., that made up the store's inventory. As with the apartment, there was nothing of any help in terms of tracking Billy, or providing evidence.

"Well, Sylvester, I agree with you. I don't believe that Billy was trafficking in stolen goods. It makes no sense."

"Exactly. It's almost as impossible as what you and your brother put forward as the reason for his disappearance." Stout paused, scratching at his scalp, creating the impression that some small living thing was trapped inside his watch cap. "Especially since Reverend Tate tells me that you've recanted and apologized for the accusations you made."

Despite himself, Frank's eyes widened, even though Tate's sharing of the news that the Tedeschi brothers had eaten humble pie was not really surprising. Wasn't that the idea in the first place? The reverend would announce—to his connection(s) in the Flowers administration, at least—that the brothers were no longer a danger. They'd *seen the light*. In fact, Tate had offered congratulations for doing just that. If he didn't add, "*I* am the light," it was probably because he considered that to be self-evident. Or so Frank had opined to his brother afterward.

He'd gone to the Holy Church of Christ alone, Rob having agreed that it was better that way. Frank would be more able to conceal his visceral disdain for the reverend. The brothers, and Fowlkes, had correctly assumed that Reverend Tate would willingly grant an audience to Frank, on hearing that he wanted to clarify and amend points from their previous conversation and that he felt more comfortable doing so in person. They knew that Frank would be frisked at the security gate—"Out of the car, hands in the air, please"—and then probably again by Cavanaugh, Tate's "security chief." And Frank should shave and look presentable, a penitent showing some respect—also showing his best face to the cameras that would likely film him from the gate on in.

The meeting with Tate lasted only ten or fifteen minutes. According to Frank, Rob was too embarrassed, too ashamed to come along. In his bereavement, his desire to do *something* for his daughter, find some justice, he'd grasped at the first straw that came his way, the only one—Frank's reports about Billy Patterson's ranting threats against Shove it Up and First Union Arena. And Frank, who'd dearly loved his niece Laureen as well, had been equally guilty of putting emotion and a desire for revenge over common sense and reason. For which he was deeply sorry.

Over the previous week, he and Rob had had the opportunity to reflect on matters. Given what he knew of Billy, and of the evidence amassed by the FBI and the CIA—the Islamic tracts found at the site, the video-taped images of the terrorists involved, FBI agent Scanlon's report, and the members of All for Allah who had turned state's evidence (their identities were being closely guarded, for obvious reasons)—it was now clear that Billy, wherever he was, had nothing to do with the attack.

The loss of Laureen Tedeschi was no less devastating to her family than it had been at first. But her memory would only be sullied by false accusations. Frank and

Rob were abandoning their misguided "investigation," which had been borne of grief. The indicated apology could properly be offered only in person. Frank had come to do just that.

"Right," he said now, his eyes fixed on Stout. "I acknowledged that we let our emotions get the better of us, cloud our judgment. That is correct."

"Well, I admire the fact that you were humble enough to admit a big mistake, and man enough, really, to apologize directly to the reverend. I know that the conference you and your brother had with him involved hard feelings all around, although I'm sure that Reverend Tate had already forgiven you, long before you asked him to do it. But where Billy is concerned, I don't know *what* to think anymore. If these FBI agents—you think that's what they really were?"

Frank shrugged. "I don't know. They haven't come to see me yet." *Or, at least, they weren't much interested in talking.* "So I couldn't evaluate that first hand, not that I'm any kind of expert anyway. But if they came to question you, using some bogus excuse…I don't know. Maybe he owes them money? Maybe he was gambling or something?"

"I had the same thought," declared Stout, nodding intently. "Or, at least, they feel like he owes them *something.*" He shifted in the plastic chair, attempting to rearrange his long limbs for maximum comfort, or balance. "At first, I assumed that Billy'd run off because of who he is, bipolar, maybe prone to relapses, drinking. Now, I'm not so certain. But my strong suspicion is that he needs help. He doesn't need to have his legs broken, or worse. Of that, I'm sure. I'm also sure that whoever those 'agents' were, I don't trust them. They were mean bastards. That much was plain. Now, I'm an old man myself. Or I'm getting there, Lord knows. And I have my work at the church, even if it's winter. I can't go looking for Billy. But if you and your brother the detective can, and are still willing to look, I'd much prefer it if you found him first. And maybe I can help you."

Frank made a small show of thinking about it. "Well, yeah, I'm concerned about him also," he said finally. "And I could probably have my father take over the store for a week or so. He's the original owner. My brother Rob, he doesn't have a personal interest in Billy, but maybe I can call in a brotherly favor. 'Course, he'd have to get time. If he's in the middle of a case…"

Actually, Rob was prepared to be docked pay, face disciplinary action, take early retirement, and work in private security. Whatever it took—and that would be the operative principle, Frank realized, as it hit him with full force that Billy was indeed alive and on the loose. Why else would Flowers's thugs be pounding the bushes for him? As younger son, Carl, might've said, "like, duh,"—except that Frank could barely contain his excitement.

"Well, why don't you get a pencil and paper, in the event that the two of you do decide to go and find Billy?"

"Good idea." Frank fairly jumped up then strode to the front of the store, where he requisitioned writing materials from the disinterested Moira. Felipe, who was helping a customer find a dual thread faucet aerator, glanced up as Frank passed on the return trip. "This young lady also needs a key made," he announced. "You saved me a trip to come get you."

"Cool," Frank replied, without breaking stride. "If you can give me a few minutes, ma'am."

CHAPTER 12

The bursts of vapor emitted from Julie's mouth, rapid-fire, merged into a small, spreading cloud of laughter. And she sounded like a hoarse bird chirping. Or so Frank had occasionally teased her, when she'd gotten off on a giggling jag and couldn't stop until her cheeks were glistening with tears. But now her laughter was sardonic, elicited by Frank's suggestion that she tell him about *her* day, like they were just another couple working on the marriage, on *listening*. As if he hadn't just told her that all systems were go, that he was off on a perilous mission to track down the real perpetrator of the worst crime in modern American history and, if things went really well, to upend the US Government, sending shock waves the world over.

"How was my day?" she repeated finally, gasping, stifling another wave. Actually, it had been half a day, point five subtracted from the ample personal leave she'd accumulated. And Frank, to Felipe's delight, had departed early, leaving him in charge of the store. The kid had been given a crash course in key making and seemed to have picked it up. Hopefully.

The Tedeschis were walking glove-in-glove along the Bronx River, which had the effrontery to run up into Westchester. Actually, it ran down *from* Westchester, north to south. But as if getting into character, it already resembled a stream of liquid sludge. Gray patches of crusted snow dotted its banks. Bordering them on both sides was Bronx River Park, a swatch of frozen earth decorated with rustic-looking wooden benches, some situated beneath leafless willow trees.

The park formed a buffer between the town of Armonk and the Bronx River Parkway. Julie and Frank were on their way to a Chinese restaurant about a mile south, a couple of long blocks off the paved trail down which they now strolled. A moderate late Friday afternoon hike followed by a leisurely dinner. An assertion that they could walk in the open like a normal—if gun-toting—couple, now that Frank had given his fingers-crossed apology to Reverend Tate.

"My day was, um, fair to middlin'. Relatively speaking. I spent most of it mentoring Rachel. The new hire out of Brooklyn College. The school had called—not Brooklyn College, duh, PS Forty-Five—to report that little Jose, kindergarten kid, has bruises on his arms and legs. Rachel, doe-eyed, like she's on the verge of tears herself, looks the kid over again then ventures to question Mom and Dad's claims that Jose just plays rough with his friends. She's fluent in Spanish herself, but all she could get out of the kid, in either language, was that he was 'bad.' When she point blank asked him, out of Mom and Dad's range, if they hit him, he just shook his head. Repeatedly."

"Could mean anything."

"True," Julie replied, "although if I had to venture a guess, I'd say they're not sparing the rod. Or the belt. Rachel finally wrote up her report, translated it for the parents, told them that however Jose got his bruises, it was their responsibility to ensure his good health. And she trusted that the school would not have to call Social Services again. Very professional, neither accusatory nor seemingly intimidated by Dad, who was a little surly—sleeveless T-shirt, under the influence of Cerveza Budweiser—and then, we get outside, and she starts bawling. I gave her a little hug, told her that she'd done fine, perfectly. She actually feared for the kid, that he'd be blamed for the visit. I told her it was just as possible that the parents would shape up, at least temporarily. And that this was a new experience for her. She had to get used to it."

"Like you," Frank said, obligingly filling in the pause.

"Yeah. Déjà vu."

"All over again."

"Well, yes and no. I mean, 'Nam was a long time ago, and we weren't married, or even really a couple anymore. Plus, you should be back a lot sooner. No land mines or booby traps—hopefully, no bullets. Even with Cowboy Rob riding shotgun."

"He'll be driving, Julie. Most of the time. If he gets tired enough, he might chance having me take the wheel."

"Right. You know what I meant, sweetheart. About Rob. And I don't want to sound blind to the dangers, either. There are those mysterious thugs who are also looking for Billy. Then there's Billy himself, who figures to be desperate. Even if he's crazy, he's gotta know that if he gets nailed for being the real perpetrator of First Union, his life is over. He'll be the most hated man in American history—whether or not that would bother him. And even opponents of the death penalty would probably flip the switch on the electric chair with him strapped in it." She shuddered. "So…Sylvester Stout thinks that Billy might've gone to New Paltz."

"Yeah, that's his best guess. Billy was living with a woman up there. Divorcee. Nancy Horowitz."

"He was living with a Jewish woman?"

"That was before he found Jesus. Besides, according to Stout, according to Billy, her disdain for Judaism was matched only by her disdain for Christianity. Her Jewish parents disowned her years ago when she married a *goy*. That's—"

"I know, Frank. Non-Jew."

"Right. And then her *goy* husband—"

"*Goyishe.*"

"Okay, goy—how do you know that?"

"Molly Passikoff. My colleague on maternity leave."

"Oh, right. The one who's big time into tap dancing. From which she's also on maternity leave."

Julie gazed over at him with raised eyebrows. "Very good, Frank."

"Thank you, my dear. Somehow, it stuck. Anyway, the husband abandoned Nancy Horowitz, left her with a young daughter. She worked two or three jobs to pay for daycare and everything else. Met Billy while she was doing the AM shift at Dunkin' Donuts. He came for breakfast every morning."

"Wow. Stout told you all this?"

"Yup. Apparently, Billy spoke to him a lot, he was like his father confessor. And Stout, he may be a little older than us, but he retains details. And relates them in *full*. I had to take a break at one point to go make a key for someone, and when I came back, Stout picked right up where he left off. Didn't miss a beat. Now, where was I? Joke," he pointed out after a moment.

"Oh, I get it."

"But you're not amused."

"Mildly."

"We do what we can," said Frank. "But supposedly, Billy was seriously fond of Nancy Horowitz. And of her little daughter. Also supposedly, Horowitz made an honest man out of him. At least semi-honest, and he contributed some money—odd jobs, house painting—provided free childcare, and a warm, sober body in her bed at night. Billy credited her with inspiring him to straighten up enough so that he could come to know Jesus."

"Which wasn't her intention."

"Far from it. So far from it that when she refused to join him in Christ, or even listen to another word about it—or go anywhere near the pastor of this church up there, who mentored Billy, I guess—then he left. Or she invited him to. Stout got different versions of the breakup at different times. In any case, Billy saw an ad for a 'Christian landscaper, will train,' down south in Westchester County, far enough away so that he wouldn't be tempted to go see Nancy Horowitz. Forsaking her love for Jesus's had not been easy, but there was no other choice. That's more or less a direct quote. If second hand."

"Speaking of retaining details."

Frank smiled. "Yeah, well, I wrote the stuff down, but it wasn't really necessary. I'm trying to play detective. Like your brother-in-law. Speaking of whom, he could barely contain himself when I told him about my conversation with Stout. He was ready to go, like *now*."

"I can imagine." Julie dropped Frank's hand and readjusted her woolen cap, pulling it over her reddened ears, reducing the visible portion of her face by about a third. This made her look endearingly girlish, an effect abetted by the white pom-pom atop the hat. He put his arm around her, and she snuggled against him, their jackets audibly crinkling. "Well," she said, "I might get religion myself, at least until you're back safely."

"Not to worry," he replied, with as much conviction as he could muster.

She disengaged. "That doesn't help, Frank."

"Sorry."

"Well, there's really nothing you can say. Other than that you'll be very careful and keep me posted. And let's hope that the greatest danger will be you and Rob being together non-stop, for as long as it takes."

"Right." He gave a throaty laugh. "We have a long and storied history."

Julie had been there for much of it—including the legendary Whitehall Street episode. It was understood that when Frank used the term "storied," he was referring to that event, which had been written up in the *New York Daily News*.

BROTHERS IN ARMS, the headline on the front page had read. The accompanying photo featured a scene from an anti-Vietnam War demonstration in front of the draft board at Whitehall Street in lower Manhattan. Not really news, such rallies were going on almost daily at that point of the war. But this one was larger scale than most. Both the Vietnam Veterans Against the War and the Students for a Democratic Society were viewed with disdain by the cops, and the feeling was mutual. Still, violence at the demonstrations was not that unusual either. But the clever reporter who wrote the piece in the *Daily News* had come up with a new angle. Human interest, sort of.

Julie had gone to the demonstration with Frank, overriding his strong objections. He'd warned her that the shit was likely to hit the fan. Nightsticks and fists might be flying. Paddy wagons would be on site. But that was a chance she was willing to take.

Before he walked back into her life—and her sociology seminar—she'd paid as little attention to The War as possible. It helped her to not think about him, an ongoing project. However, once she became a teaching assistant, she was obliged to "facilitate" discussions on the sociological ramifications of the war, specifically the disproportionate representation of minority-group members among the soldiers dying for Uncle Sam in Southeast Asia.

She was fairly adept at doing so by the time it was Frank's turn to sit among the students clustered around her in one corner of the lecture hall. He informed the group that that particular "ramification" was not surprising, since the war basically involved the slaughter of poverty-ridden, yellow-skinned Vietnamese. The powers-that-be were simply killing two birds with one stone.

At this, the mostly "liberal" students who were unknowingly grouped with the TA's ex-lover nodded agreement, although a couple later indicated to Julie in private that they'd found the statement a mite radical. None knew that he was a Vietnam vet. Outside of VVAW meetings, he was loath to talk about his experiences in-country. Still, halfway through the semester, with Julie sitting across from him in a coffee house on McDougal Street, he found that he couldn't help himself.

They weren't looking to rekindle their romance. Or she wasn't, at least. But they had a history together. Hopefully, a friendly conversation in which they caught up on the past would help her to feel more comfortable around him, more in charge of her teaching responsibilities, and less like a broken-hearted high school senior masquerading as a professor-in-training. Gamely, she filled him in on her life and family. Mom and Dad were both okay, if getting slightly antsy for grandchildren, despite the fact that she was barely twenty-two. After all, she was their only child. And they were bewildered by her dogged pursuit of degrees, of a career. School? They were old school. Oh, well.

Eventually tiring of holding up both ends of the conversation, Julie scanned the coffeehouse, which was crowded with students, with tourists soaking up the smoky atmosphere of Greenwich Village, admiring the posters of Hendrix and Dylan on the walls, nursing their cappuccinos around rickety, circular wooden tables. And Frank could've passed for a refugee from the storied *Summer of Love*. But despite the beard and unkempt hair that covered his ears, that was him underneath. Or was it?

"Tell me, how've you been?" she'd asked perkily, feeling foolish as she looked into his eyes, as if suddenly privy to everything they'd seen, spontaneous downloading.

He peered back at her, feasting his eyes on her face, which was, for some reason, topped by that short, frizzy blonde hair. But he could've been sitting with her again on a bench in Pelham Bay Park, on the evening he'd officially screwed up his life. Everything in between then and now was thrown into sharp relief. It was as if his life, or the only segment of it that seemed to matter, were flashing in front of him again. He badly wanted to put his arms around her, to erase that little gap of years. Take two.

"Well, Julie," he began, chancing speech despite the frog in his throat. "I'm hangin' in. Goin' to school, obviously, an' workin' some in my father's store, which I swore I'd never do again, but everything's relative, you know? In terms of how much it sucks. Um…maybe I should start over. Which is sort of the idea, I guess. It's…I'm getting there now, but it was rough for a while when I got back. Sort of like, I don't know, when astronauts reenter the atmosphere? Something like that. I—I killed people over there, Julie. There was no other choice, I guess. I was trying to stay alive, stay in one piece, but knowing that doesn't…I'm doing what I can now to help stop the war, I really am. But it's just something I have to..." Her face blurred in front of him. He looked away. Then he felt her fingers in his hair, a preliminary indication that she'd never really stopped loving him.

"You know," she said the next morning as they walked together from the West 4th Street subway station toward NYU, hand in hand, "I was deathly afraid of being proved right, of seeing your face in the newspaper, in those rows of pictures of soldiers killed in action. They look like passport photos." She shook her head. "Crew cut kids. I just avoided those pages. In fact, anything to do with Vietnam. You were my excuse for ignoring the war, Frank. Or trying to."

That changed the next weekend. By Sunday afternoon, her voice was hoarse from chanting, "One, two, three, four, we don't want your fucking war!" Etcetera. The soreness in her shoulder was a result of having repeatedly thrust her fist into the air. Over the course of the war, the demonstrations had become more confrontational, as it became apparent that "All we are saying, is give peace a chance," sung with arms linked while swaying rhythmically, was not going to impress LBJ, Tricky Dick, or any of the other warmongers.

About a month later, Julie and Frank were part of a huge mob on Nassau Street in lower Manhattan. They were swept along as if funneled by the skyscrapers on either side of Nassau, bordering the financial district, Wall Street, a fitting location for the draft board. When they reached the saw horses set maybe a hundred yards back from the squat gray granite and mortar Selective Service building on Whitehall Street, there was no question of stopping. It was either forge ahead or risk being trampled. But forging ahead meant running into a wall of blue. The cops were out in force, and the sawhorses were their line in the sand. Breach them, and you were violating an ordinance against disorderly conduct and disobeying a lawful order from the police, who were then duty-bound to restrain you. If that meant cracking your skull with a nightstick—justifiable force—they would do so with relish.

Frank was holding on to Julie's arm with his right hand. In his left, he carried a metal trashcan lid down low, a makeshift shield hidden from view by the densely packed crowd of demonstrators. He didn't want to attract the attention of New York's Finest. A trashcan lid held high, dully gleaming if caught by the sun, was tantamount to an invitation. On the other hand, like a good soldier, he needed to be prepared.

Almost directly in front of them, they could see a wave of blue uniforms surging. Above the chanting of the crowd from behind and the screams of demonstrators trying to flee the cops, he heard Julie's shrill, piercing cry: "Frank, look out!"

He got the trashcan lid up in time to deflect the blow of a nightstick that had been swung at him without warning, with no preliminary order to stop. The lid also briefly hid from frontal view the hard right that he landed on the bottom edge of the cop's helmet and his jawbone. The padded left sleeve of Frank's winter jacket cushioned a blow from the nightstick of a second cop—barely, but enough for him to roll with it, swallow the pain, keep his wits about him.

Julie's anguished screams helped in this regard. Having staggered the first cop, Frank took a backhand swing at the second with the trashcan lid. But he struck air. The second cop, in the process of drawing back his nightstick again, had been shoved in the chest by a third. The guy landed on the street, in a space that miraculously opened up among several demonstrators, none of whom were anxious to lay hands on him, certainly not to break his fall.

The guy jumped to his feet. "Tedeschi!" he roared. "What the fuck?"

"That's my brother, you asshole!" Rob spun, his light blue helmet glinting in the sun as if he were a giant top. He thrust himself between Frank and the first cop, who, having sufficiently recovered from the knuckle sandwich to his jaw landed by an ex-wrestler, was actually unsnapping his holster. "Sullivan, that's my fucking brother."

"I don't care if it's your fucking mother. Get out of my way," ordered Sullivan, a hulking cop with reddish stubble dotting his chin.

Rob didn't budge. "I'll throw his ass in the paddy wagon myself. Okay? But you swung on him for no reason. I'll testify to that if I have to. You wanna charge me with…whatever…be my guest." He pivoted again and stuck his face directly into Frank's. "What the *fuck* are you doing here?" he snarled. His disgust was not just for show.

"That's not obvious, bro?" What looked like a sneer on Frank's face was, in fact, a grimace. It was a tossup as to which hurt worse, his left triceps or right knuckles.

Rob, currently sharing an apartment with another rookie cop, had heard from his parents that Frank had joined the VVAW. This had troubled him enough, his whack-job brother becoming one more commie agitator. But it was still information in the abstract. Now he'd just borne witness to Frank, in army fatigues, long hair and a beard, the whole bit, slugging it out with fellow members of his Bronx precinct. They'd all been sent down as reinforcements— under the command of Sullivan, who could make Rob's life miserable. And if he got kicked off the force—this unbearable thought flashed in his head a second before he grabbed and twisted the left shoulder of Frank's jacket, causing him to grunt in pain.

"Easy, Rob," Frank said through clenched teeth. "I can still kick your ass."

"Yeah? In your fucking dreams." This retort was accompanied by another, external flash, two or three of them. Some ballsy photographer was recording the scene for posterity. Good. Visual evidence of Rob doing his job. "*Listen,* scumbag," he hissed at Frank. "Just walk. You're under arrest, and if you give me any static, I will not save your ass again when they tear you to pieces. Believe me, they would love to."

"Yeah, I'm sure. Hey, I never did thank you, did I? Think he woulda shot me?"

"Nah. Not with all these witnesses," Rob replied under his breath, not trusting the crowd's noise to cover him. "Now, move your ass."

"Arrest me too. I want to go with him," said Julie, who'd been tossed aside like a candy wrapper by the cop whose nightstick had landed on Frank's arm.

"My girlfriend. A fellow traveler."

"No shit. Actually, she looks kinda familiar. And no problem…*Julie.* Ever been in jail before?"

They walked through the parting crowd toward the paddy wagon parked at the intersection of Nassau and Whitehall, backed by two other cops from Rob's precinct. On the way a reporter—Rob could sniff them, he knew how the guy made his living even before a microphone was stuck in front of his face—asked him how it felt to be arresting his brother. Apparently, and unsurprisingly—reporters were like worms, they turned up anywhere—the guy had witnessed the brawl and its aftermath.

"No comment," said Rob, who also suggested that the reporter take his fucking microphone out of his face immediately, unless he wanted to be busted for obstruction.

The guy's piece in the *News* the next day, with its catchy headline, also referenced the Civil War. Brother against brother. Clever, maybe, even if a mite melodramatic, and even if the Tedeschis had briefly been on the same side.

CHAPTER 13

"*What?*" Albert Tedeschi gazed from Frank to Rob, and back again. Okay, Frank had been known to horse around, father and son having developed a certain ease with each other over the course of their shared involvement with Tedeschi's Hardware. Dad had ragged Frank about the music he insisted on listening to in the car while driving to the store as a teenager—"'Tryna set the night on fire?' What, he needs the insurance?"—about his driving, about his pitiful excuse for a mustache, etc.

And Frank had responded in kind: "Old Blue Eyes? Doo-bee-doo-bee-doo? That really rocks." He'd teased his father over the advertising campaign in local newspapers: "'*Tedeschi's—for all your hardware needs?*' Very imaginative, Pop."

But their bantering had rarely crossed over the line into disrespect, or meanness. Regardless, Frank would never joke about something like *this*—not that they'd ever encountered anything like this before.

Rob, to whom Dad had never been quite as close, slowly nodded. It was no joke. His own daughter had died at First Union Arena. It had almost torn him apart. The rest of his grief-stricken family had worried that he wouldn't survive Laureen by much. Yet here he was, seconding the insane assertions his brother was making, the same brother with whom he ordinarily wouldn't be caught in the same room if he could help it.

Albert Tedeschi looked at his daughter-in-law Julie, who nodded as well, offering him a tight-lipped version of that beautiful smile of hers. He gazed across the living room at his old Motorola television—currently, mercifully dark—from which the terms All for Allah and "terrorists" had issued so frequently that they'd become distorted—*terrorish, awfrilla*—mutating themselves in his brain like the first tremors of dementia.

"Billy Patterson?" Dad repeated finally in a subdued voice, triple-checking. "I was up there a few times when he was working. He never said anything like that to me. He was a little strange, yeah. Manic. Kind of like he had a bug up his ass. If I had to lift something heavier than maybe five pounds off a shelf, he'd be there like magic, like the Flash, like I was a hundred years old. Almost knocked me over once, didn't seem to hear me when I said, 'Hey, it's all right, I can handle it, I was doing this before you were born.' Didn't seem to hear much, period. I told him, 'Yeah, sure, I'm a Christian, but me and Jesus, we got our own arrangement. We don't bother each other too much.'" Albert took a quick glance at his wife, having felt the heat of her disapproval. He shrugged it off. "Ol' Billy, he would not stop trying to convince me to repent, get saved while there was still time. He could be a pain, yeah. But First Union Arena? I never heard him say anything about that."

He turned again to his wife. "Maria? We're supposed to believe this? Yeah, President Flowers lying through his teeth, that's not a stretch. Corrupt clergymen? That's nothing new either. But this is way beyond corrupt. This is…"

Maria Tedeschi gazed back at him and shook her head,

causing her new brown-dyed perm to briefly dance. She'd cooked up a nice meal for this family get-together, spent half the day doing it. Now she was at least as bewildered as her husband. "Why didn't you tell us about this before?" she chided.

Frank and Rob glanced at each other, hesitating. "We didn't wanna upset you," claimed Rob, who was not normally all that long on sensitivity. "Laureen, that was bad enough, beyond bad. But us being under surveillance, the danger involved—we didn't want you worrying, that's all."

Maria's eyes flashed. "Oh. And you don't think we're going to now?"

"It'll be okay, Ma," Rob said. "Seriously. I—we—we know what we're doing. Okay?"

"There was no other choice," said Frank. "What were we supposed to tell you? That we were going off fishing or something, and we didn't know when we'd be back? Plus, I need Pop to run the store for a while. He can do that with his eyes closed."

"Sure," said Dad. "Except you got everything on computer now, which I know sh—which I know nothing about."

"It's not much, just inventory, vendors accounts. Moira, the girl up front? She can help with that. So can Felipe. And if you're there long enough, you'll pick it up. If *I* could, believe me, you can. And, hopefully, we won't be gone that long."

"Or you might be. And by the way, thanks for the advance notice. You're leaving tomorrow morning?"

"Yup," Rob said. "The longer we wait, the farther away the bastard may get. Or the deader he might get, if the wrong people find him first. Plus, if *we* do, we got evidence now. Courtesy of Fowlkes, Frank's army buddy."

"Yeah, we had a strong connection. Stayed in touch all these years. Which is fortunate, 'cause for the last twenty or so he's been working for the FBI."

Fowlkes had returned Frank's call the night following Sylvester Stout's visit to Tedeschi's Hardware. It was somewhat late, or at least inconvenient. Frank had caught Julie in an amorous mood, which had dissipated by the time he depressed the "off" button. By then, his mind was elsewhere as well.

"Excellent," Fowlkes had said after Frank apprised him of his conversation with Stout.

"Yeah. If I didn't hear back from you, I was gonna call again first thing in the morning."

"Well, amigo, I hope I didn't interrupt anything."

"Nah," Frank replied, swallowing laughter, wondering if Fowlkes was intuitive or had just gotten lucky.

"Good. Wouldn't wanna do *that*. So…seems like Billy Boy must be alive and on the loose. Tell you the truth, I'd have bet big money otherwise. And you guys will have a head start on finding him, thanks to Stout. New Paltz, yeah, he had a post office box up there for a while—but no address, record of employment, W-Two form, nothing. He's as much of a spook as I am."

"Different kind."

"Right. Except when he's being videotaped by security cameras. I managed to access the footage from First Union Arena the night of the gassing. It wasn't quite as impossible as I thought it would be."

"*All right*," declared Frank. "I'd have bet otherwise too. Never underestimate Comrade Fowlkes."

"Damn right."

"Okay, so what's in there?"

"Well, first of all, there's the phenomenon of people going nuts at a punk-rock concert one minute and then—after suddenly realizing that they can't breathe anymore—they're writhing, like an intensification of the dancing they were doing seconds before, then falling over. The dance of death. People collapsing all over the arena, like a domino effect."

"Jesus."

"Yeah, I know. Even with all the crap we've seen—and even if it was just a video—the concert footage they've shown like a million times on TV basically just shows Shove It Up going down. No pun intended. Some people near the stage, too. Anyway, more than one person with the necessary clearance and knowledge has seen this stuff. It's classified top secret, but it holds a certain kind of fascination, obviously. In any case, like I said, it was easier to access than I thought it would be."

"Yeah? Well, that's—" Stricken by an image of Laureen choking, Frank needed a few moments to gather the necessary resources to finish his sentence. He shifted position on the bed, sitting more upright, and glanced over at Julie, whose eyes were fixed on him, questioning. "I'll tell you after I hang up."

"What?"

"Sorry. I was talkin' to Julie. Anyway, try not to mention that stuff to Rob. You know, the dance of death."

"Yeah. Understood. So…I spent at least an hour going over those tapes. The loading dock, that was easy enough, just zero in on the approximate time frame and there he is, bursting onto the platform. You can't see who it is, 'cause he's got a gas mask on, trying to get it off, and in the next instant, he's attacked by two guys with clubs."

"Whoa. Really?"

"What, that surprises you? Only surprise is that they didn't just shoot him—maybe they didn't want to leave a trail of blood? As it was, they had a hard time getting him into this white van. Your friend Billy—"

"Not."

"Okay, figure of speech. But he's a tough son of a bitch. They had clubs, and he still gave them a run for their money before they finally put out his lights and got him in the van. Unfortunately, in the melee, you can't really get any kind of clean look at him, even freeze framing."

Frank nodded, absorbing, thinking that it would definitely be best if Rob talked to Fowlkes directly. "So, why didn't they just kill him afterward?"

"I'm sure that was their intention. Shoot him, dump the body someplace where it wouldn't be found. And, I'd bet that my fellow FBI grunts—a scam of this magnitude, like I said before, you're gonna have very few people in on it. Otherwise, it explodes all over the place, you know what I'm saying? Flowers, Tate, maybe one or two higher-ups in the bureau. But the guys honestly investigating this thing, I'm sure they saw Billy, who they don't know is Billy, but they saw him get Shanghaied after he ran out of the arena, they figured it was All for Allah covering their tracks. Making sure the perp doesn't get caught, and sing. Except that terrorist groups usually claim responsibility. Maybe that was the reasoning, I don't know. In any case, he must've escaped somehow. Maybe he put that gun of his to use. There's a few moments where he's surrounded by the goons, there were actually three, before they got him in the van and slammed the doors. Locked them. I'm assuming they disarmed him, but you can't really see. And yeah, I ran the van's plates. Nothing."

"Which sounds like what we got."

Fowlkes playfully cleared his throat. "Oh, ye of little faith. We got footage from the basement. A little dim, but visible enough. Billy, if that's him, from the back, shooting the guard. The guy was sleeping, by the way—on camera, no less, not really the American hero they made him out to be in the media. But then he, Billy, spun around and looked straight at the camera, almost like he knew where it was."

"Yeah, he's probably had practice."

"I'm sure. He had this exaggerated sneer on his face, almost like a caricature of a sneer, wild look, like he was all fired up from having made his first killing, and done it personally, as opposed to the thousands more he was gonna gas from a distance. It was like he was looking into the camera and screaming 'Fuck you' to whoever might see it. Only it was '*Allahu akbar.*' Loud, man. It had to be to be heard over Shove it Up, even in the basement."

Frank tried to picture it. Soon enough, he wouldn't have to. "I don't get it. How did the FBI guys investigating this interpret—if the AFA denied responsibility, if they didn't want to have this shit pinned on them, why would their hit man be shouting '*Allahu akbar*'?"

"God is great."

"Yeah, I'm sure He is. But you understand what I'm saying?"

"Sure. They probably figured he's a fanatic and just got carried away in the excitement, thinking about all those virgins he was gonna have when he got to paradise." Fowlkes paused, sighing, as if wishing he might have just one, and if she wasn't really a virgin, that was okay too.

"Then you see him from the back picking the lock to the room with the central air intake. Then he's coming out, wearing a gas mask. And—you can't see this in the footage, but I have an acquaintance in forensics, just told him I was curious—the guard was killed with a bullet from a plastic gun. So I'm assuming Billy entered the arena through one of the gates. And he probably did, if he picked a lock to get in, he'd undoubtedly have triggered an alarm. But at any of the gates, a metal gun would've been picked up by security, detectors."

"Okay. So if we do find him, and he still has the gun—very big 'ifs,' I know—then, they can match it with the bullet. Yes?" Almost reflexively, he stroked the back of Julie's neck, knowing the effect words like *gun* and *bullet* would have on her.

"Yeah, they could. Assuming we recover the gun. Like you say, the odds at this point might not be that great. And if we do, I'll have to find someone in forensics who's willing to cooperate, since this is considered solved by the bureau, signed sealed and delivered. I'll be trying to figure out the best approach, different options, while you guys are hopefully running down Patterson.

I also spent a lot of time going over the stuff that involved footage from the corridors around the inside of the arena, where the restrooms and refreshment stands are, souvenirs and all that. A lot of territory, and crowds of people. But, eureka, I saw him coming out of a supply closet, assuming that was him. You can corroborate. He was dressed like a maintenance man. He's got this silver thermos-looking thing, which is probably the gas canister. Folded gas mask in his other hand. Work gloves. He blended right into the crowd, this was probably before Shove It Up came on, while they were tuning up their instruments or whatever. But I got an ISO of him coming out of the closet. No, I refuse to make any stupid gay jokes."

"Paul, you've changed."

"Kiss my—Anyway, I'm gonna send you the ISO. Actually, there are two good ones. Plus, I'll send the footage from the basement. And until I can get a thumb drive to you, I'll give you the site and the code, and my password, but don't open it at home, or at work. Maybe find some coffee shop where there's Wi-Fi. Then let me know if it's him."

"Good idea. I'll do it tomorrow. There's actually this place near the store, people sit there all day with their laptops, nursing a cup, but it's not that crowded mid-afternoon. I'll sit against the wall. But, Paul, do we still have to take these security precautions? Since I apologized to Tate, I've seen no indications that I'm being followed. No indications of anything."

"Okay. Well, you're still on the high priority list, you and Rob. Which doesn't mean—it's been what, a week? Less? Believe it or not, even with something like this, the wheels turn slowly. They just might not have gotten around to updating the list yet. Or—"

"Shit. Right, okay, I hear you." Frank clenched his teeth, shook his head. "Hang on for a sec. Julie, I need paper and something to write with. Please?" he said, attempting a playful smile.

She rolled over, retrieved the requested materials from the nightstand on her side of the bed, stuck the paper on top of the hardcover novel she'd been reading—which had been largely responsible for her amorous mood—and put both on Frank's lap. Then she handed him the pen.

The next day, at the Coffee Grounds in Armonk, Frank discovered that the face in Fowlkes's freeze-frame was indeed Billy's. Above the dark gray denim, or whatever it was, of the maintenance staff shirt, there he was. Brownish-black crew cut; compressed, yet prominent, forehead; a thick nose with a small bump midway, like the makeshift sled-jumps young Frank, younger Rob and friends used to erect on snowy hills in the park; dark eyes that had always seemed narrower beneath the shelf of his forehead, and in contrast with the nose.

Billy's lips were compressed in the picture, his stride long and purposeful as he joined the crowd of Shove It

Up fans moving past, hustling to their seats, or making a pit stop mandated by a couple of preliminary, overpriced beers, or maybe looking for something to satisfy those cannabis-induced munchies. He was like poison entering the bloodstream. The image on the computer chilled Frank to his bones. Freeze frame. If only it were possible to reverse the action from there. According to his understanding, this was a routine maneuver on almost any video apparatus—have Billy turn and insert that gleaming silver canister back into the supply closet, or trash it, moved by a unexpected infusion of sanity, a gift to the world from a suddenly merciful God.

The footage from the basement was as Fowlkes had described it. Billy, probably without his medication, definitely without whatever small measure of rationality he ordinarily possessed, screaming at the security camera. Son of a bitch.

Frank hit *quit,* and the pictures vanished. Just like that. It took another minute for him to lift himself from the wooden chair, after closing the computer. He really hadn't doubted beforehand that Billy had done the deed, but still…

He called Fowlkes as he drove back to Tedeschi's Hardware. "It's him," Frank said, stifling an urge to punch the dashboard.

Rob, on the other hand, had seemed gratified on receiving confirmation that their little Jihad was a righteous one. Now, he was reminded that for all intents and purposes, he'd lost both members of his immediate family.

"What about Nellie?" Maria Tedeschi said, half an accusation in her voice, unless it was his imagination. "What did you tell her?"

"Um, that I'd be away for a week or two. She barely nodded, Ma. I guess I should be grateful that she still knows who I am, although since she's been at Fran's, I'm not always sure…By the way, thanks for helping out over there."

"Of course. I just wish I could do more."

"Ma, you're not a magician. At least, you know, she's comfortable over there, back living with her sister, or whatever world she's in, in her head. Away from the house where Laureen lived. And me. And it's like, I'm not even sure she remembers her. It's like premature Alzheimer's or something. I don't think I've heard her mention her daughter's name once since the funeral. Not *once.* And when *I* do, I don't get the feeling that she knows what the hell I'm talking about."

"Rob, that's PTSD," Julie said, shifting in the metal framed, canvas "sack" chair that had recently been added to the more staid furniture in the living room.

"Post Traumatic…"

"Stress Disorder," she filled in. "Her premature Alzheimer's, as you put it, that's symptomatic."

"Yeah, so I've heard. Or so I've been told by her shrink. I've sat in on one or two of their sessions, only because the shrink, Doctor…what's her face…Rabinowitz? Maybe my mind's going too. Anyway, she thought it might help. Good luck. And good thing I got health insurance. The woman's prescribed new medications. No difference that I've seen." He glanced over at his mother, who didn't disagree. "Nellie wasn't in great shape before. But compared to *this*?"

"Spring comes, I'll try to get her to help me with the garden," said Maria. "Hopefully, you'll be back before *then.* But gardening's therapeutic. I've experienced that myself, even before I read it in a magazine. Maybe she just needs time, and a little prayer. Between your sister-in-law and me, she's in good hands."

"As opposed to professional ones?"

"Exactly. Well, she has been seeing Dr. Rabinowitz two or three times a week. But if you're talking about institutionalization, that has to be last resort, Robert. They perform no magic in there, believe me. She could even get worse, depending."

"Right. Well, I wasn't seriously thinking about that. Yet," said Rob. "She can still dress and feed herself… go to the can independently."

"Maybe we should change the subject? For now?" suggested his father. No one objected. He turned to Frank. "So, what did you tell Sergio and Carl?"

Frank took a sidelong glance at Julie, who was seated next to him on the flowery sofa. "Nothing," he replied, shrugging. "We call them twice a week each, like clockwork, although sometimes they call in-between, if they need something. Like a cash transfusion. But, as often as not, Julie talks for both of us. Maybe I listen in on the other line, or she gives me a report. They probably won't even notice I'm not there."

"Be nice if they called *us* once in a while," said Albert Tedeschi, receiving confirmation from his wife, a quick nod. "Hell, we're only their grandparents."

"We tell them to, believe me."

"Don't take it personally," Julie said, her faint smile an acknowledgement that this might be easier said than done. "College, it's just a different world they're in now, that's all. Very absorbing. If I remember correctly."

"Well, how are they doing?" asked Maria.

"Okay. Carl, to our surprise, is actually running cross-country, although they practice indoors now until the weather gets warmer. But he says it clears his head."

"Yeah, that was good news," added Frank. "Hopefully, if he really wants to keep his head clear, he'll stop—" He hesitated, as Julie shot him a look: *Mom and Dad don't really need to hear about that.* Okay, agreed, especially since it was true, from Frank's own experience, that drugs—depending upon which, and how much—would not do irreparable harm. And if Carl was not the most stable kid, at least he was now living in the insular, accepting environment of Stoneybrook University, where it was likely that at least half the student body was trying to get its head on straight.

"He's doing okay," Julie reiterated. "He's getting by academically, and I think living on his own is good for him. It'll help him to grow."

"Cross-country?" mused Albert. "Does he run with that nose ring in?"

Julie laughed. "The two are not mutually exclusive, Grandpa," she said, bringing a yellowed smile to his face. "And Sergio? Unlike Carl, who could care less about politics, he's all fired up about the supposed liberal bias of his professors. Even after everything that's happened with the Arabs—his words. He even sees this in his business professors. That's his major. You know that. And, as of now, he's still *in love*, he's—" She hesitated, glancing over at Rob as it dawned on her that reports on her offspring might have an effect on him.

"Hey, it's okay," Rob said, reading her face. A detective's skills were not really necessary. "Seriously, it's okay. What, you're never gonna talk about your kids in front of me?"

CHAPTER 14

Frank had hardly been on the Tappan Zee Bridge over the previous ten years, not since Carl and Sergio had gotten old enough to make family vacations a thing of the past. Now, with Rob driving, he had the luxury of scanning the Hudson River at length, time and distance-wise. It was a cold and clear day, late January, with a few die-hard ice floes dotting the wide, murky river, riding the current, heading for the George Washington bridge and points south.

Beyond the GW, with its hills and valleys of steel cable, Frank could make out the western skyline of Manhattan. He might've even been able to dimly catch sight of the World Trade Center towers at the far end of the island, rising out of a gray mist like some primordial manifestation of matter. Except for the fact that they'd collapsed, with a little help. Viewed from the Tappan Zee, that probably would've looked like hell erupting, down there at the end of the world. Make mine Manhattan, while it's still around.

Nine-eleven begat First Union Arena. Nine years later, people hadn't needed much convincing to believe that the Arabs had done it again. And one side effect was that Frank had become something akin to a bounty hunter—at least it felt that way—a role he'd never have wanted to play, had he ever imagined himself in it. He gazed wistfully downriver. New York. Home, once removed. Hopefully, he'd make it back in one piece, again, this time with a little extra company, an ex-employee of his, chained and cuffed into the back seat. Rob, with the help of a mechanic he knew at the Bronx NYPD garage and two hundred-dollar bills, had furnished the rear of his car with iron brackets. Billy would not need to buckle up.

Still, according to Rob, the SOB should not be left alone back there. One of them would have to ride with him. Frank was not looking forward to this. But maybe Rob would do it instead. Maybe he'd enjoy putting the fear of God into Billy, in a way that the Reverend Tate's fire and brimstone couldn't even approach. Assuming that they found and caught Billy in the first place.

"You wanna be a grandfather?" asked Rob as they followed the Tappan Zee's downward slope toward the New York State Thruway. His voice startled Frank, whose absorption in the scenery, and his own head, had been absolute. This was facilitated by the absence of conversation or music. Silence was a compromise when musical tastes were irreconcilable. And it was preferable to small talk, an art at which neither of them excelled, particularly not with each other.

"What? Oh. What Julie said last night, about my love-smitten elder son."

He paused, shifting mental gears. The broad expanse of the river had vanished. The thruway ran past high rock walls created by its own construction, by bulldozers and dynamite. Hills of stone had been sheared into striated cliffs as if via karate chops from the Almighty. Chain-link fences protected drivers and passengers against the potential after-effects, time-released rock slides. Exits flew by for subdivision towns like Nanuet and Yorktown Heights, rail commutes into the Big Apple.

"I don't really think Sergio's in a hurry to get married." Frank chuckled. "Not unless he does the cost benefit analysis…filing jointly, whatever." He idly flicked the spring-latch on Rob's glove compartment, which doubled as a clip for papers and maps. "Hell, I guess I should cut the kid some slack. Stop holding grudges. He did bring her home to meet us, Thanksgiving. Seems like a long time ago, man."

"Yeah, I know. I half remember her. What's her name again?"

"Sandra. Nice little WASP. Very polite, modestly dressed. *She* wants to get married. Or so we gathered from Sergio. She's already compromised her principles, gave herself to him, even though they're not hitched."

Rob spat out a laugh, while cutting into the left lane, the middle having been obstructed by a driver directly in front of him who was seemingly determined to obey the speed limit. He made the switch at a sharp angle, taking the opportunity to practice his evasive skills, just in case.

"*What*?" he demanded theatrically. "What planet is she from? And he told you this?"

"Told Julie," Frank replied, ignoring the flip-flop executed by his stomach in response to the unexpected swerve. "Even if she wasn't his mama, she's just—she could've gotten Nixon to come clean, without even trying. She's sympathetic, non-judgmental—"

"I don't know about that, man."

"Hey, with you, that's different. You're a serious asshole."

"Fuck you."

Frank laughed, a sort of grosser version of the rumbling in his midsection. Being in a hurry to get going, hyped, he hadn't eaten much for breakfast. "Thanks, bro," he said. "Seriously, I need to develop some of that non-judgmentalism myself—that might not be a word—

but I've built a case against her in my head. Sandra. She's a business major like him. Conservative, Young Republican." He pronounced this last word with reflexive disdain. "That's how they met."

"Ah. *That's* what it is. Politics. That figures. Personally, I thought she was nicely built. That I remember. 'Course, you're not just marrying the body, which doesn't come with a warranty anyway."

"Rob, you're too much. According to Julie, Sergio really loves her, for whatever that means. If they decide to get married, I need to get my head on straight. Accept it. Welcome her and her parents, even if they carry pitchforks, thump bibles. Whatever. Seriously, I don't wanna be like Julie's parents."

"Boycotted your wedding."

"Yup."

Out of deference to his mother, Frank and Julie were married in a Roman Catholic church—Saint Ignacio's, in a now-dying parish at the edge of Pelham Bay, abutting the New England Thruway. Frank and Rob had been confirmed there. It hadn't taken, in either case. And Saint Ignacio's had since shrunk, or so it seemed to bridegroom Frank. The air was even less breathable. Maybe it was just the tuxedo with its cummerbund, another concession to his mother. He harbored no doubts about marrying Julie, the war had done that much for him. As far as he was concerned, death would have to do them part.

After the ceremony, they had a catered reception at the Tedeschi home, utilizing the inside and the yard. Fortunately, the spring rains had abated, and a soft, salty breeze was coming in off the Long Island Sound. The ceremony and reception were attended by Frank's side of the family, and by friends, including Paul Fowlkes, who'd returned from Vietnam several months after the groom. He'd gotten soused at the reception. In this, he had a partner—Rob.

Decades later, the two men would not remember having previously met each other, despite the evidence—a photograph that Frank had dropped on the table near the end of their conference at the Forest Hills library. Rob, leaning against the living room wall, was staring at the camera with a self-satisfied smirk on his face: "Hey, check out how plastered I am." Standing next to him was Fowlkes, minus fifty pounds, with a whiskey tumbler in hand and an insane grin spread across his face. The red eyes on both men, an accident of photography, seemed very appropriate. What the reception lacked in glitz—at the preference of the newlyweds—it made up for with high spirits. A good time was had by all, despite the absence of Julie's parents and relatives.

Gerardo and Sophia D'Millio had never been that crazy about their daughter's high school sweetheart. Something about the way he and Julie looked at each other, like it took serious effort on their parts to keep their hands off of each other, even in front of her parents. The D'Millios were surprised, and grateful, when Frank enlisted. They did grudgingly acknowledge his patriotism to Julie, who responded by slamming her bedroom door in their faces.

Well, she'd get over it, and it was all for the best. Little did they know that Frank would return from the war and convert their daughter into a flaming radical. He'd caused her to be saddled with a jail record, owing to her participation in demonstrations against her own country's mission to preserve freedom at home and in the world at large. Julie's parents also accused him—the last time he'd entered their home, sporting a pony-tail and beard—

of introducing her to marijuana, LSD, and other illegal drugs. She had vehemently denied this, even as she readily admitted to using the vile substances in the first place. Hell, she'd been proud of it, as if breaking their hearts was some kind of noble rite of passage.

By the time their male grandchildren were in college, Julie's parents had been living in Florida for fifteen years. When the boys were younger, she periodically took them to visit. They returned home with tans, monogrammed sun visors, T-shirts featuring glittering palm trees and what-have-you, gifts from Grandma and Grandpa D'milio.

A mile away from the next toll plaza, traffic on the Thruway began to back up. Rob cursed and edged back into the middle lane, looking for a non-existent advantage. "Well," he said, "I guess what goes around comes around."

"Meaning? Oh, like her parents had no use for me—guess I should say *have*—and now—I told you, man, Sergio wants to marry her, I'm okay with it, if it happens. Or, I'm getting there."

In fact, First Union Arena had put everything into a different perspective. This was not really news to Frank, but the truth of it was suddenly as clear as the morning's view down the Hudson.

Rob finally tossed Frank's coins into the hopper at the toll plaza. He'd argued for splitting the tolls and gas until Frank suggested letting Billy Patterson cover their expenses, or at least a chunk of them. Billy had never picked up his last pay check. Pity. Still, the costs of Frank's association with him were yet to be known.

Did anyone pull out from the shoulder as they exited the plaza? Negative. Right along, Frank had been surveying the cars behind them, looking for company. As far as he could tell, no one had been in Rob's rear view mirror for any suspicious length of time. When Rob pulled off the Thruway at the Rip Van Winkle Service Center, north of Tarrytown, New York, Frank twisted his head around to note the cars following them into the parking lot. Negative on Ford Broncos. Later, he would check to see who was following them out. Of course, it was possible that they were being tracked on some computer screen, maybe even with the help of a satellite. Anything was possible, a notion that seemed to gain more credence as they headed north.

The service center featured overpriced gas and even more overpriced food. Mickey D's, minus the arches. KFC, Arby's, Taco Bell, all of them together under one roof, travel a thousand miles and you couldn't get away from these places. They didn't call it fast food for nothing. Still, it was almost comforting to get out and mingle with families of bleary-eyed parents and kids who were hyper from hours of sitting in the car, or cranky after being roused from auto-induced naps. Intimations of sweet normalcy—except for the headlines visible from New York City newspapers, which were available in coin boxes outside the main building and inside at the Rip Van Winkle Traveler's Store.

The typically garish headline on the *New York Post* grabbed Frank's attention first—

MO-HORROR: INFIDELS DESERVED TO DIE. It would have been surprising that Mohammar Khan, leader of All for Allah, was issuing statements for public consumption from his maximum-security jail cell at an undisclosed location, except that accuracy, or even plausibility, had never stopped the *Post.* The *Times's* front page featured a story about Iran's warning to the Flowers administration regarding the ongoing buildup of American forces in the Persian Gulf. A sub-heading quoted President Flowers as saying that any further Iranian threats against those forces, verbal or otherwise, could have "devastating" consequences.

Frank resisted the temptation to stop and read more. Better to ignore the newspapers. And he tried not to envision the headlines he and Rob might make if their mission succeeded. Undoubtedly everyone fantasized himself as a hero, at least now and then, but he liked to think that he was beyond such childishness, that he'd seen enough. *Right*. Of course, it was even more difficult to avoid contemplating the ways in which he and Rob might fail. They might simply be unable to locate Billy. Or, if they did, there could be plenty of pitfalls, fatal and otherwise.

The brothers wolfed down double cheeseburgers and even greasier fries. His mind working overtime, Frank barely tasted the stuff, except when it repeated on him later in the car. As they drove upstate, the city's far-flung suburbs finally receded. The terrain was forested, brown and rolling. On the hills flanking the thruway, only the exhaust soot collected in gray, crusted patches of snow offered evidence of human encroachment. Ahead loomed the Catskill Mountains, bulldozer-proof. The view was stunning. It was as if the roof of the world had suddenly been raised, walls eliminated. The thruway dwindled in the distance, subsumed by the mountains, its cars and trucks little more than metallic winks of the sun.

"Man, I haven't been up this way in so long. It's like a whole 'nother world," said Rob.

"Yeah, it's purple mountains' majesty. All that jazz. 'Cept they're not purple, but they are beautiful."

"I don't know. Nice place to visit. You'd wanna live up here?"

Frank shrugged. “Maybe. It’s got a nice effect. It’s mellowing, and it kind of dwarfs the shit going on in your head. I just realized that since we left the service center back there, I haven’t felt for my gun once.”

“Yeah?” Rob laughed. “I used to do that when I was a rookie, pat the thing. Sort of like, I don’t know, a weight lifter feeling up his bicep, checking it.”

“More like a nervous tic, for me. The absence of which…I’d have to say this is the most relaxed I’ve felt in a while. Which is saying something, considering why we’re up here in the first place. ‘Course, *you’re* probably used to this. Chasing after crooks. Mass murderers.”

Rob shot Frank a sideways look, of sufficient duration to discomfort him slightly, given the rate at which they were moving forward. “You think so? Man, a lot of my time is spent on paperwork, and you’d be amazed at how much of that there is, and now they want everything on computer. Unfortunately, I’m not exactly a whiz at the keyboard yet.”

“You sound like Pop.”

“You mean with the computers? Yeah, must be in the blood. But aside from cursing at uncooperative computers, a lot of my job is about trying to convince people that they’re not gonna get blown away if they talk to me, that everything’s confidential.”

“Is it?”

“Yup. It’s supposed to be. But they might get blown away anyway, ’specially if it’s drug-related. These guys have their sources. Hell, they’d make good detectives, ’cept that the pay’s a whole lot better in their line of work.”

“I’ll bet. Um, you might wanna slow down, man.” The needle of Rob’s speedometer lay on ninety-five.

He nudged the brake. “Good point. For once you might be right. These state troopers would probably not give a shit that I'm a city cop. Betcha they'd enjoy writing the ticket. Make their day." Rob paused, flipping down the sun visor above his windshield. "But anyway, when I *am* in a dangerous situation, or the possibility's there, I still get serious butterflies. Just try to control it. It's not like if you do it enough…you were in "Nam, you must know that."

"Right. I remember."

Rob passed a *Food Lion* tractor-trailer that was laboring on the upgrade then pulled back over to the right, where he would stay until he crept up on the rear of the next vehicle in front of him. "You know what though? This? I'm not the least bit nervous, whatever comes down. Think I just don't give a shit anymore, except that I want to catch the motherfucker. But don't worry, I won't do anything stupid. Just don't let me bash in his brains, if we're lucky enough to find him."

Frank nodded. "Will do."

They reached New Paltz by mid-afternoon and checked into the Super 8 Motel, economy lodgings made more so by the fact that they were sharing a room. Neither of them could guess at how long they'd be away, eating out, paying for a bed, shower and cable TV while still paying mortgages. If they got lucky, Nancy Horowitz might've been desperate enough to take Billy back, assuming he'd come there in the first place. One-stop shopping for the Tedeschi brothers. But Frank didn't think it would be that easy. Billy might have been crazy, but he wasn't stupid. And he wasn't a rookie at evading the law, nor was he just looking at a two-year rap for breaking and entering.

Rob and Frank tossed their duffel bags on their respective twin beds. Either Frank had over-packed, or his bed sagged in the middle. Well, he could always lay the mattress on the floor. That might help some. It would also put a little more distance between himself and Rob, who, if memory served, was prone to snoring. The memory in question was a Christmas dinner at their parents' in Pelham Bay, where Rob had conked out on the sofa, with the help of some spiked eggnog.

Beyond that, they'd shared a room in the Bronx apartment in which the family had lived while saving for a down payment on a house. Neither of them was particularly worried about sleeping back then. But during one of their frequent wrestling matches, the boys had actually managed to dislodge a chandelier from the ceiling of the Polish family below them. That was evidence enough that they'd gotten a mite big to be sharing a room—or the room wasn't big enough for the both of them, a description that eventually applied to any room.

The room at the Super 8 might've been smaller than their childhood bedroom, if memory served. For sure, and despite its non-smoking status, it didn't smell any better, although back then the boys were more or less immune. Their bedroom had smelled like it smelled—Eau de Locker Room.

They quickly left the motel, which featured a side view of the thruway. New Paltz proper, though, had a certain quaint charm to it—or might have under different circumstances. The State University of New York at New Paltz made it half a college town, with the attendant hippie/crafts shops, used records—the only kind left—bookstores, and veggie/ethnic restaurants lining the hilly Main Street. The other half featured strip malls, fast food, CVS pharmacy, what now passed for small town America. All of this was overlooked by cliffs that swarmed with rock climbers during the warm weather, twenty and thirty-somethings, male and female, with their ropes, helmets, and hardware. The sweep of the Hudson Valley lay at their feet when they got above the trees.

Between town and cliffs lay a few miles of farmland, which Frank and Rob were into immediately after exiting Main Street via an army-green metallic bridge. It turned out that Nancy Horowitz had rented the upper floor of a spacious house owned by a farmer who needed the money. Even if his farm ran almost to the horizon, it was not an agri-business. As Frank understood it, the family farm was going the way of the Mom-and-Pop store. Tedeschi's Hardware was an exception so far, or it had already expanded to the point where "Mom and Pop" no longer applied.

After a couple of broken U-turns, Frank and Rob located the address Fowlkes had supplied for Nancy Horowitz. They sped up a long gravel road that ran past fields lying brown and fallow on either side, past cows who didn't bother looking up from their sparse grass. Dust fanned out behind Rob's car in the fading afternoon light.

The mailbox back on the main road was a miniature tractor with the requisite plastic signal flag having replaced the vertical exhaust pipe. A hinged door atop the front wheels featured the name *McAdams. Horowitz* had been affixed beneath, likely with permanent marker. The brothers ascended the steps to the only door visible on the outside of the wooden house, a once-white colonial fronted by two cars and a pickup truck, standing amidst a weathered barn and various sheds. An actual-sized tractor was parked to one side, the treads of its giant wheels caked with dried mud.

Standing on a veranda enclosed by wooden rails, chipped green paint, Rob put the brass knocker to use, resoundingly. Half a minute later the door swung open.

"Help you?" asked a stocky hombre in a John Deere cap and soiled SUNY sweatshirt. He was in the brothers' age range, with graying stubble spread across the lower half of his moon-shaped face.

"Mr. McAdams?" asked Rob, eliciting the barest of nods. "We're looking for Nancy Horowitz."

"She expectin' you?" he inquired curtly.

Rob sighed, handed Frank the laptop they'd brought along, and took out his wallet. He held his badge in front of McAdams's face, not threateningly, but close enough to render any nearsightedness irrelevant. "I'm Detective Tedeschi, NYPD. Miss Horowitz has done nothing wrong, she isn't in any trouble, but we do need to speak with her."

McAdams hesitated then cleared his throat. "Follow me," he said, salvaging what authority he could. The foyer on the other side of the door led almost immediately to a steep, dimly lit wooden stairway. At the top, he knocked on a door decorated with school stickers: a rainbow, iridescent flowers, yellow smiley faces. It opened almost instantly.

"'Lo, Lily," McAdams said, his voice turning soft, playful. Frank could make out a little girl, maybe five or six years old. "Your mama here?"

The answer became apparent a couple of seconds later.

"Jim," said Nancy Horowitz, filling the doorframe, nodding at him.

She was a taller, shapelier version of her pixie-like daughter, starting with the brownish-blonde ponytail.

"You got visitors," he said unnecessarily, finally stepping aside.

"Miss Horowitz? I'm Detective Tedeschi, NYPD," Rob announced again, flashing the badge and a quick smile.

Post-9/11, NYPD was more than sufficient. This self-introduction was definitely more congenial than it had been with McAdams. Still, Nancy Horowitz's alarm was obvious. Her slender jaw tightened. The smooth skin of her neck pulled upward.

"This is my brother Frank," Rob added, pointing with an open hand, as if Frank's more benign nature were readily apparent, and might reassure her.

Brother Frank nodded, gratified that Nancy Horowitz was home. According to Stout, she had been working two or three jobs. Her eyes flitted toward Frank, questions passing over her face—*his brother? This is a family business?* Then she bobbed her head once in McAdams's direction, attempting to signal him that the situation was under control. No problem. Looking unconvinced, he hesitated for a second or two before turning toward the stairs.

Horowitz stepped back from her doorway. "Come in," she said, gulping. "Please."

As the brothers accepted her invitation, she instructed Lily to go play in her room. The girl didn't move. But after a second glance at her mother's face, she double-timed it toward the rear of the apartment, the pattering of her bare feet on the pine floors diminishing as she went, finally being punctuated by the slamming of her door.

The sound caused Horowitz's face to swivel involuntarily in her daughter's direction.

"Shit!" she declared, as if this oath had been jarred loose by the resounding thud of wood on wood. She glanced apologetically at Rob. "Look, I didn't mean—" She took a deep breath. "You're looking for Billy, right? Aren't you? Well, he's gone. Again. Thankfully."

Frank shot a sideways look at Rob: *Did I hear her right? Good job, Sylvester Stout.*

Rob's eyes hadn't strayed from Nancy Horowitz, whose pretty face was fraught with consternation. "Billy Patterson," he said flatly.

"Yup. Crazy son of a—came back up here…what was it?…a month and a half ago? Two? Seems like longer. Talkin' all this crazy stuff about First Union Arena in

New York. Like, *he* did it? I told 'im, Billy, the Arabs did it. They caught them already. I'm like, 'you were nuts enough before you left here—and I was stupid enough, or hard up enough, maybe both, to almost beg you to stay, even though you were makin' *me* crazy, even before you started hasslin' me about Jesus. But now, you're like completely whacked out.' He told me, yeah, while he was down there in Westchester, he was diagnosed as bi-pola—" She paused for breath, sweeping a stray strand of hair back from her high forehead. "Said at the church he was workin' at, they paid him peanuts but set 'im up with health insurance, some faith-based government thing. Something. Got some medication, an' some special attention from this famous reverend…Tate?…who thought he needed it. Shit, I could half believe that, 'cept that this was the same guy who Billy said gave him permission to gas the arena in the first place.

"But the whole thing was a set-up. I'm like, 'Oh my God,'" she said, rolling her eyes. "No pun intended. But, like, usually it's like, the *devil* made me do it, ya know? This is a new one. Anyway, I asked Billy if he was takin' his meds, like it was probably a good idea, an' he fished this empty pill bottle out of this like gym bag he had. I told 'im, like, go get the refill, *ASAP*. Like now. 'If they haven't kicked you off the insurance, and there's a co-pay, I'll cover it if need be. I'll even pay for a month's worth. Whatever they give you, you need it big time.' Not that I'm rollin' in money. But I told him I'd do it on the condition that he goes away and doesn't come back this time. I mean, he was a mess, had this bump on his head, scar over his eye like he'd been in some kinda fight. But it wasn't even the way he looked. He was just crazy, he was freakin' me out. Even Lily—" She gave a toss of her head in the direction of her daughter's bedroom. "—and she usta really like him."

"So, where might we be able to find him?" Rob asked, his baritone a stark contrast to Horowitz's breathy, agitated soprano, with its New York accent. Or so it seemed to Frank, who was trying to make himself useful, to observe and absorb details, from her body language to the ramshackle furnishings of her living room, which might have appeared that way because of Lily's toys, crayons, and drawings. They were scattered everywhere.

"Don't know," Horowitz quickly replied, shrugging. "I mean, he might be nuts. But, like, he's harmless. I mean, I'm not surprised you wanna try to find him, like I expected it, I *told* 'im if he talked all that crap about First Union Arena, probably to anyone who'd listen—or even if they *weren't* listenin', probably the government is. Big Brother's watchin'. Cops could even wind up comin' around, on the off-chance that he's not completely nuts, that he might know somethin' they don't. Didn't really believe that would happen, but like, here you are."

She paused again, taking another deep breath, releasing it slowly. "Look, if you don't mind, do me a favor, on your way out. Like, I'm not tellin' you to leave or anything. But tell Jim down there that I'm, like, not in any kinda trouble. I was lucky enough to get this place, it's like, livable, and cheap enough, and I wanna keep it. He's already complained about Lily jumpin' rope on his head and whatnot, although he's kind of taken a shine to her anyway. Wasn't crazy about Billy bein' here either, though Billy helped him out some with the farmin'. Dirt cheap. No pun intended. Jim just took some offa the rent. He didn't even know that Billy was back this last time. An' I wasn't about to let him stay long."

Horowitz shook her head, her ponytail flopping from side to side behind her, its motion augmented slightly by the shifting of her weight on bare feet. The interview was being conducted standing up. She hadn't thought to clear off the furniture and offer them a seat.

Even given the premature crow's feet in the corners of her wide hazel eyes, and the pinched set of her thin lips during her rare moments of silence, Nancy Horowitz was attractive. She had slightly buck teeth, thick brownish hair and the remnants of an air of innocence. Frank imagined her as a transplanted city girl trying to find a saner life in the country, with mixed results.

"If you're wonderin', like, what I was doin' with him in the first place—like I said before, I guess I was a little desperate, for someone's help with the rent, with Lily, with…havin' a man, or at least another adult in my life, for those rare occasions when I wasn't workin'. Plus, believe it or not, *I* can't believe it, but I sorta liked him at first. He had a kinda weird genuineness about him, sometimes. Earnestness or something. Like a puppy." She looked away, seemingly embarrassed at having uttered this little confidence.

"Yeah, he did in a way," said Frank.

"I mean, that's why he could relate so well to Lily, he could get right down—" Horowitz paused, as his comment registered. "Wait. You're talkin' like you knew him."

"I did. *Thought* I did."

Puzzled, she studied Frank for another long moment. "Tedeschi. That's what you said your name was? I should've—like in Tedeschi's Hardware? Where he worked."

"Yeah, I'm the owner. After my father, who's now just overseeing things."

"I don't get it. You said you were a cop."

"*I* am. He's been deputized. Unofficially," confided Rob, with a small lift of his eyebrows.

Frank said, "I was just like you, with Billy. I didn't take him seriously when he talked about gassing First Union Arena. If I *had*—" He tried to shrug off the pang of guilt that shot through him, despite his having talked this through with Julie, several times, and supposedly resolving it in his own head. There'd been no reason, beforehand, to take Billy seriously. Had there? "—then after the thing actually happened, and he disappeared, I started thinking that maybe he hadn't just been blowing off steam."

"So you actually think...*Billy?* Uh-uh, even if, maybe, he wasn't playing with a full deck. When he came up here again, talking about how even Jesus would never forgive him...plus I'd sort of had time to get my head on straight, after he left, like, yeah, it was clear, he was a little nuts—whatever medical term they wanna give it. But still, there's no way—"

"Miss Horowitz," said Rob, "we have evidence. Video footage, from the basement at First Union, that shows Billy shooting that guard, the one who was stationed by the central air conditioning unit."

He paused until Horowitz, mouth agape, nodded slowly, robotically: Yes, she knew about the guard, even aside from Billy's ranting, the whole story of First Union had been replayed, in detail, for weeks, on every TV channel, in every newspaper. And she understood the concept of evidence, and what Rob was claiming it showed, even if she couldn't come close to believing that Billy would do such a thing. She gazed at Frank now, as if by dint of his association with her ex-lover, he might corroborate that there was no way it could be true.

"But the Arabs did it," she said finally. "Right? You think, like, All for Allah hired Billy? And if there's evidence, why isn't the FBI, and the CIA, whatever, why haven't they been all over here, looking for him? Why is it just, like, a New York City cop, and his brother who runs a hardware store?"

"The whole thing was staged by the government," said Rob. "Elements of it. With the approval of Flowers, or so it seems. They wanted to blame the Arabs, for political reasons. Get everyone behind our fearless president. Start another war? The usual stuff."

Frank whistled soundlessly. Had these liberal-sounding words really issued from his brother? Horowitz's eyes were fixed on Rob, reflecting a deeper state of disbelief. President Flowers and his party had nothing but disdain for single mothers like her, or for the kind of working class riff-raff who would attend a Shove It Up concert. But killing thousands of them, so they could blame it on the Arabs? And with Billy as the point man? Okay, fantasy was big nowadays, movies, books if you had the time and energy. But *that*—

On the other hand, Billy's being on a hit list was not too much of a stretch. Nor was the idea that anyone in his or her right mind, let alone criminals, would be unwilling to bank on Billy's silence. Still, Horowitz cringed as Rob explained why there were goons hoping to kill Patterson.

"They already tried to," Rob said. "Which is undoubtedly why he was banged up when he came up here. But somehow he escaped, and they're looking for him."

"He's just not that easy to find," Frank added. "You said while he was up here he was working for McAdams, in exchange for rent reduction? So, in effect, he was off the books."

She gave a muted laugh, more like dry expectoration. "Yeah, off the books, that was him. Well, he was also workin' some for this, like, painter-slash-handyman in town. Off the books too. Suited both a'them, I guess."

"I'm sure," said Frank, despite the fact that he himself had paid payroll and social security taxes for Billy's part-time services. "Off the books, and off the map. But Rob and me, we just got lucky. Found out about his relationship with you from this guy he was working for at the church, who favored us with that information after he received a visit from those gentlemen who're looking for Billy. Apparently, they didn't make a good impression."

"But you guys did."

Either it was his imagination, or Nancy Horowitz was teasing them. Frank gave a quick smile. "Apparently. But like I said, we got lucky. Billy's good at traveling under the radar."

"I guess. Except that he has a hard time keeping his mouth shut. But I still can't believe it. I mean, why the hell would he ever do that in the first place? What'd they, offer him a ton of money? Even if they did, there's no way—"

Rob said, "Shove It Up—and their fans—they were anti-Christs, in his eyes. He was a fanatic. And crazy, as you've pointed out. Plus, he was encouraged by Reverend Tate, who's sort of in league with the Flowers Administration. They used him."

"I don't know if I can believe it. The whole thing, it's like outta some half-assed thriller. And, I mean...*Billy?* Dumb-head?" As if on cue, her daughter Lily's bedroom door creaked on its hinges, and Lily came sashaying down the hall, holding an oversized stuffed green turtle in front of her. "That was, um, her term of endearment for him," Horowitz said. "He usta, like, bug out his eyes and stick out his tongue when she said it. She loved it."

"Cute," Rob offered, as Lily, her smile missing both front teeth, wordlessly handed him the turtle. "What's his name?"

"*Her.* It's a girl," corrected Lily, the set of her lips conveying her opinion that this should have been obvious. "Myrtle. Myrtle the Turtle."

"Ah. Very original."

"Yeah. I made it up," Lily said primly, Rob's gentle sarcasm having passed over her head.

"Sweetie, I need to talk to these men privately, okay? Go stay in your room a little more. It won't be long."

Rob, feigning reluctance, handed Myrtle the Turtle back to Lily, his right hand cradling the stuffed animal beneath its furry yellow belly. "Thanks, Lily. That's your name, right?"

"Yup. Silly Lily." Accepting the turtle with both hands, she turned and offered it to Frank, who raised his hands, showing her his palms.

"You heard what your mother said," Frank told her, having an audio-flashback of the last time he'd uttered those words, maybe ten years ago, to his son Carl, although the context escaped him. "Maybe you can introduce me to Myrtle later."

Lily actually batted her eyes at him, licking her upper lip and jutting out one hip—to no avail. Finally, her mouth compressed and tightened, increasing her already close resemblance to her mother. She spun, flung the stuffed turtle down the hall, and then stomped after her, sending Myrtle the rest of the way to the bedroom door with an impressive kick in the rear.

Horowitz pursed her lips. "I don't know where she gets that vamping shit from, I really don't. Guess I should monitor what she watches on TV more. We only got one, but a lotta times I'm cooking or whatever an' she's playin' in front a'the thing, sorta tunin' in an' out. Plus, when Jim's daughter's watchin' her, who knows what she's got on? She's a teenager."

"Yeah. I know all about *that*," said Rob, the bottom briefly dropping out of his voice. "But, Miss Horowitz, we really need whatever help you can provide. If you knew we were telling the truth—"

"How am I gonna know that?" she asked, her pitch rising. "An' if I did, just for the sake of argument, I'd probably be too much in shock to be much use to anyone."

"Well, I could show you that video footage I was talking about before. From the security cameras at First Union Arena."

"We have a connection," Frank said. "Rob being a detective, he knew someone, who knew someone. Neither someone knew about why we really wanted to see the footage. We were trying our best to lay low, until we knew for sure. Or until we bring Billy to justice. But it's him. Before he puts on the gas mask. There's no doubt. Believe me."

"I can't. But I'll take a look. Actually, I was wondering what you were doing with that laptop."

"Now it becomes clear," said Frank, reaching for a little levity.

He unzipped an inner pocket of his open winter jacket and fished out the thumb drive that Fowlkes, complaining about the traffic he'd encountered on the way up, had dropped off at the store. Frank had had to stifle a laugh when Fowlkes had delivered the thing via a handshake.

Horowitz cleared a cardboard copy of the book *The Mouse Finds a House,* a soft plastic sheet half laden with unicorn stickers and a bag of crayons off her paisley sofa, adding them to the mess on the wooden floor, moving items around to create foot space.

She was flanked on the sofa by Rob, the PC in his lap, and Frank.

"I'm having second thoughts," she said, while watching her fingers unknot the tangled hair of one of Lily's dolls. "And third." When Lily herself, as if having sensed drama in the offing, walked into the living room, Horowitz inhaled sharply. "Lil. I thought I told you—"

"A laptop!" declared Lily, crowding in on Rob. "Can I see it?" She was already opening the PC when Rob gently plucked away her hands. They briefly disappeared beneath his thick fingers.

"Silly Lily," he said. "Now what would you like to see?"

Frank's eyes widened as he watched this little demonstration of kindness on his brother's part. Horowitz sat back, suddenly disinclined to assert her authority, maybe welcoming the delay.

"Starfall," said Lily.

"What's that?"

"You can read. Play alphabet games."

"It's a free site they use at her school," Horowitz filled in. "Nice graphics. Cartoons. She's got a computer in her bedroom too, and she loves it. Right, Lil? But I'm gonna have to put a filter…you can block 'inappropriate' sites? Lil's learning how to surf, all on her own."

"Impressive," said Rob. "But, Lil, this laptop doesn't get internet. Not here. Sorry. Maybe you can show me Starfall on your own computer?" He glanced over at Horowitz, who nodded.

So did Frank, as Rob handed him the laptop. Maybe Rob had seen the footage enough. Once had been plenty, although he'd perused it several times. Maybe he was just getting Lily out of the way. As the child towed Rob out of the living room, leaving behind a very loud silence, Frank inserted the thumb drive, opened it, and clicked on the document. Horowitz leaned forward.

The videotaped sight of Billy shooting the sleeping guard, executing him as if putting down an animal, caused Horowitz to drop her face into her hands. Frank paused the video until she looked up and managed to nod. Then she recoiled, shaking her head in disbelief, from

Billy's contorted face screaming "*Allahu Akbar.*" He could have been standing in front of her.

There were tears in her eyes when she finished watching. "That motherfucking—how the fuck *could* he?" she rasped finally, her voice almost breaking. "In my worst fucking nightmares—" She inhaled deeply. "I gotta go wash my face. Something." She fairly jumped off the sofa and strode out of the room. Seconds later the bathroom door slammed.

Rob walked backed into the living room. Frank gave him the thumbs-up sign, a gesture that felt almost obscene. "Where's Lily?" he said.

"Typing short vowels to complete three-letter words," he said, shrugging. "Piece of cake."

The brothers were sunk into the sofa, neither inclined to move, by the time Horowitz returned. Her eyes were reddened, the lines of her face sharp.

"I can give you a couple of leads," she said unprompted, after a glance at the now blank computer screen. "But I don't know how much help they'll be. And if he calls again—which I doubt, I think I made myself clear to him, but on the other hand who knows what the fuck he'll do—but if he does, I'll try to find out where he is, and let you know. But what if he comes after me? Us? What am I gonna do then?"

Rob said, "If we find him, he's not gonna know how. Assuming he escapes in the first place, which, I can guarantee you, he won't. Your name will never be mentioned, or alluded to. And along those lines, it would be good if you told nobody, not even—"

"Jim?" She tilted her head in the direction of McAdams's downstairs dwelling.

"Right. *No one.* Make up a story for him, if you need to. Ditto for Lily. A story that fits with us being cops. It's vital that no one knows what we're doing, and where we are."

Rob started taking down information from Horowitz. Fifteen minutes later, the brothers were outside, finding their way to the car, almost stumbling once or twice in the cold darkness.

CHAPTER 15

"What'd you think of her?" asked Rob, who was sitting in their motel room's maroon armchair, with its threadbare upholstery. A spot of yellowish stuffing was visible at a corner of the right arm, like elbow skin protruding from a torn sleeve, a shirt outgrown. The chair itself looked undersized for Rob, who had moved the night table from its position between the twin beds for the purpose of sticking his huge feet on it. His toes were outlined by worn white socks, the nail of the big right one straining at the cloth.

Frank sat on the bed opposite, his rear end nestled into the mattress's sagging middle. "Nancy Horowitz? Like I said before, she seemed like she was genuinely upset. And I think she told us as much as she knew."

Rob sighed. "Right. I agree. But what I meant was, what'd you think of her as a woman?"

"Ah." Frank slid farther up against the rickety bed board, in a futile attempt to get comfortable. "Well, as a woman, I couldn't say, 'cause I ain't one." Rob was unamused. Frank shrugged. "She was fine, man. Attractive, if harried. Why?" he asked, playing dumb.

"Because I wouldn't mind filling the void in her life. At least for a night or two."

"Ah. Rob, I hate to tell you this, but you're married."

"Technically. I'd probably be more of a caretaker now than a husband, if Nellie's wonderful sister Fran—I'm shocked that she never got married, *not*—but if she hadn't taken over the job. I guess I should be grateful. And proud, or something, about the fact that I've never screwed around. We were seriously rocky *before* First Union. You know that. And Laureen had a lot to do with it, true, but she also kept us together, in a way." He paused, rearranging his feet, having some comfort issues himself. "I guess you've never…"

"Nope. No way. Never even been seriously tempted. I couldn't do that to Julie, man, even if she didn't know about it. I don't think I could live with it."

"Hey. Obviously, you're a better man than I am, you know?"

Frank snorted. "Spare me the sarcasm. Okay? That's not where I was coming from, and you know it. Your situation's different, and I'm not about judging anyway. 'Least I try not to be. But—this may sound corny, whatever—but I probably love Julie now more than I ever did. We've hardly been away, and already I miss her. Might have to do with the nature of this little mission we're on, I don't know. 'Course, she's also a lot nicer to look at night than you are."

"You're a fucking riot, Frank."

"Jesus. I was joking, okay? You need to lighten up a little."

"Yeah? Thanks for your brilliant advice, bro. Next time I need some, I'll ask."

"Sorry," Frank said after a few moments, half-sincere.

Still, Rob had never been a barrelful of laughs in the first place, unless he was soused. Or maybe Frank's memory just didn't extend back far enough, pre-First Union, pre-enlistment. And probably Rob had an easier time horsing around with his cop buddies—although he'd also known whom to call on when he was desperate enough.

"Seriously," Frank added. "No more advice."

"Seriously?" Rob briefly toyed with the Gideon Bible he'd found in the night table, attempting to riffle all the pages at once, to elicit that strangely satisfying crackle one can produce from a deck of cards. But all he produced was a faint spray of dust. "Seriously, Frank. You think she's good-looking?"

"Like I said, yeah. Plus I liked her, at least at first glance, she seemed…I dunno, like someone who's doing her best playing the hand that's been dealt her. And like we used to say back in the day, I wouldn't throw her out of bed. Were it not for Julie. But you know, Nancy Horowitz comes with a daughter attached. Even if you just envision a weekend fling here and there. Assuming she was interested."

Rob tossed the bible back into the drawer from which he'd extracted it. "I don't know what I envision. Right now, even if Nellie was living at home, I don't think she'd notice I was gone. And once she gets better—assuming she does, she did seem a little more of this world, the last time I saw her—but I don't know what the odds are of us staying together. Maybe I can get her a caretaker for a while, get some of those funds they're giving away to the families of First Union victims, you could make the case that Nellie's been seriously affected. But, yeah, what was the daughter's name? Lily. You know, this might not be a big surprise,—a lotta things remind me of Laureen—but she definitely did. When Laurie was little. Same high strung, kind of bright, alert look in her eyes—like, 'What can I do next to piss Mommy off? Especially with these two bozos standing here.'"

Frank laughed. "Hell, I liked her too. Both of them." Grunting, he heaved himself from the chair, arriving at the air conditioner/heater by the window after two steps. "I'm gonna raise the heat a little."

"Cool. I mean yeah, good. And speaking of Lily's mom, I woulda told her about Laureen, if all else failed. To try to get her to help us. Could've even logged on to that First Union scroll-a-victim website, if she didn't believe me."

Frank nodded. "You could've."

The site Rob had referenced was eerily reminiscent of the Vietnam War Memorial, in video, the names of the dead drifting upward in alphabetical order. In both cases, one visit had been enough.

Frank had spent half an hour at the Washington DC memorial with Sergio and Julie, then pregnant with Carl. Sergio, two years old and exhausted from the drive down, slept in a stroller as Frank searched out the name of Julio Hernandez, his Yankee fan buddy who was blown apart a few yards in front of him by a grenade. But engraved on the black marble wall, an elegant, elongated, gut-wrenching tombstone, were four Julio Hernandezes.

The name was common enough. Frank still remembered this, and the army's attempt to distinguish between them by adding on ranks, middle initials, and hyphenated maternal surnames. But these last, in the name of economy, had been omitted from Hispanic soldiers' dog tags, not that Frank had ever made a study of Julio's anyway. Three of the Julio Hernandezes were PFCs. One of them had to be Julie-o—as Frank had teasingly, masochistically called him on occasion, experiencing sharp pangs of regret over what he'd left behind.

After a minute of gazing at the black marble, the names blurred anyway. He tried to remember what Julio looked like, the smile with the gold tooth in front, and how they used to rag each other about their respective accents, Nuyorican and Bronx Godfather.

'*Ey paisan, dju ever make it with a Latina? Sweetest gatita in the world, man, gonna hook you up when we get our asses outa this muthafuckin' jungle.*'

'*You mean back to New Djork, Julio?*'

'*Fuckin' A.*'

Julio had made it back to the Big Apple first—in a casket. Now he was a name on a wall, pick one out of three, briefly alive again in Comrade Tedeschi's head. Finally, Frank just kissed his fingertips and placed them against all three names. Then he turned to Julie and wrapped his arms around her, dripping tears into her hair.

Shortly thereafter, he'd located Lieutenant Walton on the memorial, distinguished by rank from his one other name-mate. And he'd left a lips-print—once removed—there as well, a phantom kiss that could've been all they both ultimately would amount to, Frank and his would-be murderer, brothers in oblivion.

"Glad you didn't have to," he told Rob now. "Might be a good site for Billy to visit, though. From beginning to end. Especially if they could include a little mandatory video of each person's life."

"Right. Well, I could supply one for Laurie, straight out of my head. Don't even need to close my eyes. The Laureen Tedeschi show, in living color."

"I can imagine," said Frank, searching for some supportive words, coming up with none. "Speaking of closing eyes, it's about that time. We got a big day ahead of us tomorrow. Hopefully." He stood up and slid his mattress onto the floor. "Might be more comfortable down there on that rug, scuzzy though it is. Couldn't be less."

The Church of the Redeemer, New Paltz, reminded Rob of many of the *Iglesias Pentecostal* he'd seen in the Bronx, ninety miles south. Private houses with crosses nailed above the front door, maybe a statuette of El Senor, or His Son, in the patch of grass in front that passed for a yard. As additional identification, either hand painted or commissioned at the local sign shop, *Iglesia de Milagros* or whatever, screwed into the aluminum siding. No parking lot, not even reserved curb space, such places were the churchly equivalent of the illegal immigrant: ramshackle, part of no parish or religious hierarchy, likely in violation of fire laws. Folding chairs instead of pews. Not that the congregants spent much time sitting anyway. Their arms and bodies were upraised, and they made a joyful noise, no translation necessary—for God, even for a cop on the street who wished he didn't have to work Sundays.

The Church of the Redeemer did feature a clear plastic-encased message board abutting the sidewalk. *God Allows U-turns* was the aphorism of the week, or month. Although the board also announced that All were Welcome, and the front door was unlocked, it seemed prudent to ring first. Walter Hawes, Pastor, answered the doorbell almost immediately. His slightly lop-sided smile didn't completely fade even after Rob introduced himself. Still, Hawes took more than a cursory look at the badge Rob presented. Frank thought he saw the pastor mouthing the badge number, and could imagine his thin lips working silently, non-stop, as he read scripture in his study or bedroom. It seemed clear at a glance that he worked at home.

"Detective Tedeschi?" he repeated, giving Rob's hand a firm shake as if to banish any impression that he wasn't delighted to be paid a surprise visit by a cop before eight a.m. "NYPD? You're a little far north, aren't you?"

"You could say that," Rob replied unsmilingly. "This is my brother Frank."

"And you're a police officer also?"

"I guess you could say I've been deputized."

Vaguely conscious of having borrowed Rob's phraseology, Frank gripped the hand offered by Hawes, studying the pastor's face for some initial indication of whatever he might've brought to bear in the process of selling Billy Patterson on Jesus. Some light in his greenish eyes, maybe. Hawes did seem fresh and alert, if only in contrast to the way Frank felt, having tossed and turned all night on his floored mattress.

"I see. Well, come in. Please." The pastor stepped aside. "It's cold out here. I've got some coffee brewing. Smells good, doesn't it? I'm hoping you'll join me for a cup."

Rob said, "Thanks, but we'll pass," cutting off a more affirmative response from Frank, who'd picked up the aroma even before Hawes opened the door. "We're here to ask you some questions about one of your ex-church members. Billy Patterson?"

At this, Hawes stopped in his tracks. "Billy?" The pastor's already-creased forehead furrowed, and he studied Rob, as if trying to divine Billy's crime, to determine how far he'd backslid. Hawes did not appear optimistic. He shook his head, exhaling audibly through a flat, triangular nose that more resembled a vent. His thinning black hair was flecked with gray, especially at the sideburns. Their bushiness stood out in contrast to his narrow, tapered jaw, to the economy of his face, and torso. He seemed slender and fit, ready to be of service. "Billy left

New Paltz…what?…at least six months ago. I last heard from him about a week after he left."

Hawes invited them to sit, indicating a sofa in what appeared to have originally been intended as a dining room. At one end, the space opened into the chapel—once a large living room but now packed with maybe twenty-five rows of wooden benches. They faced a pulpit that was backed by an elevated crucifix and, slightly to the side so as not to be obscured by whomever was extolling His name, an alabaster representation of Christ.

The statuette was bathed in light projecting from the ceiling. The Tedeschi brothers were positioned for a clear view of the glowing Jesus across the otherwise dim chapel.

Pastor Hawes sat in an armchair to one side, closest to Rob. "What is it? How can I help you? Is Billy in some kind of trouble? If so, I can't say I'm totally surprised. I received a call about him, maybe two weeks ago, from Reverend Maximillian Tate of the Holy Church of Christ, in Katonah. You've probably have heard of him. He's become rather well-known, as the leader of the Christian Crusade? And you probably know that Billy was working as an assistant groundskeeper at his church."

Rob nodded. "We're aware of that, yes."

"Well, Reverend Tate was concerned about Billy's sudden disappearance. The reverend was particularly worried in Billy's case, because of his past struggles with the law, and with his own mental, or emotional difficulties. Even when someone has finally come to Christ, the devil will tempt him, test him. *Especially* when one has come to Christ, been born again in His light. Reverend Tate knew that Billy was reborn here, in this humble church."

"Right," Rob replied, uninspired. "Well, as it happens, we've already interviewed Reverend Tate. After he'd already spoken with you." He omitted the likelihood that Tate was actually trying to locate Billy so as to facilitate his murder. "Mr. Tate expressed the same concerns to us that he did to you. He said that he would do whatever he could to help find Mr. Patterson."

Hawes nodded. "Yes, indeed. Hopefully, his prayers, and mine, will bear some fruition. But, from what I know of police procedures—and I am familiar with them, I've worked with many individuals who've had brushes with the law, and I've ministered in correctional facilities—I don't think you would have come up here to New Paltz purely on the basis of a missing person's report, even one that the reverend told me he filed personally."

"That's correct. We believe that Mr. Patterson was the sole witness to a double murder." Rob paused, gauging the effect of this statement on Hawes.

The pastor's face flinched slightly, tightening as if he were poised on the edge of a dangerous leap. "That's… most unfortunate. He's been through enough trials already, although I'm not ultimately the judge of that."

"Well, we'd like to see him go through just one more," Rob said with a tiny smile. "Without his testimony, we have nothing. He had a girlfriend in the Bronx. We're not sure how he met her. But her cousin was involved in drug-dealing activities. We don't know how much she, or Mr. Patterson, were aware of this. The girlfriend was a church-going individual, we've learned that. She and her cousin were both shot to death. We have reason to believe that Mr. Patterson witnessed this. That it was he who called nine-one-one from a pay phone, leaving the license plate number of the perpetrators, which he must've absorbed before fleeing the scene. In short, we have suspects, but without Mr. Patterson's testimony, we have nothing. And we believe he fled the Bronx because…well, if you're as familiar as you say you are with crime and criminals, you know what often happens to witnesses who step forward. We believe Mr. Patterson disappeared because he feared for his life."

This last statement, at least, was true. The rest had been concocted by Frank and Rob earlier that morning, over coffee and spongy bagels with cream cheese at the local Dunkin' Donuts. The notion that they were looking for Billy because he was in danger from loan sharks—as theorized by Sylvester Stout—did not sound especially convincing. And reciting insane-sounding allegations to Pastor Hawes regarding Billy and Reverend Maximilian Tate did not seem like a good idea either.

At that point, the brothers didn't know whether or not there was any real connection between Hawes and Tate. Stout had mentioned Hawes almost in passing, as the person who'd provided him with a reference for Billy. Nancy Horowitz had mentioned him as well—and had graciously provided directions to Hawes's church/residence.

"Once he heard about the double murder, and Billy's likely status as the only witness, Reverend Tate agreed with us regarding the reason for his disappearance. And he told us that he'd already spoken with you, since he thought that if Billy—Mr. Patterson—was going to turn to anybody, it would've been you, his first pastor. And if you had no idea about his whereabouts...well, it didn't look good. But we wanted to come up, talk to you ourselves, see what we could find out. We told the reverend that we'd keep him abreast of any new developments in the case and assured him that Mr. Patterson would receive around-the-clock protection if he did come forward. We can keep you abreast of new developments as well, if you'd like."

So there's no reason for you to call Tate yourself. The last thing the brothers wanted was to confirm for Tate that Frank's apology and recanting, his *mea culpa,* had been delivered with a forked tongue. As of Frank's last conversation with Paul Fowlkes, a day before leaving for New Paltz, the Tedeschis were off the surveillance list. But Fowlkes had raised the possibility that this was a ploy, intended to make Frank and Rob believe that their recantation had been bought, to induce them to let their guards down. Of course, this presupposed that they had access to the list in the first place, owing either to extraordinary computer hacking skills or some kind of connection at the FBI. The latter possibility presupposed a misstep by Fowlkes. No way, he'd asserted.

Still, safety first, as much as possible, anyway. Neither brother needed convincing in this regard. They'd as yet had no indications of any goons following them, but that meant zip.

"Yes, I'd very much appreciate it if you keep me in the loop, as they say," Hawes declared. "I only wish Billy had come to me in the first place. There's that tradition of the church as a refuge, a sanctuary. Not that I think he shouldn't testify. Quite the contrary. But the right thing to do becomes more apparent when one is closer to God, in His house." He paused, ostensibly to let this message sink in. "One person you should talk to, who might be able to help you locate Billy, is Nancy Horowitz. She was his girlfriend. He was cohabitating with her, and her young daughter Lily. I called Nancy after I promised Reverend Tate that I'd see what I could find out. She told me she knew nothing about Billy's whereabouts. That was right before she more or less hung up on me. I believe she blames me for her breakup with Billy. When he accepted Jesus into his heart, there was actually more room for her, there was an opportunity for their relationship to be consecrated in Christ, but she saw it differently. I don't think she understood that she, and her daughter, had actually paved the way for his rebirth. His affection for them opened his heart, opened him to new possibilities, to a much greater love, a higher one."

"Right," Rob said, sighing and glancing over at Frank, whose face betrayed neither incredulity nor disdain.

"I can remember Billy standing on a ladder—he was painting the ceiling in the chapel there. It was long overdue. I'd contracted with a sort of contractor/painter in town, and Billy was helping with the job—I told him to be careful. He was really working that roller with two hands, swaying on the top step of the ladder. It was like those spackled cracks, and the brownish stains from when the roof had leaked, were a personal affront to him, he couldn't cover them over fast enough. He said, 'Don't worry, Pastor, this is the first time I been in church in a *real* long time, since I was young enough for someone to force me. An' I'm feelin' it, you know? No way I'm fallin' offa this ladder. This is a ladder to heaven, man.'"

Frank snickered despite himself. Hawes's brief rendition of Billy in manic mode was dead-on, the voice, the taut face seeming to pulse in several places as he spoke.

"Billy was putting me on, of course. I'd say mocking me, but I don't think there was that much intention behind it, it was just energy that had to be released. The fire in him giving off sparks. But then the next day, after he'd been working for a while, I walked into the chapel, and there he was, on his knees in front of that statuette of Our Savior. Before he'd started painting, he'd covered it with a drop cloth. It was opaque, spread over the pulpit, the statuette, and the chapel beneath the section of the ceiling he was working on. Billy had turned off that little spotlight that you see projected on Jesus, so he could paint around it safely, paint the housing. Yet the portion of the cloth covering the statuette began to glow, as if the light were now, in fact, lit beneath it. Billy was astonished. He took off the drop cloth, and there was Our Lord, embodied in the statuette, still and contained within His normal luminosity. No glow. But when he covered Jesus again, there was His holy light, radiating through the cloth."

"Did you see this?" inquired Rob.

"Truthfully, no. But I told Billy, and I believe, that the fact that *he* saw it was a great blessing, a sign from Our Lord especially for him. An offer that he couldn't refuse. Not that he wanted to. There were tears in his eyes, gentlemen. And after that, he became the most dedicated member of this church. Never missed a Sunday. Any repairs that needed to be made, he did them and refused payment, despite the fact that he was almost desperately in need of money. He said that he'd already been compensated. He'd been saved. Forgiven. Blessed. You know that before Billy came here, he'd been in prison."

"Right. Breaking and entering," said Rob.

"Yes, well. But before he left New Paltz, he was a completely changed man. Jesus had picked the lock on his heart."

"I thought you said Nancy Horowitz had performed that trick," Frank said, instantly regretting it, even if it seemed likely that Hawes had nothing useful for them.

But if the pastor had taken note of Frank's sarcastic tone, it wasn't apparent. "She…you could say she fertilized the field, even if unintentionally, so that Jesus's love could blossom. An apt metaphor, since they were living on a farm, right on the edge of town. She's still there. And I suggest you contact her. Perhaps she'll be more forthcoming with you than she was with me."

"We'll do that."

"Good. I wish you luck. And I should tell you that when Billy decided that he could not share a dwelling with someone who rejected Our Lord, I invited him to live here. But he was also having financial issues. When he saw the ad for an assistant groundskeeper at the Reverend Tate's church, it seemed like a perfect opportunity for him. And if it was only part time, at least it was regular work. He said that he could probably supplement it with something else. According to Reverend Tate, he'd found part time work at a hardware store in the area."

Frank said, "Yes, he had."

"You've obviously been investigating. Well, I think that even had Billy not found work elsewhere, one thing about him that didn't change was his need to keep moving. His history is such that he never stayed that long in one place. Thankfully, when he left here, he took Jesus with him. If I do hear from Billy, I'll urge him to contact you. Please leave me your number."

"Will you notify us?"

Hawes considered this for a moment. "That I couldn't do. Again, I could urge him to do the right thing, to pray on it if he needs to, and to testify. God will protect him."

"And we will," Rob said. "Joint venture. God and the police department." He provided his card.

Hawes thanked him then offered his own, which Rob pocketed. "Would you let me know if you find Billy?"

"Sure," replied Rob, stifling the indicated response: *That we couldn't do.*

After handshakes all around, the brothers were back in the car, en route to the home of the other person mentioned to them by Nancy Horowitz: Herman Detweiler, general contractor/painter.

"So," Rob said, turning on the heater and sending lukewarm air up toward the windshield, which had begun to re-frost during the time they'd spent in the church. "Think your friend Billy was off his meds when he saw the drop cloth light up?'

"You're such a wit, Rob," Frank muttered. "He's not my fucking friend. I think we've discussed that before."

"Touchy."

Touchy was an understatement. For whatever reason, Frank was in a seriously foul mood, which wasn't ameliorated by the smirk on Rob's face, by his obvious satisfaction at having gotten under his brother's skin. The oily smell of the car heater didn't help either.

Frank felt a bit queasy, and he doubted that this had to do with the bagels, cream cheese, and coffee he'd ingested for breakfast. "You could say that," he replied. "You could also say that he hadn't even been diagnosed at that point, let alone been prescribed medication. Besides, I'm pretty sure that bipolarity doesn't involve hallucinations. 'Course, I could check with Julie. She'd probably know. But I'm guessing, based on subsequent events, that Billy's heart didn't really get filled up with Jesus. And did you notice that when he came back up here, he didn't even get in touch with Hawes, his Jesus guru?"

"Haw, haw."

"Yup. I'm also guessing that Billy might be a crazy, genocidal motherfucker, but he's not stupid. He's gotta know that the Reverend Tate set him up. He probably realized that with the first club that landed on him when he ran out of First Union. So maybe he's soured on 'religion,'" said Frank, putting finger quotations around the word. "And maybe he figured, like us, that Hawes might phone Tate."

"Yeah, we're all on the same page, man." Rob turned left onto Main Street, heading back in the direction of the Super 8 Motel base camp. Herman Detweiler was located on the other side, past the thruway, where New Paltz proper petered out. Scattered, rectangular homes fronted by pickup trucks or ancient gas guzzlers were interspersed with the occasional construction depot or gravel pit, Hackett's Bar & Grill and what remained of the woods, all of this flecked with patches of crusty, black-tipped snow, scored with rivulets of ice.

Like Pastor Hawes, Herman Detweiler lived at the office. Really his wife's office, since she was his secretary/receptionist, bookkeeper, and overseer of the property. Driving past a dented sheet metal sign that advertised *Detweiler's General Contracting/Painting/Carpentry* and also promised *Free Estimates*, the brothers pulled into a yard with tire tracks frozen in dirt, parking next to a drywall-laden pickup. They ascended two paved steps. There being no doorbell or buzzer, Rob knocked, hard enough to make Frank wince slightly. It occurred to him that cops probably assumed most people were hard of hearing.

Still secured via a chain, the door opened a crack. Rob flashed his badge. "Detective Robert Tedeschi, NYPD. We'd like to speak with Herman Detweiler."

The slightly chipped brown door swung open. A heavyset, forty-ish woman with her hair in curlers stood appraising the visitors. "Regarding what?" she asked, clearly unfazed by the fact that two plainclothes cops—no uniforms but a strong resemblance nonetheless—were looking for her husband.

"Regarding Billy Patterson," Rob said, in more of a retort than a reply, his curtness a mirror image of hers, if a few registers deeper. "He used to work for Mr. Detweiler?"

"Billy Patterson," she murmured, as if speaking to herself. "*That's* a shock. Yeah, he used to work for Mr. Detweiler. I'm Mrs. Detweiler, as you've probably figured out, detective that you are. Anyway, Billy came around again what, two weeks ago? We didn't have any work for him. As you can guess, if you look around, the phone hasn't exactly been ringing off the hook with demands for our services."

"So Patterson…"

She shrugged. "Gone."

"Well," said Rob, "how long did he work for your husband, back when?"

"Hell, it wasn't *that* long ago. Only seems that way. I mean, he was willing to work cheap, that was one advantage, and whenever we needed him. Cash, I still remember that. I had to keep more on hand when he was working, that was how he wanted to be paid, for whatever hours we had for him. Don't even know if he had a bank account. Had a rap sheet, though. Mr. Detweiler, trusting soul that he is, was willing to take a chance with him."

"And were there any problems?"

"Nah. Told 'im day one that he needed to stay away from my daughter. Other than that—Herman had to pick him up at first, Billy didn't have a car. Sometimes he'd bring 'im back here for lunch. My husband is a generous person, to a fault. Sometimes when I see what he bills people, I want to—"

"Mrs. Detweiler," interjected Rob, rubbing his hands against the cold. "Is your husband available?"

"He went to get some lumber and other supplies. Putting a deck on this house in town, in the other direction. So, he should be passing by this way in about ten minutes. You wanna come in an' wait, I'll give 'im a call. Hopefully, you won't need him too long."

They took her up on the offer. Frank and Rob sat at the kitchen table drinking coffee, Mrs. Detweiler having shoved aside various invoices and junk mail to make room for the cups and the brothers' elbows. They sipped tentatively, black with sugar, savoring the warmth of the cups in their hands as she punched in her husband's number on the kitchen's landline.

"There's two, um, policemen here," she said a few moments later. "They're askin' about Billy Patterson… yeah, *I* know that…no, I'll leave that to you. Just, get here." She hung up the phone and turned to Rob and Frank. "Ten minutes, like I said."

She bustled around the kitchen, rinsing off the dishes she and her husband had apparently used for breakfast, sponging surfaces. As she dipped her head in the process of reaching under the sink for a bag of Kibble, it occurred to Frank that her hair rollers resembled construction equipment in their own right.

Mrs. Detweiler set out a bowl of the Kibble, and a large German shepherd showed up almost instantaneously. The sounds of his chewing were evocative of surging water lapping against mud. He paid the visitors no mind until he emptied the bowl. Then, licking his bared teeth, he trotted over to Rob. Rob's right hand reached under his jacket, unnecessarily. The dog—Spiro, as addressed by Mrs. Detweiler in the course of telling him to get the hell away—first sniffed Rob's thigh then rubbed his head against it, soliciting a scratch. Rob reluctantly obliged him with his left hand, for the two or three seconds it took Mrs. Detweiler to drag the dog away by his collar.

Several minutes later, as Frank was examining the dregs at the bottom of his coffee cup, a teenaged girl in a floor-length white terrycloth robe appeared in the kitchen. Despite the robe's being securely tied, she gave its belt ends a tug when she saw the two male strangers sitting at the table. Sleep vanished from her blue/gray eyes instantaneously. They widened beneath pencil-line eyebrows.

"Nina, this is Detective…"

"Tedeschi," Rob filled in.

"*Detective*?" the girl repeated slowly, almost as if the word needed translation.

But then her initial uneasiness seemed to disappear, to be replaced by a fascinated curiosity as she studied the two men. A hint of a smile appeared on her plump, rose-ate face. "Someone get murdered?" Her voice and jaded tone were almost identical to her mother's. This might've been comical, had she uttered something else.

"Someone might, if you don't take care of the laundry like you said you were gonna," replied Mrs. Detweiler. "'Bout time you got up."

Nina didn't move. She absently scratched behind the ear of Spiro, who now seemed more of a big pussycat than a construction/junkyard dog. Sparks of static electricity jumped off Nina's robe when Spiro finally stopped rubbing against her. "Seriously," she said. "What—"

"They're looking for Billy Patterson. And they want to talk to your father about that."

"Billy Patterson? Oh. Isn't he that speed-freak-turned-Jesus-freak?"

Mrs. Detweiler didn't look up from the sink, where she was applying steel wool to a frying pan. "Yeah, that's him. Given your descriptive powers, it's amazing you're failing English…Language Arts…whatever the hell they call it now. There's scrambled eggs in that bowl over there. On your way back to your room to get dressed—'less you need to shower first—check on your brother. Actually, leave 'im alone. Let 'im sleep, the eggs can be reheated."

"'Bout time he got up, Ma," Nina said.

Shortly after she turned to go, Spiro bolted toward the front door. It opened a moment later to the accompaniment of loud barking.

"Hey, boy," Herman Detweiler said in a breathy voice, as if he'd been hustling to get back home. As he strode into the kitchen, his long fingers were half hidden in the fur at the base of Spiro's neck. Detweiler was rangy. Jeff to his wife's Mutt, Frank thought, unless Mutt had been the tall one. Abbot to his wife's Costello. His stubbled countenance, topped by a light blue Marlins baseball cap, was thin and angular. It featured a prominent nose that stood out all the more because of the near concavity of the rest of his face. Also, because it was red veined. Maybe he worked a lot outdoors and needed fortification, a little firewater.

"Gentlemen," he said, "I'm Herman Detweiler." He offered his hand, which Rob shook a trifle reluctantly, the hand having been embedded in Spiro's fur, maybe even licked on the way into the kitchen.

"Detective Robert Tedeschi, NYPD."

Rob flashed his gold detective's badge as if it were an ultra-hypnotic amulet, under the influence of which one could speak only the truth. Not that Rob did so himself. After introducing Frank—his brother, who was assisting in the case, as he knew Billy Patterson, having employed him at his hardware store—Detective Tedeschi repeated the same story he'd given Pastor Hawes. Billy was likely the sole witness to a double-homicide. This suspicion had been bolstered by the fact that he subsequently disappeared, undoubtedly fearing that he would become victim number three.

Detweiler frowned, further elongating his face, as he took in the story. "Surprise," he said finally, shaking his head. "Trouble still finds him, even though he found Jesus."

"Maybe he forgot the address," Mrs. Detweiler chimed in, while tying a knot on the drawstring of a bulging plastic garbage bag.

Her husband shot her a look, seemingly wondering who had invited her into the conversation. Then he turned back to Rob. "Don't get me wrong, I feel for Billy. You say his girlfriend—next in line after Nancy Horowitz, I guess—but the girlfriend was one of the ones killed? Maybe that's why he was such a wreck when he came over here. What was it, a few weeks ago?" he inquired of his wife, having need of her two cents after all.

"At least," she replied.

"Time flies, don't it? Anyway, he was lookin' for work. Did mention that he'd worked in a hardware store down in Westchester." Detweiler nodded at Frank. "Said between that and the grounds-keeping thing he'd been doing, he'd picked up a few more skills, he was a regular Jack of all trades, whatever I needed done, on and on. But I told him I didn't have any work for him, didn't expect to have much more than I could handle, at least until the springtime, if I get lucky. 'Course, even if I did need a helper, I might not've offered him the work. He was all…like, agitated…nothing new really, but he wasn't makin' much sense. He was talking all kinds of nonsense about that terrorist attack in the Bronx. Did I think the people who did it deserved to be forgiven? On and on. I told him that I thought they deserved to rot in hell, for at least a billion years. Even Jesus wouldn't forgive 'em. Not that I wanted to raise *that* subject. Jesus, I mean. When Billy was workin' for me, I had to tell him that if he didn't lay off a' that particular topic, I was gonna have to find another helper."

"Hell," said Mrs. Detweiler. "If you hadn't sent him to do that job over at Pastor Hawes's church—that's how he caught the Jesus bug in the first place."

"Amen." Detweiler lifted the baseball cap off his head, scratching at his scalp, further disheveling its sparse hair. "Still, Billy was a good worker. An' I think if he's takin' the medication he got—was tellin' me about that too, about how Nancy Horowitz staked him to enough to fill his prescription, so he was good to go, an' how he shoulda been better to her when he had the chance. You know who she is?"

Rob nodded. "We've already spoken to her."

"Ah. Shoulda figured. Anyway, what I was sayin' was, unless he's really gone around the bend, he's a good worker. Which is why I referred him over to Clyde Strezoff, over at Sharpe Reservation. Cross the river, outside of Fishkill. I did some work with Clyde a few years back, before he became caretaker, head a' the maintenance crew over there. They gave him a nice house right by the entrance. I felt like I wanted to do *something* for Billy. Called Clyde, an' he told me that they got a skeleton crew that works durin' the winter an' spring. They got four Fresh Air Fund camps there. Huge reservation, more than three thousand acres of woods. Clyde told me yeah, he could use another hand, but couldn't really pay 'im, just room and board. Little stipend, maybe. I figured Billy would say 'no way,' but man, he jumped at the idea. Said it sounded perfect."

Off the books and off the map. Frank glanced over at Rob, whose eyes were riveted on Detweiler, and wondered if he was thinking the same thing. Frank had heard of the Fresh Air Fund, in fact, remembered that once it had *Herald Tribune* affixed to the front of its name, before that newspaper followed a couple of other New York papers into a TV-created graveyard.

"Funny, it kinda fits, too," Detweiler said. "Fresh Air Fund—charity for poor city kids—Billy ain't necessarily a charity case, but you get that feeling from him. Know what I mean?"

"Sure. He's—"

Rob cut his brother off. "So Billy Patterson is living and working over there?"

"Far as I know," Detweiler replied, absently scratching behind the ear of Spiro, who wagged his tail and pressed in for more, dog, husband and wife equally oblivious to the effect of this simple response on Rob. The engine of his car might as well have been revving inside of him, straining at the emergency brake.

As for Frank, he felt a mixture of trepidation and relief. This was what they'd come for, although half of him had been hoping they'd run into a dead end. Now, he was just hoping nobody got killed.

"The way I understand it, they have some lodges, they're heated, can be lived in year round. And there's a ton of work—road and trail maintenance, plumbing, cabin repair, boat docks, what-have-you."

"And he's still over there," said Rob, shifting on the balls of his feet.

"Far as I know," Detweiler repeated. "I could call Clyde and ask 'im."

"You don't really have to do that. Please don't. On the off-chance that Patterson finds out, it could spook him. We'll just take a ride over."

"Well…sure, that's easy enough. Sharpe Reservation's not that far away. Half hour, forty-five minutes. But maybe ask Clyde to gimme a call, let me know how Billy's workin' out. Maybe if I need him in the spring some—"

"You won't," his wife said. "Not him, anyway."

"Hey, he can work, an' he's cost effective. Cheap labor. Ain't that what you told me we need, back when I needed someone? An' he's not a bad guy, just a mite mixed up." Detweiler turned back to Rob. "I know you boys are just tryin' to get him to testify. But if he does, you'll make sure he's okay? That he doesn't wind up in the Hudson River with cement boots on, or whatever the hell they do? You'll protect him?"

"Oh yeah," Rob replied. "We'll take good care of him."

CHAPTER 16

"All *right*," Fowlkes said to both brothers, courtesy of the speakerphone feature, which Frank couldn't remember using before. Or if he had, he'd never done so on the cell phone registered to his alias, Phillip Abruzzi. Owing to the transmission, Fowlkes's gravelly voice seemed to vibrate, to echo slightly—the better to set forth his enthusiasm. Paul was psyched. Frank could almost see him in the room, wedged into the armchair, a pasty-skinned, mustached Buddha with that green and white, woolen *NY Jets* cap on his head. "Fishkill? I'm MapQuesting as we speak. Two hours? I'm guessing I could get up there in an hour and a half. Just like old times, Comrade Tedeschi. Rumble in the jungle. The woods. Whatever. Get out from behind this fucking computer."

"Paul, we can handle it, man," said Rob, as Frank shot him a look: *That right? Did you consult me?* "Time you get up here, and we coordinate, it'll be easier and quicker to just get over there and bag 'im. The little fucker will not be expecting us, plus, big brother Frank here got some practice with a rifle and pistol. Local cops let us use their firing range. We're loaded to the teeth. Not that that'll likely be necessary, it should be a piece of cake. We can get over there around one or two, I guess. If you could pull up a detailed map of this Sharpe Reservation, fax it to us here at the motel, we can use it if he runs, if we need to track him down, seal off the exits—"

"Three could do that better than two, Rob," Fowlkes interjected.

Frank said, "I agree. We don't know what we're gonna find there, or even if Billy'll be there, today being Saturday. Maybe he's got a day off, or whatever. So there's no hurry, no reason we can't wait an extra hour or two. And if he *is* there, then like Paul said, come with numbers, you know?"

Looking up from the speaker phone, Frank was almost startled by his own ghostly image in the mirror. The room was dimly lit, its thick floor-length curtains having been drawn in the name of privacy. His nerves were definitely on edge.

"Yeah, but there's no point. For all we know Patterson got canned," countered Rob. "This could turn out to be just another stop, or even a dead end. And if it's not... yeah, we need to be prepared, but we also need to get over there, get in, get out with Patterson, nice and quick. Paul, you can start laying the groundwork for exposing this shit, find out who we can go to in the bureau, in the newspapers. Wasn't that the plan?"

"Yeah. But basically, I know all that already. There's a guy in ballistics, if you do find that plastic gun. We got the tapes from First Union Arena, I'd say we're good to go. Except for one little detail. Without Patterson, we got zilch. And if he makes it into the woods up there...this may sound, I don't know, like bullshit...but Frank and me, we got some experience with that kind of situation."

"What, from Vietnam? When you were both probably stoned out of your minds? For what seems like my whole life, I been doing cop and detective work, chasing down perps. I know what I'm doing. And I wanna get over there, once you fax us the map, and we get some provisions, little extra ammo, just in case. And then, hopefully, two or three hours from now, we could have the son-of-a-bitch chained up in the back seat."

"Best case scenario," said Frank. "Maybe we should put this to a vote."

Rob glared at him. "Fuck that."

"Well, yeah. You're a tough guy. John fucking Wayne, with the keys to the car."

"Damn right."

Fowlkes's sigh was audible through the receiver. "Hey, we're on the same team here. Remember? Now, what about Detweiler? He's not gonna call over there, is he?"

"Nope," said Rob. "We told him not to. And he thinks Patterson should testify. Said it's his duty to society, something like that. 'Specially when his girlfriend was one of the ones who got killed. Plus, we told him we just want to talk to Billy, try to convince him. Can't force him to do anything. Although, on the off-chance Detweiler did call over, maybe Patterson finds out and gets a running start, that's even more of an argument for moving our asses now."

"Nice little story you cooked up."

"Yeah. Did the trick. So far."

"All right. Gimme the fax number, and I should have that map up to you quick. See if I can get one that details the layout of the whole place, and each camp. You said there are four of them? And please, keep me posted. Once we do have Patterson, we want to act. The faster Flowers and his boys can be exposed, the better chance the world has of not becoming a place populated primarily by cockroaches. With him as the chief cockroach."

"Cool. Will do," said Rob, tossing Fowlkes a bone.

"That's it?" demanded Frank. "What Rob says, goes?"

"Let it be," replied Fowlkes, over some static in the reception. "If Patterson's not expecting any visitors—"

"Neither are we. What if Flowers's cowboys show up?"

Rob pursed his lips and sent a disdainful look in Frank's direction. "Man, we've had no indications, and both of us have had our eyes peeled. We're off the surveillance list. And right now we're just wasting time."

A minute later, after wishing them good luck and reiterating that he was available as needed, Fowlkes hung up. As did Frank, emphatically, the cell phone snapping shut like predatory jaws. "You know, bro, there's nothing to prove here. Seriously. Everyone already knows you're a bad motherfucker. Rambo with a detective's badge."

"Oh. Gee, I thought it was John Wayne. And you? You're big brother, the voice of reason, trying to save my stupid, shit-talking self from myself, from my need to prove what a man I am. Right? Well, let me tell you something. Yeah, Patterson killed the person I loved most in this world, maybe the only one, and I'd snap his fucking head off if I could. But still—bro—I do understand that we got bigger fish to fry here, that he was just their flunky. And if we get to Sharpe Reservation and, for some reason, I think we need reinforcements, then we'll call Fowlkes. But, at the risk of repeating myself, I know what I'm doing. And I have you to keep me in check if I lose it once I get my hands on the motherfucker."

Less than an hour later, the Tedeschis checked out of the Super 8. Shortly thereafter they were heading back down the New York State Thruway, the foothills of the Catskills rewinding, sooty patches of snow like temporary lesions on brown skin, trees devoid of leaves, imperturbable, waiting out the winter. Periodically Frank cautioned Rob to slow down, that they really didn't need to get busted for speeding. Rob complied, grudgingly and temporarily. As far as Frank was concerned, they could've kept going, headed home. That was infinitely more appealing than hunting down Billy Patterson—even if Julie was in Florida, visiting her parents.

Julie hadn't felt safe at home by herself. Probably, she wouldn't have even had she not answered the land-line and been treated to a few seconds' worth of heavy breathing before the bastard clicked off at the other end. *Unknown Caller,* according to caller ID. This usually meant someone was soliciting donations, let the answering machine pick up. Except that they'd turned it off, being leery of the friendly messages that might be left there in the aftermath of Frank and Rob's initial visit to the Reverend Tate, in the aftermath of the car chase.

Sergio and Carl could leave messages on their parents' unlisted cell phones. But Julie, multi-tasking in the kitchen, had unthinkingly answered the phone without bothering to check the ID screen first. Still, it was possible that this caller had just been a random, garden-variety pervert, someone who would have been all the more titillated had he known how much he'd scared the owner of that soft voice. Maybe this hadn't been another attempt to make Frank think twice about the project he and Rob had embarked upon.

Regardless, he concurred wholeheartedly when Julie told him that if he was heading upstate, then it was good time for her to fly to Florida. He'd actually been on the verge of suggesting it himself. She hadn't seen her parents in a while. Plus, she could use some warm sunshine. She could use a little freedom from fear, or at least the freedom to worry exclusively about *his* safety, rather than hers as well. For however long the mission took—and

Julie had a ton of unused leave time—it would be nice to be in a place where she had some company at night besides the television, a place where a phone call, or some unexpected, unfamiliar noise, would not cause her heart to jump. A place where foamy surf sank into the sand.

ॐ

Frank stared down at the Hudson again, crossing it this time from the opposite shore. They were heading east on the Newburgh-Beacon Bridge, a little erector-set number compared to the Tappan Zee. Still, it afforded a nice view of this more northern stretch of the river. He could make out cattails waving in the breeze, whipping around as if trying to get free from the ice that immobilized their lower portions. A gleaming, contiguous layer formed a shelf along the rocky shoreline. The unfrozen expanse of the river flowed beneath and past them. Postcard worthy, green and serene, for maybe five seconds. He was thinking about what lay ahead, trying to consider all the possible outcomes, despite insufficient information. Intermittently, his mind was also replaying the day. It had been an incredibly long one already. Not only had they interviewed Pastor Hawes and the Detweilers and conducted the conference call with Fowlkes, but they'd put in a half hour on the firing range of the New Paltz police force, in-between.

ॐ

The local cops had seemingly been impressed by Rob's gold badge. NYPD. New York, the city of, where the caca hit the fan every five minutes, and Rob was a plainclothes detective. The New Paltz PD, comprising five cops and one clerical, had converted a small abandoned warehouse outside of town—conveniently located not far from the Detweilers—into a facility for target practice. Sergeant Ahearn took a cursory look at Frank's gun license before ushering the Tedeschis inside and providing them with ear protectors.

The pot-bellied Ahearn had magnanimously provided the non-cop brother with some basic instructions regarding sighting, body position, bracing of the shoulder, etc. Then he stood back a safe distance. But after five minutes or so, Frank was nailing the human-in-outline in the heart, head, balls or wherever Rob directed. Pistol or rifle, target in motion or otherwise, it didn't matter.

Rob was wide-eyed. Ahearn was slack jawed. Frank's only pleasure, though, was in the fact that he had no flashbacks. Other than that—the incident with the thugs in the Ford Bronco had been one thing, fear and adrenaline easily obliterating any resolutions he'd once made, any qualms about taking up the gun again. Plus, he'd been shooting at a car. But standing there and leisurely filling a simulated human body with bullets while Rob tallied the damage, his geeked-up voice piercing the ear protectors—*sonuvabitch now has five assholes, man*—Frank could think of plenty of other things he'd rather be doing. Still, he realized that he needed to prepare himself. Billy would likely be armed, he had to know that he was being hunted, even if he didn't expect his former employer to be on the other end of the gun.

After the last dollars from Billy's unclaimed paycheck had covered the toll on the far side of the bridge, Rob made a dogleg turn on Route 9 and headed up Snook Road. It featured several hairpin, mercifully ice-free curves that he took with squealing tires. Around one of them, in a break in the woods a couple of miles up the road, stood the entrance to Sharpe Reservation. Beneath its faux-tree bark sign dangled six smaller ones, skeleton-like: Camps Anita, Bliss, Coler, Hayden, Mariah, and Tommy. To the left lay what looked like a garage/maintenance facility. Beyond that, atop a snow-flecked hill, stood a brick house fronted by a large satellite dish.

Both of the garage's bay doors were open. A pickup truck laden with pipes and fittings stood in one of the bays. The other contained a metal canoe with a badly dented front, two motorized lawn mowers that resembled golf carts, a tool that looked like a giant toilet augur and numerous other pieces of equipment. Moved by ingrained habit, Frank was standing beneath the door and mentally cataloging some of the smaller items, the ones carried by Tedeschi's Hardware, when a baritone voice caused him to jump.

"Help you?"

He turned to find Rob, his hands held far enough away from his body to make it obvious that they were empty, tentatively approaching a stocky Caucasian positioned a good ten yards back from the garage. The guy held a rifle, roughly at a forty-five degree angle to the ground.

"Afternoon," said Rob, with as much affability as he could muster. "I'm Detective Tedeschi of the New York City Police Department. I'm going to reach inside my jacket and take out my badge to show you. I'm telling you that just so there's no misunderstandings, no jittery finger on that rifle. Okay?"

"Um, sure. Just take it out nice and slow."

Frank wasn't sure if he'd imagined it, or if Rob had snickered slightly over this little cowboy-movie line. With exaggerated deliberateness, Rob removed his wallet from an inner pocket of his jacket. He held it open to show the badge, and the rifleman motioned him to come closer. After a sidelong glance at Frank—who was standing with his palms out in front of him, a caricature of non-threatening—the guy studied the badge for a moment and then pointed his rifle straight down.

"NYPD?" he said, almost bemusedly. "What're you doing up here? The cops from Fishkill, or state cops, in uniform—them I was expecting. Had some stuff stolen from the shed in there. They broke the lock. Now the idiots who work here want to make it easy for them. Don't even shut the doors on their way out."

"You got a license for that rifle?" Rob's deferential tone had vanished.

"Sure do." The guy dropped the firearm so as to fish in his pocket for his wallet, quid pro quo. He squinted down at the plastic sleeves, flipping them impatiently. "Okay. Here it is," he said finally, double-checking before handing the license to Rob, who made a little show of studying the attached photo, his eyes shifting to the live, frowning face in front of him and back again.

"So, Mr. Strezoff. You're—"

"Head of maintenance here. Year-round. Live up there." He tilted his head—which was covered with a fur-lined hat reminiscent of an old-time football helmet—in the direction of the brick house.

"Yeah. Figured," said Rob, finally lowering the license. "I need to see your driver's license also. Match them up."

Strezoff hesitated for a few seconds, steam coming out of his mouth, his jowls quivering slightly as he fixed his eyes on Rob. He'd come down from his house with the aim of exercising his authority. He hadn't planned on being carded. Still, he handed over the driver's license, which Rob scanned. So did Frank, curious as to Strezoff's age. Sixty-four. He appeared younger in the picture, which was also deceptive because it was close-cropped. Looking at it, no one would guess that Strezoff was a bear of a man, an impression augmented now by his puffy black jacket.

Rob handed back both licenses. "Now as for what we're doing up here," he said with a close-lipped smile, a small peace offering. "That's a good question, Mr. Strezoff. True, we're far afield. But that's because we're working on a very important case. Before I explain that to you, though, we need to know if Billy Patterson is still working here."

"*Billy?* If you mean Will Patterson, yeah. That's what he likes to be called. He's a good worker, even if he forgets to close the goddamn garage doors. I need him. So I hope you're not—whaddya want 'im for?"

Rob recited the same story they'd given Pastor Hawes and the Detweilers. Strezoff listened intently. Finally, he gave a soft whistle. "*Wow.* Guess you're used to this kinda thing, though. Life in the Bronx, right? Lotta the kids who come up here in the summer, two weeks at a time, they come from there. Future customers of yours, some a'them. But Patterson, yeah, I knew there was something up with that poor bastard. No wonder he never even wants to leave the reservation. Only one jumps at the chance to work Saturdays, which he is today. Herman Detweiler was right, he sure pulls his weight, even if he's a strange bird. I hope you're not gonna—if he agrees to testify, he wouldn't be gone that long, right? I need him here. Pipes freezing, repairs needed all over the place. Even if it's winter, we got a lot to catch up on before camp starts."

"Mr. Strezoff, all we can do is talk to him, encourage him to do the right thing, and explain to him that he'll be protected. No one even knows he's up here. It took *us* a while to find him. And if he does agree to testify, he should only be gone a few days."

Strezoff fished a cell phone from his jacket pocket. "Okay, let me call 'im, and—"

"Better not to, Mr. Strezoff." Rob's tone made it clear that this was more than a suggestion. "Like I said, it's his decision. But we don't want him getting skittish, maybe even running, before we get a chance to talk to him."

"Mr. Strezoff, Billy knows me. He used to work for me at my hardware store. That's why I came along, to reassure him," said Frank, working up a smile, trying to look the part. "Now, if you could just tell us where he is, we won't be long. And we can let you know what's going on afterward. Or Billy will."

Vapor drifted from Strezoff's mouth as he mulled this over. "Okay," he said finally. "I'll take you there."

"Just give us directions. We need to be able to talk to him without any outside influences. He sees you, he might think, 'There goes my job.' He trusts me, Mr. Strezoff. He told you he used to work at a hardware store?"

"Um, maybe. Yeah, I think I remember that."

Rob said, "We'll have him call in to you, let you know what's going on, soon as we finish talking to him. Trial won't be for a while yet anyway. It's not like he's not gonna finish the job he's working on now, or he'll be gone by nightfall or anything like that. This is the way it needs to be done, Mr. Strezoff. Period. As a courtesy, though, like I said, we'll have Billy call you. If you call him, tell him we're coming, and he runs before we get there, you could be liable for obstruction of justice. Now, where is he?"

Strezoff cleared his throat. "Listen, I'm supposta take my missus shopping, in town. But I'm gonna wait 'til I hear from Will. Try to make it quick," he said, shooting a defiant look Rob's way. Then he turned and pointed at the road that ran past an empty guard booth and into the reservation. "You go straight up that road, up the hill—actually, you're going up a dam then past a lake—Camp Tommy's on other side of the lake. To the left. You'll see signs, you can't miss it."

"Camp *Tommy?*" said Frank. "What—"

"Usta be Camp *Pioneer.* Boys, ten to thirteen or so. Tommy Hilfiger—the fashion guy—he donated a ton of money. Just like when they name them stadiums after banks or corporations, you know? Money talks. But like I said, Will's over there, workin' in the mess hall. Which is there on the right as you turn left into the camp. Believe me, you can't miss it. He's fixin' a burst pipe."

"You don't shut off the water in the winter?"

Rob shot Frank a hard look: *What's up with all this chatter?* If Strezoff noticed, it wasn't apparent. "'Course we do. But the boy scouts use the place sometimes. Did last week, and our friend Will forgot to shut the water down again. Made a little extra work for himself."

"Okay, good," said Rob. "Just, let me have your number in case we can't find the place." Strezoff complied. "Now, you gonna lift that arm?" The edge to Rob's voice was plain enough. He pointed to the diagonally striped wooden slat that blocked the road beyond the guard booth.

"No problem. 'Cept it'd come down again in ten seconds. I'll just deactivate the thing, so I don't have to be here to let you out. Tell Will—or I'll do it, when he calls—to come down when he's done fixin' the pipe and activate the thing again after you get out."

Strezoff climbed into the guard booth and the wooden arm lifted. Endgame. Frank willed the butterflies in his stomach to dissipate. He felt for his gun, double-checking. Rob nodded curtly at Strezoff as he drove past the booth.

The wintry silence of the place enveloped them almost immediately, leafless trees allowing views deep into the rolling forests on either side, an ice-rimmed stream following them along. Sharpe Reservation was intended as a refuge from the city for kids whose most common experiences of nature probably involved rats and stray dogs, the occasional tree. Frank could appreciate the logic. But the place felt nothing like a refuge to him now. Keeping himself grounded, he intently identified each landmark they passed, the model farm, the turnoff to Camp Mariah, verifying the accuracy of the map faxed to the motel by Fowlkes. After they rounded a bend and came to a crossroads at the base of the dam, Rob pulled over.

"Lemme see that," he said, snatching the map from Frank's lap. "Okay, like we saw before, this road is the only way into and out of the reservation. We're here—" He nailed the spot with his finger. "—there's Camp Tommy, there's the mess hall, straight up. Nice and simple. Thing is, if we go in together, in the unlikely event that Patterson gets past us—obviously, hauling pipe, he's up there with a vehicle, probably a pickup—but if he gets away, he's gone down the road, out of here, not even that stupid fucking wooden arm to slow him down.

"So we park here—" Rob pointed to a spot behind what was labeled *Staff Lounge* on the map, roughly a quarter of a mile below the mess hall. "—then I walk to the mess hall, hugging the side of the road, going through the woods, whatever, I'll scope it out, lay low. That way he won't hear anyone drive up, or see me. After I have the motherfucker on the ground, with my gun pointing at his head, I'll call you on the walkie talkie. You drive up, and I'll cuff him. In case he does get lucky and get past me, you're guarding the road with the rifle. You shoot out his tires, windows, do whatever you have to do to stop him. You'll know he's coming, maybe get behind a tree or rock on the side of the road there, it'll be a piece of cake, especially given the way you were nailing those targets in New Paltz. But I doubt it'll come to that."

"Rob, maybe we *should* go in together, man."

"Uh-uh. Trust me. This way, we got a plan B, other than trying to chase him down, with you pegging shots at him while I drive. That shit might look good in the movies, but if he gets out of the reservation, he knows these roads better that we do, obviously. He makes it to the highway, he's gone. He's workin' on piping? He looks over when the door opens to that mess hall, he's lookin' down the barrel of my gun."

"Mess hall's likely gonna have two exits, Rob. Fire laws, I think. We come in two ways, I don't see how he gets away. It's even possible that if he sees me first, it might give him pause. Just the surprise, like what the hell is *Frank* doing here? Plus, he thinks I'm a bleeding heart liberal—"

"And he also knows that he blabbed to you about gassing the arena then vanished afterward. And you *are* a bleeding heart liberal, but if he saw you with your gun out, which is the way you would have to come in, I'm guessing it would disabuse him of any idea that you were there to reason with him."

Frank sighed and stared up at the dam, beyond which only clear blue sky was visible. The ability to fly had never seemed more attractive. "Look, I hate to repeat myself, but come with numbers, you know? If he runs—maybe he doesn't give a shit, maybe he wants to die, who knows—we shoot his legs."

"Or he runs into the kitchen, maybe there's a door back there, a window. I know what I'm doing, Frank. We get closer, and I think we need to adjust, we can do it, we got walkie-talkies. But we need to get up there *now*, before he maybe finishes the job, gets back in his truck. If he comes barreling down that hill—" Rob nodded up at the road in front of them, which paralleled the long, steep slope of the dam. "—sees a car he doesn't recognize, and he's paranoid, which he oughta be, and he's got a pickup, he's got *Ram Tough* or some shit like that—"

"Okay. I still think we should go in together, it seems obvious to me. Maybe we can disable the truck first, let the air out of a tire or two, depending. But…okay, fine, we'll do it your way," said Frank, stating the obvious. Rob had already tuned out, in profile. Frank tried to swallow his fear as his brother shifted into drive. "Just don't try to be a hero, okay? Better to err on the side of caution."

"Gotcha. Grab that rifle from the back seat."

Frank reached behind him and under a duffel bag then set the rifle on his lap. The engine of Rob's car whined as the grade steepened. At the crest of the hill, Frank could see Deer Lake—so labeled on the map—to his left. It appeared to be frozen solid, a huge field of blinding light, veined by the shadows of limbs and branches on the shore closest to the road. The afternoon was beginning to wane. The shoreline grew more distant as they drove, the lake's ice winking at them through a widening stretch of forest. The map could've been an aerial photograph, it showed the layout of the reservation with amazing accuracy, down to each twist and turn of the road.

The staff lounge of Camp Tommy came into view around a bend just like it was supposed to. Frank could see that the place was carved and colorfully painted with slogans from summers past: *Tommy Guns Rock, Tom is da Bomb, Bienvenidos Y'all, Arriba Camp Tommy.* A huge, graffitied log cabin. He also noticed a sudden, distant glare on the asphalt ahead, as if the reflected sunlight had high-hurdled off of the lake and was now glinting from a windshield. A pickup truck was coming their way.

It briefly slowed, as it would have to in order to get by safely, the road was not exactly a four-lane highway.

"It's him. *Gotta* be," Rob asserted, hitting the brakes, pulling halfway off the road onto the dirt shoulder, as if inviting the driver to pass. "Get out. *Now.* Shoot out his tires!"

"What if it's *not* him? Did Strezoff say that Billy was the only one working up here today?" Any uncertainty as to the driver's identity vanished before the words were completely out of Frank's mouth. The pickup veered to its left, screeching to a halt perpendicular to the road. Broken U-turn.

Frank jumped out of the car, sighted, and fired, aiming for the rear tire. But the truck lurched backward. The bullet lodged in the metal below its bed. The report from his next shot, which glanced off the rear fender, seemed louder. It took him a second to realize that Rob was leaning out of the driver's window and firing also. To no avail—fortuitously for Billy, the glare was now coming off his rear window and mirrors. Sunglasses would have helped the Tedeschis, but two pairs now lay uselessly in Rob's glove compartment. The pickup darted ahead, leaving rubber.

"Get in!" barked Rob, his left hand pegging another useless shot as his right shifted back into drive. He'd floored it before Frank could close the passenger door. Frank tumbled over into him. The rifle's butt smashed against the dashboard, its barrel against the windshield. Frank felt his finger involuntarily press against the trigger, which he'd never released. His teeth clenched in anticipation of the explosion, of the glass shower. Nothing. He finally exhaled as Rob shoved him off, cursing.

Still, within seconds they were gaining on the pickup. Its bed was loaded with heavy equipment. And the glare was gone, the road had turned in their favor. Even more helpfully, it straightened and elevated again. Frank leaned out of his window with the rifle. It was nearly torn from his hands by the speed-generated, arctic wind. Still, gathering and bracing himself, he fired—and got lucky. The pickup had crested the hill, lifting its rear tires, presenting two fat—if fleeting—targets. He saw the right one explode, heard it a split second later.

"All right!" Rob screamed, leaning forward as if that might increase their velocity. As they approached the crest, they saw the pickup swerve right. It crashed into a stand of trees, at the edge of the woods bordering the intersection of the main road with the one that ran through Camp Tommy. The now-forgotten mess hall stood to the left, a trickle of solid ice extending, tentacle-like, from the front door, beneath which water had flowed from the broken pipe. Not that either brother noticed this detail, or the mess hall itself, as they leaped from the car, preceded by their firearms. The driver of the pickup—it had to be Billy, even if Frank couldn't yet see his face—stumbled out of the driver's door, shielded by the body of the truck. He ducked beneath its hood. Above, Frank saw the glint of a gun.

"Get down!" he yelled, hitting the asphalt and shielding himself behind the still-open front passenger door of Rob's car. Billy rose up and fired, his bullet ricocheting harmlessly off the curve of the car's front fender. Frank's return shot, intentionally—if marginally—wide of the mark, lodged in the truck's hood, the sound of it echoing Billy's ricochet as if they were engaged in a high-powered ping-pong game.

As Billy ducked back down, Rob darted forward and crouched behind the rear of the pickup. Frank noticed this on the periphery of his vision. His astonishment at his brother's audacity was a mental footnote to the imperative of pulling the trigger, of making it most dangerous for Billy to again stick his head above the hood. But Billy must've also seen that he'd just been flanked. He pegged a shot in Rob's direction. Frank's heart jumped as he heard the pickup's left taillight shatter. In the next instant, Billy broke for the woods.

Frank shot at his legs. The back one disappeared behind a tree a nano-second before Frank's bullet hit the trunk, spraying bark through the lower end of the steam cloud left by Billy's breathing. Still, Billy appeared to be stumbling or limping. *The crash?* Frank scrambled to his feet and plunged into the woods in pursuit.

"Stay low!" he shouted unnecessarily as his brother tore through the underbrush on the far side of the pickup, the sound of branches cracking underfoot twice obliterated by the report of Rob's gun.

Frank was briefly slowed by the rifle and by thorns lodging in his gloves and jacket. But once he got beyond the thickets bordering the road he was into pinewoods. Clear sailing, although he was keenly aware of the possibility of a bullet coming from up ahead, where he could hear Billy's work boots snapping twigs.

Rob was barreling ahead on Frank's left. Suddenly that was the only sound audible in the otherwise silent woods, until Frank heard his brother hiss, "Get down!" Rob was crouched behind a boulder maybe twenty yards to the left, peering into a large clearing. Frank bellied forward on the soft carpet of pine needles.

"Think he's in one of those cabins," said Rob, pointing, exaggeratedly mouthing the words as he whispered. "Heard a door close. Did you?"

Frank gazed into the clearing from behind the trunk of a thick pine. Cabins indeed. Roughly the same shape as those shown in miniature on the map, nine of them, grouped in threes, situated across the main road from the mess hall and Camp Tommy proper. They vaguely resembled Noah's ark with a roof, beneath which rectangular openings provided ventilation, filtered by screens. Several of these, in the closest cabin, were connected by spider webs to the shingled roof, which slanted down equilaterally from the apex in the middle. The three cabins in the clearing were clustered around log benches and a circular fire hole surrounded by stones.

No, he hadn't heard a door close, but he took Rob's word for it. "He could've opened and closed it but not gone in," he replied, with some lip-signifying of his own. "Could be laying for us behind a cabin. Or back there in the woods." Frank indicated the far side of the clearing with an inclination of his head.

Emitting wisps of vapor, Rob uselessly scanned the area. "Maybe. Maybe not. He wasn't that far ahead. If he kept going, we probably would've heard 'im."

Frank pointed to himself and made a circular motion, eliciting a nod from Rob, then began crawling away, around toward the back of the camp site, taking pains to move quietly, to avoid snapping any twigs or even crushing a pine cone. The steam from his mouth, that couldn't be helped. He'd already been breathing hard, and crawling in winter apparel while dragging a rifle was not easy. Except for the sound of his own respiration, the silence around him was absolute. It seemed possible that the gunshot reports still echoing in his head could be audible. The notion further unnerved him. He glanced back at Rob, who was taking aim, his leather glove curled around the butt of his gun. Crows scattered, cawing loudly, as the shot rang out. A hole was torn through the screen in the door of the nearest cabin.

Billy returned fire, one shot. There was no secondary sound, no thud borne of a bullet lodging in wood, no pinging off of a rock. And Rob wasn't hit. Clearly, the shot had come from one of the cabins. The report had seemed compressed, deadened.

"Billy!" Frank called, tilting his head upward, acting on impulse. "It's Frank Tedeschi!"

"*Shut the—*" Rob was staring at him wide-eyed. Frank lifted his free hand, palm facing his brother, conveying reassurance, or trying. His sudden conviction that he had a plan seemed vindicated by the fact that the sound of his voice didn't draw a shot.

"Bullshit!"

From behind the door of Rob's car, Frank had only caught fleeting glimpses of a target in a black watch cap, with a beard and mustache. The Billy who'd once worked for him was clean-shaven. But any doubts that this was their man were removed by the voice—based on two syllables, even from within a cabin, it was unmistakably Billy's. High-pitched, harried, halfway between a whine and a snarl when he was agitated.

Frank took a deep breath. "You were good at cutting keys, but you had problems with the Medecos. You told me that we should get one of those paint-mixing machines like they have at Home Depot, so we could expand our operation. And when you talked about gassing First Union Arena, I told you to relax, that you just needed a babe with large breasts."

There was no response for a few very long seconds. "*Frank*?" Billy's incredulous voice rang out, probably from the middle cabin. From his current vantage point, through trees and underbrush, Frank could see the near cabin in side view, the steps leading up to the middle one and most of the front of the third. "Boss? You came all the way up here in the woods? Came to kill me for what I did? Didn't think I would, right? Live and let live, right? You like to say that, right? Jesus saves. 'Cept he didn't save those poor kids in the arena, right? An' I fucking deserve to die, roast in hell, but you're gonna hafta kill me here, I'm not goin' back, have the whole world know what a fuckin' scumbag I am, the world's worst sinner. They'll think I'm insane, lock me in the nuthouse. Or fry me in the fuckin' hot seat, right? Then I'll fry again. Uh-uh. I'm—"

"Billy!" Frank yelled again, temporarily cutting him off. "You takin' your medication?" This seemingly solicitous, and ridiculous, question—the first that had popped into his mind—earned him another quizzical look from Rob.

"*Medication*?" Billy demanded in a shrill voice. "Who told you that? The Reverend fucking Tate? But he said I don't need it, right? That how you found me? Stout? Good ol' Sly. He thought I was just bullshitting, just like you. He point you up this way? Nancy? Even Lily? Jesus. They know what I did? Detweiler? Strezoff? Oh, Jesus. I told Nancy, I swear I did, but she didn't believe me, right? Thought I was fucking crazy. She got that right, even though I was tellin' her the truth. Never lied to her. She just loved me too much to believe it, like she couldna been sleepin' with the devil. Shit, she was just as horny as me anyway, but, like, I shouldna never left her, all this woulda never happened, right? I'd never do it again. *Never*. But you told her? And Lily? You—"

"*She* doesn't know, Billy," Frank said, blasting his voice through Billy's frenetic narration—which, unmistakably, was issuing from the middle cabin. "And the others—we told them that you were the only witness to a double homicide in the Bronx, and that you ran because they wanted to rub you out, keep you from testifying."

"Shit, Frank, there's *some* truth to that, it's—whose 'we'? Thought there was two of you, maybe three, thought you were the same bastards who—"

"Just me and my brother're here, Billy. He's a detective with the NYPD." Frank glanced over in the direction of Rob, who nodded. *Fine. Good, keep talking to him. He's coming with us, one way or the other.* "His name is Rob. His daughter died at First Union Arena."

"Oh, Jesus." Billy's voice was subdued, briefly. "I'm so fucking sorry. I can only say, like, forgive me, 'cept it would take Jesus to do that, an' I don't think He's gonna do it either, even though they set me up, I swear to God. Fucking set me up, the bastards were waiting right outside of the arena, that's who I thought you were. They tried to kill me, threw me in their fucking van. Took all three of 'em to do it, an' even then, if I hadn't had that gas mask on—they were gonna take me someplace an' waste me, dump the body. I was already half dead from their clubs, layin' on the floor a'the van, which turned out to be a good thing, 'cause the back doors locked into the floor, two rods going down from the handle, you know what I'm talkin' about, boss? An' the compartment with the jack an' tire iron was back there, I used the iron to pry up one a'the rods. There was this partition behind them, they could look through it, but I was just layin' there, hopin' they'd think I was still out cold, which they musta, plus they had my gun, or they just weren't thinkin'. Shit, it didn't take me long. Jumped out an' ran."

Billy paused, refilling his lungs. "Didn't even hear me prying, 'cause sirens were goin' off all over the place, ten times louder than Shove It Up, guess it was bein' televised, monitored, or whatever, or maybe even someone outside the arena heard the place just go dead quiet an' called the cops."

"Dead is the right word, Billy. Seventeen thousand, including my niece. Rob's daughter." Frank's voice cracked, abetted by the fact that he was shouting across a distance. "And, yeah, you were set up. Those goons were workin' for Reverend Tate, or the government. Probably both."

"Yeah, boss, I'm with you. I seen the news, connected the dots, they used me, then they were gonna fuckin' kill me and toss—"

"They did use you," Frank interjected, omitting the fact that the idea had been Billy's in the first place. "Still, you put that gas in the vents. And you know it was wrong. You say you wish you could be forgiven. Well, you can't undo what's been done, and you can't avoid the consequences. But you can atone, Billy. You can help nail Tate and the bastards he was working with in the government. And that way, maybe you can even *save* some lives, stop them from starting another war, invading Iran or whatever. You can atone. You can testify."

"Amen, boss. Yeah, I could testify, sing like a bird. 'Course they ain't gonna believe me anyway, I'm just some ex-con who thought he found Jesus an' then—they ain't gonna—"

"Dammit, they'll *believe* you, Billy." Frank mentally kicked himself for the display of irritation. The prospect of Billy going off on another high-pitched ramble was more than he could deal with at the moment. Still, he was conscious of trying to perform a juggling act, to impress upon Billy that following instructions was his only option, while at the same time keeping him in a cooperative frame of mind. They had a common score to settle, they could be on the same team again, sort of. But Billy's bipolarity had to be factored in, as well as his unpredictability—not to mention his status as a man with nothing to lose.

"We got the security camera tapes from First Union. Rob's a detective, he knows some people, we got ahold of them. They show everything. They can zoom right in on your face, even got your voice."

"*Allahu Akbar*. Billy Jihad."

"Right. So, I wouldn't worry about not being believed. It's probably only a few people who are in on this thing, Billy. Once the truth gets out there—with your help—Tate and his friends will get what they deserve."

"Not in this life they won't. Neither will I. We'll all roast in hell together. The Christian Crusade. Yeah, shit, Frank, I still got the number a' the guy who I got the gas from. An' the gun I shot that guard with? *Fuck* me. Plastic job, like a little fuckin' toy gun, think they got it offa me just before they locked me in their van. Shoulda fucking shot me with it."

"Right. I mean wrong. But…the gun that you got now?" Frank slowly rolled up off his stomach, so that he was lying on his side, leaning on his elbow, his head propped up. Even if his location could have been pinpointed by anyone with ears, he was probably still invisible to Billy, with the near cabin between them. Regardless, he was starting to suspect that he was more likely to die from hypothermia than from a gunshot wound. Getting halfway up off the frozen ground helped a tiny bit. "You could just throw it out of the cabin. Take out one of those screens and toss it out. The gun. Then come out of the cabin."

"Slow. With your hands up." The unexpected sound of Rob's voice caused Frank to jump slightly, his elbow scraping the dirt. Such had been his absorption in his catty-cornered, shouted conversation with Billy—who evidenced no awareness that these last instructions had not issued from Frank.

"Yeah, boss, I know the drill. Least I remember. Thought I'd left that part a'my life—shit, most of it—thought I'd left it behind, but hey, once a sinner…'course, 'sinner,' that's chickenshit compared to what they're gonna call me."

Frank heard the muted clatter of a metallic screen tossed on the floor of the middle cabin. Seconds later, Billy's gun bounced off the cabin's bottom step and landed in the hard dirt. Then he limped down the stairs. The difficulty of his descent was exacerbated by the fact that his hands were raised.

As Billy moved toward the fire ring in the center of the campsite, Rob jumped from behind the boulder. Within moments, he was bursting through brush into the clearing, preceded by his gun. Frank followed suit, his rifle trained on Billy.

"I'm gonna cuff him, Frank. Point the rifle at his head 'til I'm done."

Rob stood a couple of feet from Billy, gazing for the first time on the face of Laureen's murderer. Frank saw his brother's jaw tighten, his fist clench. He imagined that if the vapor from Rob's breath were permeated by the poison inside of him at that moment, Billy might've expired on inhaling it. Finally, Rob reached into his jacket pocket and extracted silver handcuffs.

"Turn around. Put your hands behind your back," he commanded, his voice low and harsh. He yanked down each of Billy's gloves far enough to expose his wrists. "Now put them together."

Billy complied meekly. The cuffs fit over his wrists with a cold, metallic click. Detective Tedeschi's hardware. As Frank lowered his rifle, he flashed on Billy suggesting that they stock firearms, get a license to deal guns if necessary, there was good money in it. His reply had been, *no way.* Little had he known that before too long he would be spitting lead, with his born-again assistant as the target.

It seemed now like Billy had worked for him in another lifetime, some long-ago yet vivid waking dream in which Billy had regularly called him "boss" with a mixture of sarcasm and camaraderie. *Hey, where'd you hide the toggle bolts? Boss, got a friend I wanna introduce you to, usta work as a carpenter, he's my real boss, just like that bumper sticker, 'My boss is a Jewish carpenter.' Yours too. Can't get around that. Boss, you seen that invoice? I think they shorted us on carpet tacks.*

And even now, now that the gunfire had been turned off and the adrenaline was beginning to subside, Billy's face—despite the beard, mustache and watch cap—was familiar and non-threatening, with its high cheekbones and prominent nose, the eyes seeming smaller by contrast, intense black irises that never seemed to stop moving. A face that had reddened slightly when he started ranting about what he was going to do to the heathens at the Shove It Up concert—out of the earshot of customers, he was possessed of that much self-awareness. Hadn't he just been talking out of his head? It didn't seem possible that he'd really done it. Except that he had. This pushy but not unlikable misfit had turned First Union Arena into a morgue with corpses stacked to the roof. Lying room only.

Billy grimaced when Rob grasped his shoulders and spun him back around as if he were a mannequin. But he nodded animatedly, as if compensating for the lack of mobility now afflicting his shoulders and arms, when Rob informed him of his rights: "You have the right to remain silent, and to the counsel of a lawyer. Anything you say may be used against you in a court of law."

"Lawyer? Shit. Public defender, ain't nobody gonna donate to the Billy Patterson fund. I'm just pleadin' guilty anyway, which is what I am, there ain't no—"

"Listen, Patterson," Rob hissed. "Right now, you need to call…what's his name?"

"Strezoff," Frank said.

"Right. You'll tell him that everything's fine, you've

agreed to testify when the trial eventually comes up, and you'll lower the arm down there at the gate after the cops leave. He can take his wife shopping, or whatever. Use your cell phone, if you got one. Better that it comes from yours. I'll dial."

"Don't have to. Just press 'one,' it's like the only number I got on speed dial, ain't no one else I call, Nancy don' wanna hear—"

"Neither do I, Patterson. Where's the phone?"

"Pants pocket. Left front. You're gonna hafta fish it out."

It might have been Frank's imagination, or he might have seen Billy smirk beneath the beard, as if he were slipping, from distant memory, into some reflexive, wise-off-to-the-cop mode. Frank took off a glove, shoved his hand into the indicated pocket and pulled out the phone. He depressed "one," heard the phone ring and held it to the side of Billy's face.

Billy's remarks to Strezoff, delivered in a relatively subdued tone, were more or less as instructed. He became animated only when Strezoff—whose loud voice Frank could hear through the receiver—questioned him regarding the status of the broken pipe.

"Hell yeah, boss, it's good to go. And yeah, the water's off, I couldn't a' fixed the thing with it on, right? Boy scouts can have their little pow-wow next week, I'll have the whole thing set up."

He frowned and shook his head at length, seemingly in silent commentary on Strezoff, although it also might have dawned on him that someone else would have to set up for the boy scouts.

Rob reached over and took the phone from Frank. "Mr. Strezoff, this is Detective Tedeschi. I want to thank you for your cooperation." After clicking off, he added,

"And sorry about the truck." He stuck Billy's cell phone in his own pocket.

Per Rob's instructions, Frank retrieved Billy's gun, hustling over toward the middle cabin, stamping his feet, trying to get some blood flowing in the direction of his toes. He picked up the gun by its handle, using his fingertips, as he'd seen cops on TV do before sticking the evidence into a plastic bag. "What should we—"

"Just hang on to it for now," said Rob. "We should get back to the car, set Billy-boy up. I'm fucking freezing, and it'd be good to get on the road, take Patterson to his new home." He pointed to a trail through the woods, leading away from the clearing. "That take us outta here?"

"Yeah, it goes to a dirt road, takes you down to the main road, by the mess hall," said Billy.

Of necessity, they walked single-file, a steaming but slow-moving little caravan winding through the woods, crunching pinecones, patches of hardened snow and the occasional acorn. Billy, in the middle, was limping, and further hampered by the cuffs. Other than explaining that he'd hurt himself when the pickup crashed, his right thigh having been forcefully jammed against the shift, he was silent, withdrawn, as if his own engine had been turned off, as if he'd switched poles.

Frank brought up the rear, with his rifle—at Rob's insistence—trained on Billy's back. When they reached the dirt road, which was studded with rocks, Frank could see Sharpe Reservation's other lake to the right, or at least the portion of it visible beyond the road's upgrade. One more field of ice, a showcase for the soon-to-be-setting sun. They turned left. Rob latched on to Billy's arm, both to move him along and to keep him from falling on his face as they strode down the pitted, uneven road.

Rob's car and the truck stood as evidence of Billy's last break for freedom. The pickup was parked roughly at a forty-five degree angle to the main road's asphalt. Its fender and right headlight were smashed. The driver's door lay open, as did the glove compartment. Billy had probably kept his gun there, Frank realized. Rob's car, its bottom half stained with rock salt, was parked half on the frozen dirt shoulder and half on the road, only slightly askew. The huge map—it had been faxed in several sheets and then taped together—lay strewn across the front passenger seat and the floor, in the wake of Frank's hasty exit. Over Billy's shoulder, he could see the brackets and chains that would help convert the car into a prison-on-wheels, a paddy wagon in miniature. All that was needed were arms and legs on which to clamp the shackles.

Rob opened the rear door on the driver's side. "Once he's in, you keep the rifle on him, I'll go in on the other side and chain him up." After hustling around the back of the car, Rob saw that his brother and Billy were still standing where he'd left them. "Frank, you gotta put your hand on his head, push down so he can get in? You haven't seen this in cop movies?"

Frank hesitated—something about this went against his grain almost more than the gunplay—then palmed Billy's head and shoved it beneath the top of the doorframe. Billy went along meekly, even as his watch cap slid down over his eyes like a condemned man's mask. Grimacing as his legs bent, he fell over onto the back seat, landing on his cuffed hands. Frank obediently kept his rifle trained on him while Rob leaned into the car on the other side, unlocked the handcuffs, and then ran a chain around Billy's waist, to which he began affixing the cuffs, so that Billy's hands would now be attached to the chain in front. Finally, as an afterthought, Rob jerked the watch cap up from Billy's eyes, uncovering most of the thick hair atop his head.

Probably because he'd been intently monitoring this whole process, Frank didn't notice two men emerging from the woods a few yards down the road. A third had already crept around the far side of the pickup truck.

"Drop the fucking rifle!" he snarled, causing Frank's heart to almost stop. "Don't even turn your head around, motherfucker."

Doing so would have been almost impossible anyway, since the guy had what looked, peripherally, like some kind of semi-automatic gun pressed to Frank's temple.

The rifle clattered to the ground. Per instructions, Frank braced his hands against the roof of the car and spread his legs. He could see Rob backing out of the rear of the car with the help of one of the other thugs, who gripped the collar of Rob's jacket with one hand and pressed a gun into his back with the other. Hands in the air, he was shepherded around to Frank's side of the car and ordered to assume the same position. They were both frisked. As the gun was ripped from his shoulder holster, Frank tried not to shake, an effort that was made more difficult by the fact that the position itself was conducive to muscle tremors. He knew that somehow he had to try to stay strong, stay as calm as he could, given the fact that any moment stood a good chance of being his last.

The third thug had removed the chain from Billy's waist, reattached the handcuffs frontally and dragged him out, covered by one of his buddies. Screaming and cursing, Billy was slammed face down over the car's hood, the cuffs clanging then screeching as they landed, scoring the paint. He and the Tedeschis were now braced against the side of the car that lay on the road, guns at their backs.

"I don't think you're escaping this time, Patterson."

The gruff voice was tinged with menace. Frank couldn't make out reflections in the car window of any of the faces behind him, only his jacket, inflating and deflating as he gulped for air.

"Then fucking shoot me," roared Billy. "You think I give a shit?"

"Actually, yeah, I think you do. That's why you're gonna tell us who else you ran that big mouth of yours to, someone who might not realize how fucking crazy you are. And you, Tedeschi—both of you—you're gonna tell us who you're working with. Or working *for.* Bet you didn't know you were workin' for us too, did ya? The screw in the upper right hand corner of your license plate? That's actually a microchip. Looks just like the other Phillip's head you got in there, right?" The guy gave a taunting laugh. "Sorry, we didn't save the original for you. Some fucking detective you are. But, hey, you did find Patterson for us. Even cuffed him. We got here a little late. Fucking traffic. Outta the city, you don't expect that, you know? So we just laid for you over there in the woods. You shoulda moved your asses getting back here, though. It was fucking cold, lemme tell you."

"It's just us," Rob said, his voice shaky. "We're not workin' with anybody. Patterson blabbed his mouth to us, beforehand. That's about it. And my daughter died at First Union. That's why we're here."

"Well, you're gonna have to do better than that, Tedeschi. Or you're gonna be with your daughter real soon."

"He's tellin' the truth, you shithead. He—" This assertion on Billy's part was cut short by the butt of a gun, which smashed into his knee, almost as if the bastards knew that his leg was already contused. He screamed in pain.

"That was *nothing*, Patterson. Believe me. Oh, just

outta curiosity, what happened to your pickup? Your boss over here shoot out the tire? Maybe that wasn't a lucky shot when you put our Bronco outta commission…Frank. We shoulda sent you the bill. But you're gonna pay now."

The gun was pressed more tightly against Frank's temple. He winced and clenched his teeth, bracing for the shot. Unexpectedly, he had a vision of Julie, a trip they took once to Niagara. He had to fight down a sob. Then he heard the report of a gun. In the next instant, it occurred to him, in some hitherto dormant region of his mind, that he was already dead, or crossing over—that was why the shot had sounded so distant.

He fell to the ground. Everything went dark. But the jarring impact of his fall on the asphalt—simultaneous with the clattering of the semi-automatic as it landed next to him, and the fact that his skull seemed to still be intact—these things led him to realize, with the sliver of rationality that he had somehow retained, that he was not, in fact, dead or dying. The heavy weight beneath which he lay belonged to the inert body of the bastard who seconds previously had held a gun to his temple.

Another shot sounded, equally distant. Frank managed to heave his shoulder against the bleeding mass atop himself and roll free, in time to see a second thug go down, the one whose gun had been trained on Rob. Still prone, Frank grabbed the weapon from the guy's hand. It came free with no resistance. The third gunman spun away from Billy, dropped to one knee and fired several times in the direction of the mess hall, maybe thirty yards away. Then he attempted to get up and run, only to flop back over when Rob kicked him in the head.

Rob ripped the gun from his hand, spun, and pointed the thing at one thug on the ground and then the other, as if it were a scanning wand, capable of both detecting life and snuffing it out. Both men were bleeding from the head, their woolen caps soaked through with blood. Neither moved, or seemed likely to. Rob put a bullet in each one's neck then turned to the third ex-gunman, who had struggled to his feet. The guy was clearly woozy. Rob pointed the gun at his head.

"No!" yelled Frank, despite being somewhat stunned himself, unsteady on his feet, an aftereffect of having landed on the asphalt beneath maybe two hundred pounds of jacketed meat. The delayed echo of his voice surprised him. In the next instant he realized that it wasn't, in fact, an echo, but the voice of Paul Fowlkes, who was hustling toward them from the direction of the mess hall, hampered by his girth and a scoped rifle.

CHAPTER 17

"Whatdya think, I was gonna shoot him?" Rob said.

This attempt at nonchalance, at black humor, was betrayed by the abnormal thinness of his voice, by a laugh that sounded more like air escaping from a puncture. Frank, still stunned and wobbly, didn't reply. And the surviving hit man was likely not convinced that he wasn't about to have his skull blown apart. Hadn't he just seen Rob pump bullets into the necks of his two companions, on the off-chance that they had not yet breathed their last?

The answer was, in fact, unclear. It depended on the degree to which the guy was still in possession of his senses. For sure, even were his glazed eyes not looking down the barrel of his own semi-automatic, which could inflict a far more lethal kick in the head than that administered by Rob, he didn't seem like a threat to make a break for it. Neither did Billy, who'd sunk to the ground, cursing, after attempting one step on his battered leg.

Frank noted all of this in a very long moment or two. Perhaps time had slowed down. Fowlkes, at least, appeared to be running in slow motion. And his totally unexpected appearance—he was still lumbering toward them now, with his magic rifle in hand—lent credence to

Frank's suspicion that he himself was actually, mercifully, at the tail end of a very bad dream.

Fowlkes walked the last few steps, breathing hard, materializing out of smoke. "What would make anyone think you were gonna shoot him, Rob?" he gasped, casting a fast glance at the two bodies bleeding on the road, maybe wondering whether Rob or himself could ultimately take credit for the kills.

Being still focused on his prisoner, Rob chanced only a sidelong glance at Fowlkes.

"Very funny Paul," he said, appearing to be addressing the thug. "Still, I don't know how to thank you for ignoring what I said over the phone. About staying put in Queens. And for saving our asses."

"Yeah. Well, it's good to get out once in a while."

"Comrade Fowlkes," said Frank, his voice seeming to originate from someplace outside of himself. "I don't know how to even be around you anymore. I owe you too much. How many times are you gonna save my life?"

Suddenly choked up, he stepped forward and wrapped his arms around Fowlkes, no small trick.

Fowlkes clapped him on the back once then moved him away. "Find me a buxom wench, and we'll call it even."

Frank snorted. "A wrench, maybe. Half price. But seriously, how the hell did you—"

"I'll tell you about it later. Just got lucky. Dumb luck, got here at the perfect time, saw them without them seeing me. Right now, we need to get rolling. First, we should question this scumbag. Which would've been hard to do if his brains were blown out," he added, turning to Rob. "Although the impulse is understandable. To put it mildly."

"Right," Rob growled.

Frank was unsure whether his brother's tone was intended to instill some more fear in his prisoner—Rob did move the barrel of the gun an inch closer to the guy's face—or to serve notice to Fowlkes that saving his life was one thing, but giving him a pep talk, like some commanding officer who'd taken a seminar in human relations, was another.

In any case, Fowlkes appeared unfazed. "Okay. We need to shackle both of these guys." He glanced over at Billy, who sat rocking his upper body on the asphalt, arms pressed against himself as if trying to stay warm. "Frank, take my rifle and keep an eye on Patterson. That's him, right?"

"It is. And his leg is not in great shape."

"Yeah, I saw this douche bag over here smash him in the knee with the butt of his gun. You're some real tough hombres, you and your friends. Or your ex-friends. I think they're dead."

After handing the rifle to Frank and removing a small pair of binoculars from his jacket, Fowlkes drew handcuffs from the same pocket. "Whatdya think, Rob? I'll cuff him to that protective bumper, whatever the hell it is, on the pickup. The side that didn't get smashed up."

Rob considered this for a moment. "Sounds good."

With his thumb, Fowlkes directed the thug toward Billy's truck. When he didn't hop to it, Rob gave him a hand—or foot—leaving the impression of his right shoe on the guy's ribs this time. Even if this kick was flat-footed, and cushioned by his winter jacket, the thug grunted heavily. Then he gasped for air, vapor escaping from his mouth like dust from a beaten rug. Finally, he gritted his teeth and gave Rob a hard look. But he was also glaring down the barrel of the semi-automatic. Still bent over, he walked with small quick steps to the designated spot at the front of the pickup. While Rob covered him, Fowlkes jerked down the guy's gloves and cuffed his left wrist. He then ran the other cuff around two of the bumper bars above the fender. Finally, he clicked it shut on the other wrist, after yanking the prisoner's arm into the right position. The guy tried to sit down on the frozen dirt. This attempt nearly caused the dislocation of both of his wrists.

"Ow! Shit! *Cocksucker.*"

"Gee. You must have a death wish," said Fowlkes. He turned away, leaving the ex-hit man shackled to the pickup like a dog leashed to a lamppost, except that he was probably less comfortable, being unable to either stand upright or sit. Rob and Fowlkes rejoined Frank, who was pointing the scoped rifle down at Billy, both men avoiding eye contact.

"I was gonna cuff Patterson here to a waist chain in my car, " Rob told Fowlkes. "That genius over there re-cuffed him in front."

"I know that, Detective," replied Fowlkes. He flashed a quick smile, while trying to shield his eyes from the sun. Low in the west, it shone through leafless trees, glinting on the darkened lenses of Fowlkes's tortoise shell glasses. "Or at least, from my little hiding place, I saw you guys take him out of the woods, cuffed behind his back. Proper cop procedure. Not that you have to explain anything to me, man."

"Yeah," replied Rob, looking away from the sunlight, squinting. "That's a point."

Fowlkes turned and glared at Billy. "Patterson," he said, nodding. "It's not every day you get to meet a mass murderer. Think we'll cuff you to your truck over there too. Fresh Air Fund," he read off of the side of the pickup. "Ironic, no? After what you did at First Union Arena."

Billy said nothing. The side of his face lay drooped against one shoulder. Rob jerked him to his feet, or at least half way, then dragged him over to the truck, grunting with the effort. As Frank kept Billy covered, Rob unlocked one handcuff, which he ran through the trailer hitch at the back of the pickup before reattaching it to Billy's wrist.

Then Billy gingerly managed to get his behind back down on the asphalt. The listless set of his cold-reddened face altered only when he grimaced in pain. The brothers rejoined Fowlkes, who was conversing with their other prisoner, in front. The guy was stamping his feet, trying to ward off frostbite. He was bent over as if he were about to open the pickup's hood. It was not difficult to imagine him frozen in that position, or listing to one side, dead but unable to join his ex-partners on the ground.

Rob shook his head disdainfully as he observed the guy's tap dance. "Did you Miranda him?" he said to Fowlkes. "We don't want to deprive him of his rights."

"Excellent idea. We just got as far as introducing ourselves. Why don't you repeat your name again?" Fowlkes said to the captive. "Or your alias. Whatever." No response. After several seconds Fowlkes backhanded the guy in his ear, knocking the watch cap askew on his head.

"Ow, fuck! Son of a bitch!"

"What?" Fowlkes threateningly drew back his gloved hand again. "You know," he said, after the prisoner flinched, "I don't know how many more blows your head can take, without you suffering damage to that scholarly brain of yours. And if you turn into a blubbering idiot—as opposed to what you are now—you'll be of no use to us. Now, where were we? Your name?"

"It's Barton, okay?" The guy exhaled a cloud of vapor. "Steve Barton." Frank squirmed as he watched this brief demonstration of enhanced interrogation. He reminded himself that Barton didn't deserve much sympathy. This helped, some.

"Okay," said Fowlkes. "Steve—or whatever the fuck your mother named you—you have the right to remain silent. Anything you say may be used in a court of law against you. And, you have the right to consult a lawyer. Remaining silent is not something I would recommend, though." Fowlkes flashed him a thin smile. "So, who are you working for, Barton?"

"This game sound familiar?" Rob demanded.

Again, no reply. His nose leaking, Barton stared at the ground then lifted and rotated his head and shoulders, seemingly trying to relieve the pressure on his neck. His face was thick, unshaven. Reddened and scowling, it looked like a caricature of itself, Popeye's nemesis Bluto with a watch cap on, dark eyes peering out beneath.

"Listen," said Fowlkes after several seconds, nudging Barton's head with the semi-automatic, which he'd borrowed from Rob. "Don't think for a minute that any one of us would hesitate to waste you. We'd have to draw straws for the privilege. You're a fucking hired gun, some punk who kills for whoever will pay him. Think anyone would miss you, or your friends? Whoever you're working for—and I could hazard a guess—they're going down. You could precede them to hell. Or, maybe after a few years in the joint, you're in the witness protection program."

Barton sneezed, the force of it jarring his head and neck. He grimaced in pain. "McMahon," he blurted out finally, as Fowlkes exerted more pressure against his temple with barrel of the gun. "I'm not the direct link. Eberhardt over there is." He shifted his eyeballs as best he could, in the direction of the two corpses. "Was. Shit, I wasn't even supposed to know that. That McMahon was the guy."

"McMahon," repeated Fowlkes. "First name Walter? FBI?" With an effort, Barton nodded.

Fowlkes shook his head. "Motherfucker. Homeland Security division," he informed the brothers, over his shoulder. "Scanlon's supervisor. Probably supervised his murder, too. Or delegated it. That McMahon, he's a big fucking patriot. Just ask him. Probably altered Scanlon's reports, played those little games with your names on the surveillance list. That sonuvabtich."

"Probably supplied Tate with the contact for the poison gas, too," said Rob.

"Tate?" murmured Barton.

"The Reverend Maximilian," said Fowlkes. "Mass murder in the name of Jesus. Now, that plastic gun you took off of Patterson, the one he used to kill that guard? Before you and your buddies tried to kill *him*? Any idea where that might be?"

"Might still be in the glove compartment of the van. Might not."

"The van you and your ex-friends threw him into at First Union. At the loading dock."

"Right. But I'm fucking freezing. You want me to sing, I'm gonna have to have a fucking lawyer first, and a deal. But it ain't gonna happen if I freeze to death."

"Yeah. That would be a shame. Well, Steve, if you can hang on for a few more minutes, while we confer in private, then we can get you on your way to your new cell. And don't worry. You'll get plenty of heat there. More than you bargained for."

Frank, Rob, and Fowlkes sat down in Rob's car, and he turned on the engine. It took a while for the thing to warm up, even though the Tedeschis hadn't jumped out of the car that long ago—it only seemed that way. Frank was actually surprised that Rob had thought to turn off the ignition in the first place. He couldn't remember him doing it. He was also surprised when Rob, a couple of moments after sitting down behind the wheel, popped his trunk and stepped back out of the car.

"Be a second," he said.

In the rear view mirror, Frank saw Rob extract a screwdriver from the trunk then slam down the lid. "Ah," he said. "The microchip."

He stepped out himself. Fowlkes followed, grunting with the effort. Rob was already taking out the "screw" that fastened the right corner of his license plate to the rear of the car. The head of the thing turned out to be a porous, metallic mini-disc overlain by a detachable, plastic Phillip's-head cover—a little piece of sophisticated technology that had nearly cost them their lives.

He turned to Fowlkes. "Any reason not to destroy this thing?"

"Uh-uh. Not that I can see. These guys were using it to track you, yes?"

Rob gritted his teeth. "Yup."

"Okay, then the computer that it's been transmitting to has got to be the one I saw in their car, which is over there behind the mess hall. Ford Bronco. Still chasin' you, Frank. Or were."

"Hope they enjoyed the trip."

"So, we'll play with that computer—email or text McMahon, something—I might even be able to access his cell phone, although maybe not the one he's been using to contact these bozos. Barton over there might be useful in that regard. Gotta let McMahon know that the mission has been accomplished."

Frank gazed over at the two ex-bozos lying in the road, as he was struck again by the surreal nature of the whole situation. Not so Fowlkes, whose tone was almost matter-of-fact: "That way, maybe he won't start destroying incriminating evidence. Of course, it's very possible that he's long since done that. But the microchip? *That* could be destroyed, yeah."

Rob smashed the thing with a grapefruit-sized rock that he picked up from the side of the road, overkill. "Shit, never did like technology all that much anyway," he confided, shot-putting the rock back into the woods.

Frank said, "Um, you don't think Billy, and or Barton, are gonna freeze to death if we leave them there too long?"

"*We* might," said Rob. "Car might be halfway warm by now. And maybe we can turn on the truck, in case we need it to thaw one of them out."

"Exhaust is gonna be right in Billy's face."

"Good. Give 'im a little taste of his own medicine. Besides, if we have to warm him up, the exhaust might do it. And the heat of the engine might do the same for Barton."

The key was still in the pickup's ignition. Frank turned it on, and the engine kicked off, seemingly having suffered no damage from the crash. The smoke from its exhaust pipe subsumed the vapor emitted by Billy, who sat impassively, idling, hands cuffed to the trailer hitch.

Frank joined Rob and Fowlkes back in the car. Rob had turned on the heat full blast. Despite its slightly toxic smell, the warmth was amazingly welcome, even if it pointed out for Frank, by contrast, the depth to which he was chilled. The condensed moisture on the car's windows began to slowly vanish.

"Rob says that Patterson realizes that he was set up and wants payback," said Fowlkes. "He's gonna cooperate."

"Yeah, that's what he says. He's, um, erratic, but he knows that they tried to kill him, twice. That's hard to miss. And he doesn't appreciate being a sacrificial lamb for the reverend. So—"

"So I think we're in good shape here." Fowlkes nodded, his woolen Jets cap bobbing up and down. "I'll probably go to Ulrich first. He's second in command of the bureau, and we go back a ways. When he sees Patterson, sans the beard and mustache, and looks at the videos from First Union, he's gonna know who he's lookin' at. Maybe we'll have the plastic gun, evidence from ballistics. And when he hears Patterson's story—"

"Paul," Frank interjected, "I know you're planning ahead—and that's good, real good, and I'm sure you were even doing that on the way up here—but what do we do about those two dead bodies over there?"

"Get rid of them," replied Fowlkes, obviously needing no time to mull this over. "Their car too."

"I agree," said Rob. "Otherwise, what? We need to call the local troopers, deal with that added complication. Or Strezoff would, after he saw the little presents we left him."

"Strezoff?"

"Yeah, he's the maintenance chief here. Lives up by the gate. We gave him the same story, about Patterson being the sole witness. Strezoff took his wife shopping, or some such, after Patterson called in and said everything was cool. Didn't mention that a gun was pointed at his head. Anyway, I don't think Strezoff saw our three visitors come in. The arm by the gate was up, and timewise, they had to have come in before Patterson spoke to him over the phone. If he'd seen them, he'd likely have said something to Patterson. In any case, we should give Strezoff a call later. When he sees that Patterson's gone, the truck's smashed up, and there's blood in the road…we can tell him that we didn't want to alarm him, that Patterson was actually a wanted felon, tried to run, got injured in the crash. Which would explain the blood."

"'Cept there's none in the truck," said Fowlkes. "But that can be changed."

"Yeah, so it can."

"And when that bastard McMahon understands what we have on him—and, hopefully, we'll be able to connect the dots several different ways, starting with Barton—I don't think he's gonna worry too much about what happened to his goons. They just got disappeared, that's all. I mean, this is the Flowers administration, right?"

"True," said Rob, as he turned down the car's heater. "Plus, if worse comes to worst, we have two eyewitnesses—even if one's a mass murderer and the other's a hired gun—who can testify that those clowns were about to kill us. One of 'us' being NYPD. And the other being, um, a reputable hardware store owner."

"That's me." Frank chuckled and shivered, the two actions feeling like one and the same. He was thawing out and had little desire to leave the car, especially not for the purpose of hauling bloody corpses around.

"Throw me that map, Frank," said Fowlkes. "There's another lake, isn't there?"

"Right up that dirt road. We saw one end of it when we were escorting Billy down here."

"Okay. If that's Beaver Lake, the side abutting the dam used to be a quarry. They filled it in some, but the bottom's still deeper there than the rest of the lake. I did a little research on my computer. Sharpe Reservation, history of. Quarry was deserted, Fresh Air Fund took over the land, re-forested the area around the quarry, built the dam. Which is beside the point, I know."

"And the point is?" asked Frank.

Before Fowlkes could reply, Rob saved him the trouble. "We stick the bodies in the Bronco and sink it in the lake," he said, nodding, as if thinking out loud. "The lake freezes over it. You know, I like the idea."

"Glad to hear it," Fowlkes said. "Assuming that the Bronco will break through the ice."

"Well, if we send it off from the top of the dam, depending on how the thing's configured. And maybe we load the car up with stones first, just to be sure. Whaddya think, Frank?"

"Um, yeah. Sure," he replied, unwilling to vocalize what he really thought: *What the hell are we doing?* "Rolling heavy. Think that's an expression. Whatever, a little extra weight couldn't hurt. The road was plenty rocky, and they might've used bigger stones on the dam."

"Well, only thing is, you guys would probably have to do that part yourselves," said Fowlkes. "We don't want Barton to know what became of the bodies of his comrades over there. Patterson doesn't need to know either. I'll baby sit them, up by my car, while you guys put the corpses in deep refrigeration. Then we should get Patterson and Barton locked up. You've heard rumors about secret overseas prisons and all that jazz. CIA? FBI has 'em here. I can arrange to have both of them socked away while we get everything ready for McMahon. And the reverend. If it doesn't ultimately lead to Flowers, I'll be very surprised."

"Actually, sinking that Bronco into the lake might be a pleasure," said Frank, riding his own train of thought. "Just have to forget about the passengers."

"Yeah. Well, it's parked up there on the other side of that mess hall. *I'm* parked up the road a ways, around that bend." Fowlkes jerked his thumb back in the direction from which they'd all come. Frank, his head twisted around, peered through the fogged rear window and saw nothing except fading daylight. Fowlkes filled up most of the back seat. Between the green and white watch cap, the glasses and thick mustache, his round face could've belonged to some oddball who ran a newsstand, dined on large quantities of fast food and spent his evenings channel-surfing sports. For sure, no one would have mistaken him for an action hero, even with the scoped rifle sitting on his lap.

"I came around it nice and slow. Saw those three clowns nosing around the pickup and your car, Rob. Fortunately, they didn't see me. Least I didn't think so. In fact, I had dumb luck all the way through. I was on…what is it?…Snook Road, the road leading up to the entrance to the reservation, and I saw the Bronco turn in. Perfect timing, pure luck, like I said. I'd hauled ass up from the city, after I faxed that map, researched this place. The arm at the gate was up, I drove in myself after they were out of sight. When I saw the three of them, I reversed back around the bend, parked off the road. Snuck around through the woods, and behind that staff lounge, praying they wouldn't see me. Or if they did, maybe they'd think it was just a bear lumbering through. Nah. Jets cap woulda given it away."

"Also the fact that you were lumbering on two legs," Frank said.

Fowlkes smiled. "You might be giving them too much credit. So anyway, then I didn't see *them* when I peeked. I figured they were laying for you, it made sense. Got around behind the mess hall. Good cover, easy shot."

"You waited 'til the last second, man," said Frank. "Not that I'm complainin', you understand."

"Right. Problem was, both of them were right in front of you, and Rob. I was afraid I'd hit you. But when that fool stuck his gun to your temple, it made things real simple. There was no other option."

Rob said, "Man, between you and Frank, I could stick an apple on my head, let you fire away and not break a sweat. Seriously. But we got a lot to do now before it gets dark. Also, it would probably be good to get out of here before Strezoff gets back."

"Yeah, you're right, we should definitely get a move on. Let's get the keys to the Bronco first, then maybe you can shuttle me, Patterson, and Barton over to my car, help me get them secured over there. Figure I'll wind up taking Barton down to the city. You guys can take Patterson. Yes?"

"That was the plan," Rob said.

"Well constructed. And while Frank's waiting for you, he can smear a little blood on the front seat of the pickup. Bring the Bronco down, get the computer out of there—I saw it on the front seat—load the corpses—"

"Oh, goody."

"Lift with your legs, Frank," Rob said.

"Very funny."

"Hey, I'll probably be back before then anyway. And if not, seriously, don't strain. They're big. Dead weight."

"That's *real* funny." Frank opened the front passenger door and heaved himself out and upright. Rob did the same, performing a little jig in order to avoid stepping on either of the bodies lying outside of his car. As Fowlkes locked the rifle in Rob's trunk and began patting down the corpses, the brothers walked into a noxious cloud of exhaust coming from the back of the pickup.

Billy Patterson's eyes didn't even lift as the handcuffs were unlocked from around the trailer hitch. He did wince as Rob yanked him to his feet by one arm, while Frank levelled a gun—Billy's own. Frank's was probably on or near the person of the thug who'd ripped it out of its shoulder holster. Rob re-cuffed the prisoner, after jerking his arms around behind his back. Seemingly, Billy could barely stay upright on his contused leg. He did manage to hop some on the good one as Rob, unsympathetic, began dragging him toward the car, passing Fowlkes on his way to the pickup.

Fowlkes flashed Frank a thumbs-up sign. He'd found the key to the Bronco. This he surreptitiously dropped into Frank's hand, slapping him five. Then, groaning, he stretched backward from the waist, a maneuver seemingly intended to mitigate the aftereffects of having been bent over two dead bodies.

"Frank." He sighed, twisting his torso left and right, "I need some coverage. Need to liberate our friend Barton."

Grunting, he hoisted himself up into the cab of the pickup and turned off the engine. Frank trained his gun on Steve Barton as Fowlkes gingerly descended and unlocked the handcuffs from the bumper guard. Barton inhaled sharply and grimaced as he futilely attempted to stand upright. When Fowlkes grabbed his arm and yanked it backward, Barton howled.

"Ah! Jesus! Shit!!"

Frank could actually sympathize, having been through lower back problems of his own in the past. On the other hand, Barton *had* smashed the butt of his gun into Billy's knee, into the leg that he'd already been limping on. And he'd have killed Billy, Frank, and Rob without blinking, if he didn't have to share the murdering with his buddies. Still…

"*Move*," Frank commanded, inching the gun closer to Barton's head, trying to banish his own misgivings. The prisoner was re-cuffed now but seemingly rooted to the spot by back spasms. His forehead was dripping sweat, a residual effect of the heat of the engine, and/or a byproduct of excruciating pain.

"Go 'head," he gasped, lifting his eyes to Frank's. "Fucking shoot me."

His bluff called, Frank pocketed the gun. Besides, if he was going to drag Barton, he needed both hands. The guy was huge. Frank took one arm, Fowlkes the other. Together they hauled him, shrouded by a triple cloud of vapor, eventually managing to force him into the back seat of Rob's car. They were spurred on, if anything, by his cries of agony, wanting to get him inside and shut the door.

Billy, who was sitting behind Rob at the other end of the seat, finally came to life with the entrance of Barton. "Get that bastard away from me!" he demanded.

Fowlkes slid into the front passenger seat and twisted himself around with surprising dexterity, leveling the gun that he'd requisitioned from Frank. "Listen, douche bag," he said in an even voice. "You don't shut up, we can tranquilize you. But you'll wake up with a very bad headache. He'll be on the same seat with you for maybe half a minute, looking down this gun. And he's fucking crippled anyway. We're going maybe a few city blocks," he added, as Rob backed across the road. "Then we'll get you both resituated."

As Rob and Fowlkes drove away, Frank took a fast glance down at the corpses. The blood was beginning to congeal—on both faces and necks—probably helped by the sub-freezing temperature. For a long second, he absently pondered the fact that Fowlkes had gotten each of them in the head. Probably he'd aimed high, since Frank and Rob had been bent over the car.

Frank pulled off two blood-soaked watch caps. He looked away from the shattered skulls, protruding brains. Hadn't he seen all of this before? But that was a long time ago. And he hadn't become inured then, even after more or less accepting the fact that he was probably going to die in the mud of southeast Asia.

The dead men he was dealing with now had been scumbags, undeniably. Still, he had no desire to gaze upon their gaping mouths, or fish-like eyes. Wishing his gloves were latex, disposable, he closed two pairs of eyelids. Then he hustled over to the pickup and smeared blood on the driver's side of the front seat.

After retrieving a rag—once half of a towel—from the floor beneath the glove compartment, he made himself soak up some more blood from the head of one of the corpses. He dripped several drops onto the running board beneath the driver's door then wrung out a path leading to the dried puddles of blood by the bodies. Hopefully, no one would study this too closely. Hopefully, no one would try to match blood samples with one taken from Billy.

Suddenly, Frank was beyond caring, or worrying, enveloped by fatigue, physical and otherwise, now that he was alone. But he roused himself, taking a length of pipe from the bed of Billy's truck and ramming it into the window above the driver's seat. The webbed glass thus produced looked convincing enough. With a perverse pride in his work, he imagined Strezoff pondering the fact that Billy hadn't been wearing a seatbelt, and concluding that criminals probably didn't bother with such precautions, having a fondness for living dangerously.

Running as fast as he could—this amounted to a trot, an attempt to generate some internal heat—Frank reached and circled the mess hall. There was the Bronco around the back. With a click of the remote he was inside, briefly surveying the trash that bore testimony to the final days'—or weeks'—worth of consumption for three hit men.

McDonald's wrappers, peanut butter/cheese crackers, coffee cups, Budweiser, an overflowing ashtray. And there was the laptop on the front seat, which had been an unseen, unwanted companion to the Tedeschis, tracking them as if they were unwitting participants in some extended video game. Kill Bill. Frank wondered if there was a microchip attached to his car as well. Fowlkes could probably ascertain that on the computer. For now, it was a moot point. Resisting an urge to smash the laptop, Frank started up the Bronco and drove over a low grass embankment onto the main road.

It took a few nervous seconds for him to visually confirm that that was indeed Rob's car coming toward him, moving through lengthening shadows on the far side of the staff lounge. Frank parked the Bronco alongside the bodies, half on the asphalt and half on frozen dirt, facing the road up to Beaver Lake. Rob pulled up behind him.

"Like your new wheels, Frank," he said. "You're probably not gonna get much mileage out of it though. And…Fowlkes only pulled the car keys, right? Lemme see what else these boys have in their pockets. Fish around for wallets and what-have-you. Could be something useful in there. Then, I guess we'll toss them in the back. Like fucking sides of beef."

"Put down the back seat first."

"Right."

"Okay, good. I'll stick the laptop in your car, see what they might have in the glove compartment of the Bronco. We need to rock 'n roll here."

"Definitely."

A few minutes later, having retrieved cash, license, credit and identification cards—bogus and otherwise—from the corpses, Rob slid his hands under the jacketed armpits of the larger one. One glance at the brain matter protruding from the guy's skull was seemingly enough to bring him to the edge of nausea. He sucked air then looked away, grateful that he was only expelling vapor.

Frank squatted and grasped the undersides of the knees. Either they were seriously arthritic or rigor mortis had begun to set in.

"On the count of three," gasped Rob.

"Lift with my legs?"

"Oh, yeah."

Both of them heaved, grunting in synchrony. They managed to get the corpse halfway in, its butt resting on the Bronco's edge, sneaker heels propped on asphalt. From there it was easy. The legs were like two-by fours. Rob used them to shove the body, while Frank—who'd graciously switched ends—pulled up on the armpits, easing the head, neck and upper torso over the folded seat. Then they slid the guy to one side to make room for his friend.

One heave, together, was sufficient to get the second corpse fully inside. Frank quickly tossed in the almost-frozen watch caps and the rag with which he'd spread the blood around. Then he slammed the hatchback, now the rear door of a makeshift hearse, or tomb.

He jumped back behind the wheel of the Bronco and drove as rapidly as he could up the rocky, pitted dirt road, with the two bodies bouncing around behind him. Rob followed in the car. They pulled up at the crest of a downgrade above the lake. To their right was the dam. As they'd hoped, it was fortified by rocks, down to the water's edge.

"We fill it up with rocks, drive it back up here. When we send it back down, we gotta somehow generate as much speed as we can, so that when it hits the lake, maybe it hits with more force, maybe gets out from shore a bit before it goes through the ice," Rob said.

"Yeah, assuming it breaks through. We don't have a lot of time for a Plan B. And I don't think either one of us is gonna want to have to have to go out there and retrieve the thing, drive it back. Assuming we could even get it back up over that drop-off at the edge. But, given the drop-off, and the weight, hopefully, she crashes through, and sinks."

"Hopefully. And Fowlkes said the water's supposed to be deep at this end."

"Right. Okay, so we send it from up here," said Frank.

Standing next to Rob, he surveyed the stony terrain and expanse of the frozen lake. The scenery was undeniably, incongruously beautiful. It had been made more so by the vanishing of the sun behind the wooded hill on the far side of the lake. Left behind was a silver and gray winter tableau overlain by a darkening blue sky. The ice appeared several shades lighter, as if having absorbed the waning daylight. It was a field of absolute stillness—which they hoped to shatter, literally. Still, at another time, maybe zipped up in an Eskimo parka, Frank could've admired the vista at length, even snapped a picture or two. But he doubted that he'd be back to visit.

Rob said, "Sounds good. For sure, we can't send it off the dam. Too high up. Probably just crash on the rocks."

They drove as close as they could to the dam's base. Rob hefted large rocks and passed them up to Frank, who slung them with two hands into the back of the Bronco. This bucket-brigade style was dictated by the angle of the dam and adjoining terrain.

After the first few times, Frank became less squeamish about dropping weighty, bone-crushing stones on top of the two thugs. And the exercise actually felt good. They worked up a sweat. Even more so than when they'd hefted the corpses, it was necessary to work without gloves. If their hands got nicked and scratched, that was a minor inconvenience.

And if they removed fifteen or twenty mini-boulders, hopefully, the dam would hold up anyway.

As the brothers slid back into the Bronco, Frank's cell phone rang. "*Que pasa*?" inquired Fowlkes, over static.

"We're loaded. They're both buried under rocks. We're about to send it into the lake. Hopefully to the bottom." He began driving back up, away from the shoreline.

"Good. I'm standin' here outside my car. It's fuckin' freezing, too. Patterson and Barton are both cuffed in the back. Rob told you that, I'm sure. Heat's on, an' they're just like ignoring each other, starin' outta opposite windows. And at my gun, at least Barton. And Patterson, shit, he may even be nodding out, believe it or not. Be a shame to have to wake him, but hey…anyway, I was thinking, if you have a blanket, even a couple of floor mats, might be good to tie them to Rob's rear fender, erase the tire tracks on the way out."

"That's a thought," said Frank.

Rob slapped the dashboard. "This should do it."

It took Frank a second to reorient, to realize what Rob was talking about.

"Okay, man," he replied, circling the Bronco around to face the lake, pointing the wheels straight ahead and coming to a stop.

"Okay," echoed Fowlkes. "And good luck. Lemme know how it goes when you're done. Then, hopefully, you can take Patterson, and we can hit the road. See you soon."

"What's a thought?" asked Rob. He shrugged after Frank told him. "Could, I guess. Dunno what kinda materials we got, or what kinda tracks we'd leave. It's rocky, you know?" He took a fast look in the rear view mirror, leaned out of his window and twisted his head around. "Hell, worry about that later. I'm thinkin', we put it in park, put on the emergency brake, then wedge a large rock against the gas pedal. Floor it. We release the brake, throw it in drive—"

"And lose a fucking arm, at the least, whoever's lucky enough to be leaning in to do it."

"That's a point. Well, maybe we could...okay, I got battery cables, and maybe some rope in my trunk. If not, we use belts, or jacket strings. Could even borrow their shoelaces," he added, indicating the dead bodies with a jerk of his head. "We clamp on to the shift, run the rope through the rear window, jerk back, let go. Bye-bye baby."

Frank considered this for a moment. "Let's do it."

Rob did turn up the rope. This saved them several minutes. He tied it to the battery cable, which Frank clamped on to the release button of the Bronco's automatic shift stick. The engine was revving, approximating the sound of an army of angry hornets, amplified. The large rock depressing the gas pedal had been wedged in well enough to hopefully prevent its dislodging on the run down to the lake.

After Rob ran the rope through the back window, Frank gingerly leaned into the Bronco and released the emergency brake. Then he jumped away, as the thing lurched forward. He slammed the driver's door. Simultaneously, Rob jerked back on the rope, pulling the shift through Reverse—the rope had been long enough to provide him with a little safety margin—and into Drive 1. Blastoff.

With the rope dancing behind it like a tail, the Bronco thundered downhill, bouncing over rocks, gas and gravity flinging it over the drop-off at the shoreline. For a very long second or two it was airborne. Then it crashed down onto the ice, seeming to careen forward even as its back end began to sink.

EPILOGUE

Good thing you accumulated all that vacation time," Frank murmured, leaning back in his beach chair, feeling like he was starring in a commercial, the one in which vacationers became incensed because the sun had the nerve to go behind a cloud for a couple of seconds.

"The weather was much better yesterday," complains a bikini-clad female, her skin glistening with suntan lotion. She flips down her shades and contentedly lays back in her beach chair as the sun comes out again.

Frank was fine with the day's weather, with the gently swaying palm trees and the line of foamy blue surf melting into the sand, just like the one before it. Idly, he picked at the remaining dead skin on the borders of the scar from one of the more substantial scratches he'd sustained while heaving rocks atop the remains of two paid killers. The scar was evidence that all of it had really happened. Not that such evidence was necessary.

Daily headlines concerning the aftermath jumped off the front page of the *Miami Herald.* Still more vivid were the flashbacks—dust off the projector, take out those faded slides of Vietnam, click in Sharpe Reservation—even if they'd begun to diminish, both in amount and intensity, diffusing into the endless, hazy expanse of the ocean.

"If I didn't have it, they'd have given it to me," replied Julie, sliding over the left strap of her one-piece and applying sunscreen. "Strickland was a caseworker for twenty years, before he became management. He knows all about untenable home situations—even if it's not usually about media people making the place unlivable." She capped the tube of sunscreen and tossed it back into her oversized straw bag. "And even if I just got *back* from vacation…what, two and a half weeks ago? Three? I'm entitled to special consideration, wouldn't you say?"

"I would. In fact, I already have. So have you."

She laughed softly, a sound even more soothing to him than the rustle of palm fronds, or the lazy rhythm of surf stroking sand. "Well, still, it's true. After all, my husband is a national hero. International."

"Yeah, right. If that description applies to anyone, it's Fowlkes."

"I totally disagree. But if nothing else, you're *my* hero." She leaned over and kissed him.

He smiled. "Okay. I'll buy that."

She hadn't been all that smitten initially. Anything but—especially since she'd been led to believe that things had gone smoothly. On the way back down the Taconic State Parkway, in his first phone call to her—post Sharpe Reservation—he simply said, "We got 'im."

Billy Patterson was in the car with them, chained up in back. The crazy bastard was snoring like…like a ratchet in need of oil. *Hardware metaphor, sorry.* And yes, her lovin' husband, was okay. Fine, absolutely. So was Rob.

"Well, good," she said, after a few moments' pause. "Great. And we'll see what happens now. Hopefully, the head bastards, starting with Reverend Tate, will get what's coming to them. Hopefully, there won't be another war. And hopefully, we can live like normal human beings again. Eventually. For a start, now we should be able to feel safe in our own home again. Yes?"

"Definitely," Frank replied, with more conviction than he felt.

"Wonderful. Excellent. Well…like I told you the other day, my parents are managing. Even though Mom's probably in the early stages of Alzheimer's."

"And your father's in the early stages of denial."

"That's true. Hopefully…am I overusing that word?…they'll be okay. For a while. I'm more than ready to come home. And I can't wait to see you."

Frank had picked Julie up at the airport three days later. He'd actually worked two of them, wanting nothing more than a return to the ordinary. His father, who'd been supervising at the store in his absence, insisted on lending a hand. Albert Tedeschi had taken a shine to Felipe, Billy Patterson's replacement. And "working" in the store, or looking up from the newspaper and lending his expertise as needed—in his estimation, mostly—had proved to be an agreeable way to spend part of his day.

His retirement—brisk walks in the park with his wife, television, *bocci,* even winter excursions to the tropics, an overdose of relaxation—could now revert to a semi-retirement. Plus, he had a gut feeling that his son could use a little support, that despite Frank's emphatic disclaimers, the manhunt for Patterson had taken something out of him.

Actually, Frank could've been an automaton, a new technological advance in place at Tedeschi's Hardware. He'd been programmed over many years. He could cut a key with his eyes closed. But the mundane operations of the store and the concerns of its customers now seemed absurd, farcical. *Anyone need a brain bucket? Blood sol-*

vent? Make your driveway look like new. Plus, he knew that as he was discussing the most effective methodology for dealing with cockroaches, Fowlkes was laying the groundwork for indictments that would astonish the world, with the possible exception of the leadership of All for Allah. No, check that—they'd be astonished that the truth had ever come out. Assuming that it did.

Having spent half an hour anxiously peering down the portion of the airport corridor that was visible to the side of the security apparatus, Frank was overjoyed when he finally saw his wife. She appeared on the heels of a crowd of other arriving passengers, many having slid into welcoming embraces, as if the lines of vision established by their initial sightings of their loved ones were tangible, elastic things pulling them in, connections of beaming faces.

Frank felt his own light up. Julie—tan and beautiful, conclusive evidence that he had indeed made it home intact—was soon wrapped up in his arms. Eventually, he had to let go, lest she think that something was amiss. She used the sleeve of her jacket to wipe her eyes. He sneaked a dab at his own.

"Woman," he said, kissing her. "You look like you've been laying around in the sun."

"I'd rather be here, sweetheart. Believe me. It wasn't exactly a relaxing trip."

The lingering joy on her face vanished a couple of hours later, when Frank finally acceded to her request to give her the details of the capture of Billy Patterson. He'd stalled, saying that they should eat first and enjoy the meal. She could fill him in on their sons, both of whom were blissfully ignorant of the fact that their father the hardware store entrepreneur had just returned from a perilous manhunt. Theoretically, she could. Neither Carl nor Sergio was much into sharing with Mom, Sergio being particularly evasive where the odds of his getting married were concerned.

Leaving the restaurant, Frank suggested a walk around the neighborhood. The house was not bugged, never had been, Fowlkes had assured him of that. And the microchips that had been attached to both his and Rob's license plates were purely for the purpose of tracking them. Having been shown the technique by his brother, Frank had unscrewed and stomped the innocuous-looking little contraption soon after arriving home. Still, he felt more comfortable talking about matters outdoors. It was actually warming up a bit, no? Maybe not like Florida, but still…

She impatiently cut him off. "Frank, you're losing me here. So you were being tracked. But whoever was doing the tracking—maybe the same guys who you shot at that time when they tried to run you off the road?" Her voice trembled slightly. "Then they must have tracked you up to Sharpe Reservation, yes? I mean, they had this microchip on Rob's car too. Right?"

He sighed. "Right."

"And?"

Fortuitously, the Number Six Train rumbled overhead, postponing the inevitable for ten all-too-brief seconds, maybe. They turned away from the *El*, and from Westchester Avenue. They had taken a slight detour off the Thruway on their way back from the airport to dine at Bruglio's, their favorite restaurant in the old neighborhood, still in business, evidence that his parents weren't the only *paisans* who'd eschewed white flight.

He took her hand as they headed down a side street. *Buhre.* He'd actually had to check the street sign to make sure. Apparently, the layout of Pelham Bay was no longer engraved in his brain, or engraved in stone, as Rob had ragged him in another lifetime, when they were teenagers.

"Julie, it was a mess. Seriously. You really wanna hear about it?" he said finally.

"No, I don't. But, Frank, I need to. Whatever happened, I need you to tell me about it, even if I freak out at first." She squeezed his hand. "I can't *not* know. It's like, I am you, and you are me. If that sounds like the Beatles, whatever, I'm sorry. But…you understand what I'm saying?"

He swallowed. "Yeah. I think so." He cleared his throat and told her, leaving out nothing. Once he started, it poured out of him, in living color. By the time he finished, they were well into Pelham Bay Park. He had no idea how they'd gotten there.

Julie's eyes were brimming. "Frank," she managed after a couple of false starts, "we may have to pop into church once in a while. Otherwise, we're gonna run out of miracles. No, check that, we're not gonna need any, because that is the last fucking time you're going off on any such adventures with Rob, or even your guardian angel Fowlkes."

Laughter sprayed through Frank's lips. "Sorry," he said. "I just had this image of Fowlkes as an angel—if you could *see* him—but in any case, I totally agree. No more adventures. Believe me. It's the last thing I want. I just want to hang out with you, Sweetheart. That's all. Until such time as you have to spoon-feed me mush through my toothless gums. Except, that I'm *not* goin' to church. Unless maybe if Sergio gets hitched."

She was unamused. "Maybe I should appreciate that you're trying to joke about it, make me feel better. Or at least divert my attention. Hell, in the movies, they look death in the face and laugh about it. *Isn't this fun?* But I don't think I'm gonna be laughing about this for a while, Frank. How the hell I'm supposed to erase this image I have, already, of you spread-eagled against Rob's car with some sociopath pressing a gun to your head? About to pull the trigger? Frank, I…" Her voice gave. He turned and wrapped his arms around her.

"Hey. It's okay. Really. I'm fine, especially with you here. You can see that. The bad guys are dead, or locked up. And their supervisors are about to get what's coming to them. From what Fowlkes tells me, everything is moving along real well. He was right, it was just one crooked higher-up in the bureau—Homeland Security, no less—but that's encouraging. Seems like most FBI agents, whatever their politics, or religion, they don't look kindly on murdering seventeen thousand people. Even if part of it's about screwing over the Arabs. They—Fowlkes has some people working on this with him now, his drug trafficking investigation has been delegated to someone else—but they recovered the gun that Billy used at First Union.

"And Cavanaugh? Remember I told you about him, Tate's security chief? Well, seems he was surreptitiously taping the reverend's office conversations. Little hidden microphone, hey. Never got around to destroying some very damning evidence. Like Billy discussing with the reverend this brilliant plan he had, and then receiving authorization."

Julie shook her head. "Unbelievable."

Fingers intertwined, they headed back toward Frank's debugged car, retracing their path through the park. The place was more littered than he remembered it. Some of its benches were broken down and/or graffitied. And unless it was his imagination, the salt air bore a hint of sewage. Their old stomping—or necking—grounds had seen better days. Still, maybe someday they would take their grandkids there: *This very bench—I think—is where Grandpa told Grandma that he was going off to war. And then she told him where else he could go.*

They crossed over a footbridge above the New England Thruway. Traffic heading north was heavy with the beginnings of rush hour. "So," she inquired, "these hit men you and Rob sent down to the bottom of the lake—at least you didn't put concrete boots on them, *Goombah* style—although the idea's kinda the same. But is that gonna come back to haunt you? Even if the killings were completely justified."

"Well, according to Barton—the one who survived, who is now salted away in some FBI dungeon—these guys were not exactly family men. No surprise there. But it's not that likely that anyone's gonna miss them, even file a missing person's report. But even if it did come up—"

"As in float to the surface?"

"*That's* not gonna happen, I promise you. And in any case, Fowlkes says not to sweat it. Given the circumstances, nobody else would. In the unlikely event that it became known in the first place."

"Well, okay. I guess. Right now, I can't worry about that too much, since that presupposes that I'm firmly convinced that all of this is real. Although like I said, the image of you—your eyes shut tight, your teeth clenched together in anticipation of your head being blown apart—*that's* as vivid as can be. It's like I was *there.*"

"It does almost seem like that. At least based on that description. And damned if I didn't have an image of you. Niagara Falls. Right when I died, or thought I did."

"Ah. Well, Frank, you were in my head, and heart, practically the whole time I was in Florida." She dropped his hand, and her arm encircled his waist. He pulled her close. They were waiting at Westchester Avenue for the light to turn green: *you may proceed with your lives*. The car was parked a block or two away, on the other side. "But speaking of Fowlkes, maybe you should tell him to try to keep your name out of the papers when the story breaks. First Union Arena, revised version."

"Good idea. I agree, one hundred percent. I don't know if Rob'll be on the same page about that. No pun intended. But I'll talk to him. And regardless, I'll talk to Fowlkes about it. Maybe I should've before, it just never occurred to me."

It turned out that it was too late. The story, featuring the Tedeschi brothers, had already leaked out. Fowlkes was not sure how. He'd wanted to forestall that until he and his team had connected all the dots, had all the evidence in hand. The idea was to give the reverend, the FBI's McMahon and whoever else was involved as little time as possible to react, to try to cover their tracks.

Frank and Rob wound up doing the talk show circuit. Their names and pictures were already all over the newspapers, TV, and the internet. Rob was a public service employee, but it was a mystery to Frank how the media had come up with photos of himself so quickly. And from the first day the story broke, the Flowers administration's propaganda machine had been employing all of its resources to paint them as mendacious tools of America's enemies.

Larry King, The Today Show, etc., were cost-free venues for setting the record straight, and for reinforcing the perception that the men who'd been responsible for uncovering the administration's bald-faced—if still "alleged"—lying about the worst terrorist attack in US history were just ordinary Joes, a cop and his brother who represented the best of America, who'd mounted a two-man revolution against a corrupt and murderous government—make that a three-man revolution, with the identity of the third actor still classified information.

Frank had been unfazed by the interviews with famous personalities, by the studio audiences, and the knowledge that millions more people were watching him on the tube. Rob felt the same way. Looking into a camera, or several of them, was light stuff compared to staring into the barrel of a gun, or feeling its cold metal against your temple.

And Rob had managed to discuss Laureen without breaking down, without "embarrassing" himself, as he put it beforehand. In fact, the brief cracks in his stony-faced dignity, and the pauses he needed to retain his composure, had registered with digital clarity on the screen. It was obvious that this was a man who'd loved his daughter. So said Julie, and Frank saw it again on tape. Freeze-frame.

After their first joint appearance, he figured that the chills he felt sitting there next to Rob, despite the heat of the bright lights, were the result of his own feelings for Laureen. But it was also true that their status as brothers now went beyond the purely biological. The wordplay of that newspaper wag, long ago, had come to be true. They were brothers in arms.

"She was a beautiful kid," Rob had declared, while gazing into Oprah Winfrey's limpid eyes—*tear magnets,* he'd termed them afterward. "Even if she tried to hide it, with the cynical attitude, the nose rings, kohl around her eyes, Dracula coat, whatever. Yeah, it was an act, sure it was, but maybe she also understood, maybe the way only kids can, that there's a lot of bullsh—sorry—a lot of hypocrisy, that America the Beautiful can be seriously ugly too. And that people who claim to have God on their side are not to be trusted. I mean, she wasn't political. Thought that was baloney too. Maybe, probably, she was just rebelling for the hell of it. But, and I never thought I'd say this, but I learned a lot from her. And from her death. Not that—the fact that I loved her, regardless—that I knew right along."

Oprah nodded, her face almost a caricature of empathy, of compassion. "And that love was the motivating force behind the mission that you and Frank undertook."

"Yeah, you could say that."

They'd already discussed with her the genesis of the "mission." Billy Patterson, who'd worked at Tedeschi's Hardware—Armonk, New York—had actually served notice to Frank about what he was going to do at First Union Arena. Ranted about it. Disappeared afterward. And he was nearly disappeared for good by three hit men, who'd nearly killed the Tedeschis as well. It was only timely intervention by an FBI agent that had saved them. The thugs had likely been working for those who were, in fact, responsible for the terrorist act at First Union—allegedly—individuals high up in the government, in league with a fundamentalist preacher. A very thorough FBI investigation was currently underway. Unfortunately, two of the hit men had escaped, but the one who had been captured was being interrogated.

The television appearances had only exacerbated the problem that soon resulted in Julie Tedeschi's return trip to Florida, with her husband in tow. Not only was their house besieged by reporters, but Frank's face was recognized pretty much whenever he ventured outside—as was Rob's. Tedeschi's Hardware was actually losing money. The volume of media people and curiosity-seekers was such that it had become very difficult to service customers. Frank's father, both distressed and energized by the hubbub, had practically kicked him out of the store.

Julie and Frank now sat at the ever-shifting water's edge on a private beach. They were there owing to the generosity of one of Julie's associates at work, who offered her the use of a time-share. Rob, having used up his accumulated personal days in the hunt for Billy Patterson, had also been granted a bit of extended leave. Extra paid vacation, courtesy of the commissioner of the NYPD. After all, the department was basking in Lieutenant Tedeschi's reflected glory, as it became clear—the leaks to the media having turned into a torrent—that he was a hero of the highest order.

He'd headed up in the direction of New Paltz and Nancy Horowitz. His wife Nellie, still living with her sister Fran, was no better off than she'd been prior to Rob and Frank's departure. Worse maybe. Her tenuous, drug-induced equilibrium had been compromised by the media commotion surrounding Rob, despite her sister's best efforts to insulate her. And the mass-murder that had obliterated her daughter's life was back in the news again, after coverage had finally begun to abate.

Rob and his sister-in-law were contemplating the institutionalization of Nellie, at least on a temporary basis, until things returned to "normal." But Rob's personal status quo was close to untenable. The crack he'd made at the Super 8 Motel about filling the void in Nancy Horowitz's life should now be amended to include the void in his own. Or so he'd informed Frank, a day after speaking with Horowitz on the phone, a day before heading north. Sex would be nice, undeniably. But it was not reason numero uno, not anymore. Not that the trip back to New Paltz would necessarily amount to anything. But she'd indicated that she would be happy to spend some time with him. He could only hope that it turned out to be true.

Frank himself had no desire for any such adventures. He and Julie were sleeping late, waking up to fresh Florida orange juice and the *Miami Herald*. Its front page, over the previous week, had featured one screaming headline after another. The wife of Agent Scanlon was more than willing to testify that her husband, contrary to the Flower's Administration's claims, had uncovered no plans for acts of terrorism during his infiltration of All for

Allah. And she was now convinced that he'd been rubbed out by his own government.

As Fowlkes had predicted, the circle of conspirators was not that wide. But it involved very prominent individuals, who were taking turns ratting each other out. Singing for their lives, as Rob put it, quoting the host of an extremely popular "reality" show—one that Rob, not so long ago, would never have confessed to watching.

After maybe half a minute of watching a large tanker drift across the horizon, Frank picked up the *Herald* again from the beach blanket. He knew what he'd seen there ten minutes previously, and half an hour before that, but he needed to check again. His eyes had played tricks on him before in his life. It was still there on the front page, above the sub-heading *President Facing Indictment*, a huge headline which, once he found the energy to get up, he just might replicate in the wet sand: *FLOWERS RESIGNS.*

The End

About the Author

Howard Levine is the author of one previously published novel, *Leaving This Life Behind.* A former public school teacher of special education and English as a second language, he lives in suburban Washington DC, where he hikes, bikes and volunteers at a soup kitchen.